The Echo Rewritten

The Echo Rewritten

Book One of The Echoes of Bridgefall

R.M. Kiser

Summit & Shore Publishing

For permissions, subsidiary rights, foreign rights, media inquiries, or bulk purchase discounts, contact:

Summit & Shore Publishing Kingsport, Tennessee www.summitandshorepublishing.com rights@summitandshore publishing.com

Special discounts are available for bulk purchases by corporations, organizations, educational institutions, book clubs, and promotional use.

Published by Summit & Shore Publishing Cover design by Laurel & Stone Design Interior formatting and typesetting by Summit & Shore Publishing Edited by Larkin Vance Proofread by Silas Adkins Illustrations by Thornwick Illustration Author photograph by Chinquapin Portraits

ISBN — Paperback: 979-8-9933274-2-6

ISBN — eBook: 979-8-9933274-0-2

First Edition Book One of The Echoes of Bridgefall

Paperback edition first published September 23, 2026 eBook edition first published September 23, 2026

Printed in the United States of America

10 9 8 7 6 5 4 3 2 1

Visit the author online: www.rmkiser.com

Join the reader list: www.rmkiser.com/mailing-list

Dedication

Epigraph

"For now we see through a glass, darkly; but then face to face..."
— 1 Corinthians 13:12 (KJV)

The Echoes of Bridgefall

Book I — The Echo Rewritten

Book II — The Echo That Burns

Book III — The Echo Misheard

Chapter 1

Eleven minutes into the stormglass installation, Vael's palms began to register it.

Not grief. Not yet. Something that existed before grief — a low-frequency dissonance traveling through the bones of her hands the way a cracked bell corrupts the air around it, wrong at the origin, wrong in every direction outward. Her hands stayed at her sides. The crowd pressed in from all directions for warmth, their breath rising in small clouds through the morning mist, and the cold blue-white light from the plinth-mounted installation drained the color from every face surrounding her until the crowd looked like entries in the same official register: emptied, present, accounted for.

The Charter mandated attendance at commemorative installations. Five years. The Glass Bridge collapse, fifth anniversary, lower ward square, eighth bell. Her work name appeared on the attendance roll. She had come.

On the plinth, the official stormglass replay cycled through its sequence with the frictionless smoothness of something polished until all grain had been removed. The bridge rendered in cold light. A crowd watching — another crowd, five years prior, a different morning. The shudder that passed through the bridge's span in the seconds before the collapse. And then her father's face.

She had not expected her father's face.

The recording placed him at the southern anchor tower, which aligned with the official account: checking load tolerances, performing his duties, present at the site of failure. His face angled slightly away from the capturing crystal, giving her a three-quarter profile, and the angle was wrong.

The angle was wrong.

The dissonance in her palms sharpened — the same low hum, but now she had language for it, now she understood what her hands had been registering for the past eleven minutes. The recording showed her father at the southern anchor tower. The light falling across his face came from the northeast. In the official record, the collapse occurred at mid-morning, when the sun sat low and eastward. Northeast light at mid-morning at the southern anchor tower meant the recording had been made at a different time than the timestamp declared, or the crystal's orientation had been altered during encoding, or both.

Neither possibility was an accident.

She breathed. Around her, people wept or stood in the fixed posture of required attendance — faces arranged into appropriate solemnity, eyes forward, mouths set. A woman to Vael's left pressed a folded cloth against her mouth. A man behind her stood with his eyes shut. The cold blue-white light moved across all of them and rendered them into documents.

Vael looked at her father's face in the wrong light and did not move.

She did not move. This was the architecture she had constructed for herself across three years in the Underbrim: the counting. Not the counting of grief — the counting of physical properties. The specific weight of the dissonance in her palms, which she could now place somewhere between 40 and 60 hertz, the range associated with secondary frequency interference when a primary encoding has been laid over a prior one. The temperature of the air against her face, cold enough to water her eyes but not cold enough to account for the slight imprecision gathering at the edges of her vision. The texture of the flagstone beneath her boots — old dark granite of the lower ward square, gone slick in the morning mist, each stone dipped and hollowed at its center where the foot traffic had pressed for decades.

She counted these things. The counting was not calming. She counted these things.

The replay moved into its final sequence: the collapse itself, rendered in the officially sanctioned version — the span failing at the central load point, the fall, the debris field spreading across the Gorge Floor below. Forty-one dead. The official account listed them by name at the close of every commemoration, a recorded voice reading each name into the square. She knew those names. She had read them so many times they had become something other than names — a frequency, a pattern, a list of forty-one absences the official record had given a shape to.

The rope bridge was visible above the rooftops to the south, its lines dark against the grey sky. Coal smoke rose from the chimneys of the lower ward and settled into the mist above the square; below it came the smell of the river, that particular silt-and-iron the Sill pushed up through the gorge each morning. The crowd around her exhaled together as the collapse sequence completed, a collective breath that was almost a sound.

Vael left.

She did not run. She moved through the crowd's edge with her pace measured, her shoulders easy — the walk of a person heading back to work, a health errand, anything the warden stationed at the square's eastern exit would not bother to interrogate if she did not look like she was fleeing. She did not look like she was fleeing. Three years of practice had made that much reliable.

The warden was a young man she had not encountered before, which was either good or bad depending on whether unfamiliarity meant she fell outside his recognition file or simply outside his current rotation. He watched her pass. His gaze moved across her face with the specific quality of professional notation — not curiosity, not suspicion, but the automatic recording of a face for the rotation log that would feed, by end of day, into the Council's surveillance assignment queue.

She kept walking.

The dissonance faded from her palms as she moved away from the installation. This was how it always worked: the closer she stood to altered stormglass, the more clearly her hands registered the falsification, and the further she moved, the more the signal degraded until it became indistinguishable from the ordinary low-level hum of a city built on and around stormglass infrastructure. Two years she had spent believing this sensitivity was a malfunction. A symptom of the failed calibration that had ended her archival appointment and begun her exile. Something to be managed, suppressed, filed alongside the other costs of being what she was.

It was not a malfunction. She had come to understand this. It was the thing the Council had labeled a malfunction because the certification board had handed back her results without comment, the senior examiner turning the frequency log face-down on the table before she left the room.

The Underbrim's damp flagstones carried her north through streets that narrowed as they descended toward the Gorge Floor's influence — buildings pressing inward, upper floors leaning toward each other overhead until they nearly touched, the sky reduced to a grey strip between rooflines. She knew this geography the way she knew the counting: not by choice, but because three years of moving through it had made it part of her. The raised texture of painted-over wall inscriptions she did not touch today. The basement brewer's smell of fermented grain announcing her building before it came into view.

She turned a corner and stopped.

A narrow street. The Registry annex's brushed-metal door standing open. Three wardens — one more than standard procedure called for. And an elderly man in a coat slightly too large for him, standing at the annex entrance with his arms loose at his sides, his chin up, his feet planted as a man's feet go when he has stopped deciding.

A public re-calibration. In progress.

The warden nearest the old man had a hand on his elbow — the left hand, trained position, leaving the right free. The grip was gentle. It was always gentle. She had witnessed this gentleness before and understood it was not kindness; it was a performance of care precise enough that the watching crowd could keep their faces still and their opinions to themselves. If the wardens were gentle, there was nothing to object to. If there was nothing to object to, the crowd could remain the crowd rather than become something else.

The crowd watched. Eight, maybe ten people, standing at the distance that said they had noticed and decided not to have an opinion about what they had noticed. No one spoke. A woman near the far wall had turned slightly sideways, as though she had stopped on her way somewhere else and had not quite committed to stopping.

Vael watched too.

The old man turned his head slightly, and she caught his face in profile — jaw loose, eyes open and level, the look of a man who has set something down. His coat was dark wool, worn at the elbows. He had dressed for the commemoration, she thought. He had put on his good coat.

The warden guided him through the door. The brushed-metal door swung shut behind them.

The crowd dispersed, one person at a time, each departure timed to avoid the appearance of collective movement. Within thirty seconds the street was empty except for the two remaining wardens and Vael.

She was standing still. Her hands were flat against her thighs.

She made herself walk.

The contempt was familiar — she had been filing it under survival for three years, the way her jaw set when she kept walking, each time she kept walking, the slight shortening of her stride, the pressure of her thumbnail against the side of her first finger until the skin went white. It was the correct choice. She had no cover that would survive the attention a public objection would draw. No resources, no allies, no institutional standing. A work name and a salvage shelter and the sensitivity in her palms that the Council had decided was a malfunction. Keeping walking was the correct choice.

She filed the contempt. She kept walking.

The shelter was a single room above the basement brewer, accessed through a separate entrance off the alley — a timber door, plain, with a gap at the bottom wide enough for a folded paper to pass through. She had chosen this building for that gap.

The notation was on the floor just inside the door.

She saw it before she had fully entered — a fold of paper, pale against the dark floorboard, the kind of folded notation an archivist would make in the field when stormglass was unavailable. She closed the door behind her. The room held the smell of the brewer's fermented grain rising through the floorboards, and the cold that pooled in from the gorge below, working up through the foundation stones the way cold does in low places, and the particular silence of a space that had been empty for some hours and was now occupied.

She did not pick it up immediately.

Her salvage kit sat wrapped in oilcloth on the shelf above the pallet. The clay jar sealed with wax rested beside it. No stormglass visible — she kept nothing visible, nothing that would tell a search what she was doing or what she could do. The single window faced the alley and admitted the grey morning light in a narrow rectangle that fell across the floor and stopped two feet short of the notation.

She crouched and picked it up.

The notation system was one she recognized before she had language for recognizing it. Not her own — she had developed her own notation system in exile, a compressed frequency shorthand that occupied less space on paper and resisted reading without the key. This was different. Older. She had seen this system used once, twice, a dozen times in the years before the collapse — seen it without being taught it, the way a child absorbs a parent's habitual gesture, taking in the shape of the thing without the explanation of the thing.

Solen's system.

Her mother had developed it before Vael was old enough to learn it formally. The notation recorded frequency signatures in a way that was illegible to anyone who hadn't watched it being made — not encrypted, exactly, but embedded in a visual logic that required knowing how Solen thought about frequency before you could read how Solen wrote about it. Vael had watched her mother use it for years. The watching was not the same as being taught. And yet.

The notation on the paper indicated a frequency range she could identify: secondary band, in the range the Council's archivists never bothered to monitor, because the secondary band was an artifact of early stormglass manufacturing that had never been officially documented. A redundant encoding layer considered a flaw. Her mother had known about it. Her mother had used it.

She read the notation three times. It did not change.

Someone who knew Solen knew where she slept.

The room was very quiet. The brewer's machinery was still at this hour — fermentation ran overnight and the morning was for settling. Outside, the alley carried the distant sound of the Gorge Floor's river, the Sill, transmitted through the stone of the building's foundation as a low vibration she registered in her feet rather than heard with her ears.

She stood with the notation in both hands and did not move.

This was the other kind of stillness — not the stillness of the counting, not displacement, but the stillness of something under load, the stillness that preceded a frequency read when her palms were pressed against glass and she was waiting for the signal to resolve. Her body had already processed what her mind was still catching up to. The notation was dangerous. It was also the first thing in three years that pointed somewhere other than further down. She had kept herself invisible so the dangerous and the necessary would not find her. They had found her anyway — not this morning, not at the commemoration, but sometime before all of it, before the wrong light on her father's face, in the gap of time her invisibility had failed to cover.

The question was not whether she would follow this.

The notation was in her mother's handwriting system. Someone had been inside Solen's encoding logic — had carried that logic to the Underbrim, had pushed it under her door. Which meant someone had known where to look. Which meant someone had been looking. Which meant her three years of invisibility had already ended before this morning, before the commemoration, before the dissonance in her palms over the wrong light falling across her father's face.

She read the notation a fourth time.

The frequency it indicated was a location as much as a signal — a secondary band address, encoded in Solen's system, pointing to something that had been filed somewhere and was waiting. The way her mother had always filed things. Not hidden, exactly. Filed where only the right hands would know to look.

Vael set the notation on the shelf beside the oilcloth kit. She stood in the poor morning light with her back to the door, her palms open at her sides, and understood that she would not sleep first.

Chapter 2

The assignment form arrived at the third bell, slotted into Davan's intake tray between a routine frequency-irregularity report from the Gorge Floor and a re-classification notice he had already processed twice under different reference numbers. The redundancy was a filing error, not a test — he recognized the difference without needing to consider it. He set the re-classification aside and lifted the assignment form.

Clipped to the upper left corner in standard format was the warden's notation: face-log from the commemoration, fifth-anniversary rotation, lower ward square. The automated cross-reference system had flagged the subject by comparing commemoration attendance against the active monitoring list. Davan read the name. He read it a second time. He placed the form flat against the desk and studied it with the particular quality of attention he reserved for things that required him to be careful about what he appeared to notice.

The Council's operational offices occupied the Spire's lower two floors — low ceilings, brushed-metal stormglass panels throwing steady light that carried no warmth, a faint metallic taste in the air from the Registry's frequency management systems running beneath the floor. Nine years in this room had taught him its silence: it absorbed rather than reflected, which meant conversations did not carry and footsteps landed without echo. The building suited a certain kind of work, and he had become suited to the building. At the far end of the room, the supervising archivist moved through transit logs at a steady pace, pulling each folder, scanning it, setting it aside — his hands certain before his eyes had finished the page. He did not look up.

Davan opened the subject file. It had been amended three times. The original intake dated from three years prior — a standard post-incident review, the kind generated automatically when an archival appointment was revoked. That original document had run to eleven pages. The first amendment, filed eight months after intake, had reduced it to nine. The second, filed eighteen months after that, had brought it to seven. The third, filed six weeks ago, had left five pages.

He turned through them with deliberate evenness. A file that thins with each amendment is not being updated — it is being managed. He was experienced enough to know the difference, and the difference was the kind of thing he had learned, over nine years, to register without marking.

The five remaining pages documented what the Council's systems were prepared to say about Vael: exile status, Underbrim residential zone, salvage-work classification, no registered frequency access, no current institutional affiliation. The archival appointment revocation appeared without explanation. *Appointment terminated following calibration assessment.* Their language. He had written it himself, in other forms, without examining it. The calibration assessment that had ended her appointment was not described anywhere in the remaining pages — its findings absent, its authorizing signature missing.

He turned back to the first page.

The original intake carried a standard Registry seal. The first amendment bore a Council administrative mark he recognized as Maerath's division. The second amendment carried the same mark. The third — filed quietly six weeks ago, the one that had taken eleven pages down to five — carried a designation he had to look at twice before placing: infrastructure review, fiscal cycle, a classification code applied to archival materials deemed inactive.

She was not inactive. She was in the surveillance queue. Someone had classified her as inactive six weeks before the commemoration flagged her as present.

Davan set the file down and looked at the assignment form. The standard hunter form had twelve fields. He filled in eleven of them with the careful fluency of a man who had done this many times and had no reason to do it differently — name, residential zone, last confirmed location, flagging event, assigned operative, reporting cadence, priority classification. He marked priority as standard rather than elevated, because elevating it would route the assignment through secondary review, and he did not want secondary review before he had finished reading.

The twelfth field was location.

He left it blank.

This was not a decision. It was the absence of one — which was different — and he set it aside in the same way he had set aside the re-classification notice. Not discarded. Not acted upon. Placed where he could return to it.

The supervising archivist looked up. "Assignment processed?"

"Filed," Davan said. "Standard monitoring cadence."

The archivist nodded and went back to the transit logs.

Davan closed the file. He stacked it with three others in his outgoing tray and looked at the stack for a moment. The stormglass panel above his desk cast its steady, colorless light. The metallic taste of the Registry air was, as always, most noticeable when he had been sitting still for some time. He had been sitting still for some time.

He picked up the re-classification notice and processed it correctly.

After his shift ended, he went to the ruins — which was not irregular. He had clearance for the site. Using clearance for personal visits fell technically outside standard protocol, but the clearance records showed only that access had occurred, not the reason behind it, and he had never been asked for a reason, and he had stopped expecting to be.

This was the fourth visit this year. He knew because he remembered each one without effort, the way a man remembers things he has never set down. The first had been in early spring, when gorge fog still lay dense enough to obscure the Sill below the grating. The second in summer, the air dry and hot against his face, the stone baking where it caught the gorge-filtered light. The third in autumn, leaves from the Plateau's ornamental trees finding their way down the gorge walls and collecting against the iron bars in small damp clusters. Now this — the tail end of the year, the cold that settled at the gorge base regardless of season sharpening toward the kind that left moisture on every surface by morning.

The grating was set into the Plateau's edge where the bridge's anchor tower met the cliff face, iron bars spaced close enough to prevent passage but open enough to see through. Below, the Sill ran dark and fast. The shattered stormglass from the bridge's collapse had been working into the riverbed for five years, and on clear nights — this was clear enough — the bed caught what light came down the gorge walls and held it, fractured and multiplied, so that the river appeared to run over a shattered brightness, not the ruin beneath it.

Davan stood at the grating with both hands wrapped around two of the bars. The iron was cold. It was always cold.

The stanchions on either side were the bridge's surviving anchor hardware — iron and stormglass composite, the glass components embedded in the iron housings at regular intervals in the way the original engineers had specified. Most of the glass had cracked in the collapse. What remained carried no active frequency, no official encoding. The Council's archivists had certified this in the post-collapse survey. Five pages. Carefully signed. The stanchions produced a hum. He had not reported this.

The hum reached his chest before he registered it.

Not a sound — he had listened for it as a sound the first time and heard nothing, which had confused him until he understood that hearing was the wrong sense. It arrived through the iron bars into his palms and from his palms into his sternum: a vibration at a frequency below what the ear processed, the kind of resonance the body registered as pressure rather than pitch. The stanchions produced it. He had not reported this. The post-collapse survey had certified no active frequency in the surviving hardware, and he had read the certification, and the certification was five pages, carefully signed, and he had stood here four times and felt the hum and had not reported it.

This was not a decision either. It was the same absence.

At the base of the anchor tower's exterior face, below the grating, someone had placed small objects against the stone: a river-smoothed pebble, a folded paper already dissolving at the edges from the gorge damp, something that might have been a piece of glass salvage wrapped in cloth. Similar arrangements had been there on his previous visits. He had not been able to determine, from this angle, whether the arrangements changed between visits or whether he was misremembering the previous ones.

The smell at the grating was ozone and old burning — stormglass under heat stress, a smell that should not have been present in hardware the post-collapse survey had certified as inactive.

He stood for a while. The hum continued at the same register, neither increasing nor decreasing. The Sill ran over its luminous bed. A wind came down from the north and struck him through the bars — cold, tasting of the high gorge walls and whatever lay above them — and he turned his face into it for a moment, something he could not explain to himself or to anyone else, and did not try.

He left before the Warden rotation reached this section of the Plateau edge. He had timed this correctly on each previous visit. He filed nothing about the visit. The clearance record would show his access code at this location at this hour, a pattern legible to anyone who thought to look. He had thought to look. He understood the pattern was there, and he had not altered it.

He walked back through the Plateau's service streets with his hands in his coat pockets. The hum in his sternum went on for a time, then didn't. He did not mark the moment it stopped.

His rented room sat on the Plateau's lower residential tier, above a cartographer's workshop that kept irregular hours. Inside: a pallet, a shelf, a table, a single window facing an interior courtyard. He had furnished it for function and had been living in it for six years without accumulation — nothing on the walls, nothing on the shelf that was not operational, the pallet made each morning with the precision of someone who expected the room to be searched and wanted the search to find nothing remarkable.

He lit the candle on the table and sat down.

From his coat's inner pocket he took out the assignment forms and spread them across the table: the hunter form, the subject file's five remaining pages, the warden's notation from the commemoration. He arranged them in the order he would need to work through them and looked at the arrangement for a moment.

The candle threw a small, steady light. Below, the cartographer's workshop was quiet.

He worked through the forms methodically — checking each field against the subject file, verifying internal consistency, confirming that no field contradicted another, that the assignment as documented would survive a routine review without flagging. This was the work he was good at. Nine years of it, and the goodness was not something he questioned, because it was simply what he did and he did it well.

The hunter form had twelve fields.

Eleven of them were correct.

He looked at the twelfth field for a long time. The candle had burned down an inch. The blank there was not the blankness of something not yet filled in — that kind was provisional, expected, a line waiting its turn. This was something held open on purpose, and he knew the difference the way he knew the difference between a filing error and a test. A door not opened rather than a line not crossed. It pressed against his sternum the way the hum had, below pitch, below naming.

He thought about the file. Eleven pages reduced to five across three amendments, the last filed six weeks before the commemoration placed her in the surveillance queue. Someone had classified her as inactive. Someone with Maerath's divisional mark had done this twice. The third time, someone had used an infrastructure code — the kind applied to materials considered closed, finished, no longer requiring management.

She had been at the commemoration. The warden had logged her face.

A file that thins is a file someone has been watching closely enough to know what to remove.

He was not the first operative to receive this assignment — he understood that now. The file's thinning was the record of previous assignments, previous reviews, previous decisions about what to leave visible and what to take away. Someone had been managing this for three years. The assignment had come to him because the commemoration had placed her in the queue, and the queue had routed to him because he covered the Underbrim district, and the routing was automatic and had not been examined by anyone who would have reason to consider whether he was the right person to receive it.

His hand rested on the reporting sleeve without picking it up.

He slid the forms into the reporting sleeve — hunter form on top, subject file beneath, the warden's notation clipped to the upper left corner in standard format — and set the sleeve on the corner of the table where he would pick it up in the morning. The candle held its small light. The twelfth field held its blankness. He had not filled it in. He had not torn it either. Technically, he was in violation of nothing yet — and he knew it. He sat with that knowledge the way he had stood at the grating: hands around something cold, the hum already in his chest, waiting to see what he would do next.

Chapter 3

The Sorrow ran pale at this hour — the way it always did in the grey before first light — almost luminous, the riverbed beneath carpeted in shattered stormglass that caught what little light existed and held it, so the water appeared to move over something still burning. Vael had been coming here for two years. She knew the current's pull at the southeast grating, knew the specific resistance of the bar that had worked loose from its weld at the lower corner, knew the smell that rose from the water near the main collapse site — ozone and cold iron and something older underneath, a frequency-adjacent smell she had no technical name for but recognized the way you recognized a voice before the words reached you, before the meaning of it settled.

She moved through the Warden rotation's gap without hesitation — sideways through the grating, the loose bar dragging across her shoulder where it always dragged, familiar enough now that her body had stopped anticipating it. Forty minutes between the Plateau-side pass and the river approach. She had timed it first on instinct, then on confirmation, then repeated it enough times that the counting had gone quiet. She was inside the restricted zone before the sensation had finished registering.

The ruins occupied the gorge's lower shelf in a way that had always struck Vael as less like collapse and more like interrupted motion — the two anchor towers still standing on either side as though waiting for instructions, the surviving cable sections sagging between them in loose arcs, and the debris field on the riverbed below arranged as things arrange themselves when they fall from a great height and the Sorrow's current decides the rest. She had salvaged this field for two years. She knew which fragments were worth pulling — Council-origin glass, frequency-dense and legible to the underground market — and which were decorative ruin, the bridge's structural glass that had never been encoded and never would be, beautiful and useless in the way of most beautiful things.

Tonight was different. She had known it would be different since she stood in her shelter holding the notation, reading her mother's frequency shorthand in the gap between one breath and the next.

The notation had specified a depth and a bearing. She had been turning both over since she found it, running the coordinates against two years of salvage knowledge the way she ran her palms over stormglass in the market — not searching for anything specific, letting the dissonance announce itself. The depth was deeper than she had gone before. Not beyond the debris field, but into it — into the silt beneath the main collapse site where the heaviest fragments had worked themselves down through five years of current and seasonal pressure, embedding at angles that made recovery nearly impossible without disturbing the surrounding material and triggering the kind of frequency cascade that the Council's sensors, even dormant ones, were calibrated to detect.

She had thought about this. She had weighed it against the notation's specificity, against the fact that someone with access to her mother's encoding logic had placed it on her floor, against the fact that she had been invisible for three years and was apparently not invisible anymore — and so she had already stopped taking the long route home. She had reached the conclusion she always reached when the calculus shifted: move.

She picked her way down the debris field's upper slope, placing her feet on the larger glass panels that had settled flat against the riverbed's upper layer — the ones that didn't shift, that had been there long enough to have become part of the surface rather than objects resting on it. The Sorrow moved around her boots, shallower here at the field's edge, the current slower where the debris broke its momentum. The ozone sharpened as she neared the water. The stanchion residue — she had noticed it on her fourth visit and had been noting it without filing it ever since — hummed at a frequency she felt not in her palms, where she felt most frequencies, but somewhere further back, in the joint where her jaw met her skull, a vibration too low for sound, the kind that comes off stormglass that has been bearing load too long.

This was not routine salvage. She had told herself it was routine salvage for the forty minutes of the Warden rotation gap, and she had believed it with the part of herself that needed to believe it, and she did not believe it with any other part.

She went deeper.

The water reached her knees at the collapse site's center. Cold even now, cold the way the Sorrow was always cold at this depth regardless of season, fed by the gorge's north-running channel where the sun never reached long enough to matter. The riverbed underfoot was soft here — silt accumulated over five years, stormglass fragments embedded at all angles, some still catching the pre-dawn light from above in ways that made the bottom of the river look like a document half-buried in sediment, text still legible at the edges. She moved slowly. Disturbing the silt would cloud the water and reduce the frequency differential she needed to distinguish Council glass from archive glass, the encoded from the inert.

The notation's bearing put her slightly east of the main collapse point, toward the secondary anchor line's former position. She adjusted. The water was at her thighs now where the riverbed dipped, and the cold came up through her legs in steady increments — depth, position, how far she had come — information her body kept without being asked, leaving her attention free for the larger work of feeling.

She found it before she expected to.

Not through sight — the silt was too disturbed from her approach, the water too pale with suspended material — but through her right hand trailing in the current, fingers spread, the way she had learned to read salvage without looking at it. The fragment was small, smaller than the notation's coordinates had suggested, and the first thing she registered was its temperature: warmer than the water. Warmer than it should be, warmer than any piece of stormglass submerged in the Sorrow for five years had any physical reason to be.

She closed her hand around it.

The amber was the color she knew from her mother's calibration samples — not the yellow-amber of Council archive glass, which ran toward gold and produced a clean, frictionless frequency when read, but a deeper color, almost brown at the center, the color of resin that has been accumulating around something for a long time. Solen had kept four samples of it in her workshop, in a row on the lower shelf, and Vael had been seven or eight when she first touched one and felt the warmth and asked why it was different from the other glass and Solen had said —

Solen speaks. The calibration chamber is lit by two gas lamps, both on the north wall, and the light falls at an angle that puts the filing cabinets in partial shadow. The date on the wall register reads morning, four years before the collapse, and Solen is cross-referencing two files simultaneously — one open on the table, one held in her left hand — her head bent, jaw set, the stillness of someone taking exact measure before she commits to what she has found.

The file on the table is a stress analysis report. Secondary anchor line, eastern approach. The file in her hand is a load distribution record from the same date, same structure, different encoding origin. Solen holds them both and her face does not change but her hands — Vael knows her mother's hands, has watched them her whole life, knows every register they operate in — her hands have gone still, the fingers flat, not moving, the way they went when the numbers in front of her did not agree.

She sets the held file down. She picks up the encoding stylus. She opens a third file, a blank one, and begins to write, and what she writes is not a report — the formatting is wrong for a report, the header fields are empty, the classification marker is absent — what she writes is a notation in the secondary frequency band, the redundant encoding layer the Council's current archivists do not know to look for, and she writes with quick, deliberate strokes, the kind of pace that means she knows the window for this is short and that the window for doing anything with what she has written will be short in a different way, on a different timeline, one she cannot currently see the end of.

She writes: the load distribution figures were altered between the original survey and the filed version. The alteration is consistent across three separate reports, same hand, same filing date. The secondary anchor line was flagged as critical in the original survey. The flagging does not appear in the filed version. Someone filed a suppression order against the original survey. The suppression order has no authorization signature.

She stops. She looks at what she has written. She looks at the two files on the table — the stress analysis, the load distribution record — and she looks at the blank header fields on the notation she has just created, and something moves across her face in the lamplight: her mouth tightens, her eyes go somewhere past the papers, and then she pulls them back.

She opens the encoding stylus again. She adds: I am filing this in the secondary band, under the Eastbridge maintenance cycle, third inspection log. I am not filing a formal report. I know what happens to formal reports on this subject. I know because I have seen the suppression order and I know whose mark is on it and I know what the mark means.

She pauses. The gas lamps hiss. The calibration chamber is very quiet.

She adds: the bridge will not hold the eastern load under winter pressure. The calculations are clear. The —

The amber went dark.

Vael stood in the Sorrow with the water at her knees and the cold working up through her legs and the shard in her right hand. The eighteen seconds were over. The calibration chamber was gone, and her mother was gone, and what remained was the particular silence that follows a frequency's termination — the room still shaped by what had been in it, the air not yet settled back to ordinary.

She did not move.

The Sorrow moved around her.

The stormglass on the riverbed caught the first thin light of morning, grey and cold, and the fragments angled right threw it back in small, irregular patterns across the water's surface. The ozone smell came up sharp from the current. The jaw-joint hum continued at its low register, indifferent to what had just happened.

Eighteen seconds. Solen's hands moving over the files. The load distribution figures altered between the original survey and the filed version. The secondary anchor line flagged as critical in the original survey. The flagging absent from the filed version. A suppression order with no authorization signature, and her mother's face in the two-lamp light of the calibration chamber, tightened at the mouth, eyes drawn somewhere past the page.

Vael's hands had gone still — not frozen, not shocked, but flat and unmoving, the way her mother's had gone still over the files. The shard sat warm in her palm, warmer than the water, but the warmth was already going, the crystal cooling toward the temperature of the river around it, and she stood there and let it cool and did not move.

Not *negligence* — their word, not hers. Not *negligence*. Not *span failure* at the central load point, the official cause, the language of the commemoration, the language of the stormglass replay she had stood in the lower ward square and watched with her father's face in the light. The secondary anchor line had been flagged as critical. Someone had removed the flagging. Someone had filed a suppression order against the original survey without signing it.

Her father had been at the secondary anchor line. The light in the official replay had been wrong — northeast light, mid-morning at the southern anchor tower — and she had known for five years that the replay was falsified, had known it in her palms at every commemoration she had been unable to avoid, and had not known until eighteen seconds ago what the falsification was covering.

The secondary anchor line. His position had been moved in the record. His position, and the flagging, and the load distribution figures — all moved in the same direction, all filed on the same date, same hand, same encoding origin.

She stood in the Sorrow for a long time.

When she moved, she moved carefully, her joints stiff from stillness, the cold having worked deeper than she'd let herself register while she stood there. The first grey of actual morning was pushing in above the gorge wall — she could see it in the change of color on the water — and she had maybe twenty minutes before the Warden rotation completed its second pass and the restricted zone's approach became visible from the Plateau edge. She cupped the amber shard in both hands for a moment — the warmth nearly gone, the crystal cooling to ambient — then wrapped it in the oilcloth she kept folded in her salvage kit's outer pocket and placed it in the false bottom beneath the kit's visible contents.

She worked her way back up the debris field the way she had come, placing her feet on the settled panels, keeping her movements slow enough not to disturb the silt. The Sorrow moved around her ankles, then released her as she reached the field's upper edge and the riverbed rose toward the grating.

She was through the grating and moving back through the service streets before the Warden rotation reached this section. She had timed this correctly. She had timed it correctly every time for two years, and she timed it correctly now, and the correctness felt like nothing — functional, procedural, the step taken after the thing that mattered.

Her shelter was above the basement brewer, alley entrance, timber door with the gap at the bottom. She went through the grating gap, up the alley, and inside before she let herself think about anything other than the route.

Inside, she set the salvage kit on the table and opened it. The amber shard sat in the false bottom, wrapped in oilcloth. She left it there. She moved to the shelf above the door where she kept the secondary pieces — fragments recovered on salvage runs and held without knowing why, glass that didn't fit the market's appetite or her own immediate use, things she kept because her hands had wanted to keep them.

The Council-origin fragment was there. She had recovered it three months ago from a different section of the debris field, frequency-dense in a way that had made her palms register something she couldn't parse — not the clean frictionlessness of managed Council glass, not the warm resistance of archive material, but something between those registers that she had no category for. She had kept it without knowing why, setting it on the shelf the way you set a thing down when you know you aren't finished with it yet.

She needed the false bottom. She needed the space the Council-origin fragment was occupying in her working kit.

She crossed to the loose flagstone near the door — she had identified it in her first week here, before she had any specific use for a secondary hiding place, because identifying secondary hiding places was the kind of thing she did before she needed them — lifted it, and pressed the Council-origin fragment into the gap between the flagstone's edge and the foundation stone. She set the flagstone back. Its edge sat slightly proud of the floor where her haste had not quite aligned it, a small imprecision she registered and did not correct.

She was already moving toward the door.

The amber shard was in the false bottom of her salvage kit, wrapped in oilcloth, cooling toward the temperature of the room. The flagstone near the door sat slightly proud of the floor. The secondary fragment was beneath it, frequency-dense and unread, placed without significance in the haste of a morning she could still feel in the cold dragging at her wet boots.

She did not know yet what the fragment was. She knew only what she had been standing in the Sorrow holding — her mother's hands, and the stillness they had gone to — and the specific shape of a thing that had been waiting under the grief for five years.

She put her hand flat against the door.

The timber was cold. She held it there for one breath, then pushed through into the alley.

Chapter 4

The frequency analysis had been filed at the fourth bell. Someone had been awake to receive it — which meant the detection was not routine. Maerath read it standing at the Ledger Room's long table, the document cradle angled toward the ceiling light. When she set it down, she placed it precisely at the table's edge — not carelessly, not with emphasis, but at the edge, where it would remain visible without requiring her to hold it.

"The signature," she said.

Archivist Tenne, standing to her left, already had the secondary frequency report open. "Consistent with pre-Charter archive glass. The primary band reads clean, but the secondary register —" He stopped. Not from uncertainty, but from long practice with her — he turned a page and waited.

She did not complete it. She looked at the report.

The secondary register had produced a frequency signature the Registry's current readers could not fully parse — not because the equipment was inadequate, but because the encoding logic belonged to a manufacturing stratum the Council's standardization program had, three decades ago, classified as obsolete and filed accordingly. Pre-Charter archive glass. The kind pulled from circulation specifically because its secondary band was undocumented, its encoding behavior inconsistent with controlled archival practice, its frequency outputs legible only to archivists trained before the standardization. Few of those archivists remained. The ones who did were, by and large, accounted for.

The location was the lower bridge district. Specifically, the river approach to the secondary anchor line's former position.

"Duration," Maerath said.

"Eighteen seconds. The signature degraded to ambient within thirty seconds of initial detection." Tenne turned a page. "The encoding was active, not passive. Something was played back, not merely accessed."

She held the information still in her mind. Eighteen seconds of active playback from a pre-Charter secondary register, in the lower bridge district, in the pre-dawn hours, at the river approach to the secondary anchor line. The location was not coincidental. Locations of that kind were never coincidental — the debris field had been generating investigative interest for five years, and that interest had been, until now, manageable. Individuals who went looking for things in the Sorrow tended to find fragments, and fragments tended to find their way to the grey market, and the grey market could be monitored. Pre-Charter archive glass was different. Pre-Charter archive glass could carry encoded testimony from the original survey period, encoded in a frequency band the Registry's current readers would flag as anomalous without being able to read its content.

Anomalous — their word. She had used it herself, in reports, in the years immediately following the structural event, when the language of the situation was still being established. She had found it useful. Useful words were not dishonest words; they were precise in the direction that mattered.

"Who else has received this report," she said. Not a question — she knew the distribution list, had set it herself — but a check on whether the list had held.

"Standard distribution. The two senior Wardens. The frequency monitoring desk." Tenne paused. "The monitoring desk filed it as a routine anomaly log. They did not flag it for escalation."

"No."

"No," he agreed. He turned another page. "They lack the reference library for pre-Charter signatures. The secondary register read as noise within acceptable parameters."

Noise within acceptable parameters. She looked at the report again. Eighteen seconds of active playback from a pre-Charter secondary register, and the monitoring desk had filed it as acceptable noise — because the monitoring desk did not know to look for pre-Charter encoding logic, because the Registry's standardization program had made that knowledge unnecessary, because she had ensured it was unnecessary, because unnecessary knowledge was the specific category of knowledge that produced the specific category of problem she was managing now — she set the report down and returned her attention to it.

The room held its quiet. The Ledger Room always did — the walls swallowed sound at the edges, the stormglass installations sealed in their brushed-metal casings doing something to the acoustic register that she had stopped trying to name. The ceiling light was even and cool. The table was pale stone. Everything in the room had been chosen to keep the mind orderly, to hold questions at the correct distance from their answers.

The two senior Wardens stood at the room's far end, near the door. She had not asked them to sit. They had not asked to sit. This was the correct arrangement.

"There is a surveillance asset currently assigned to the lower bridge district," she said. "Davan."

"Yes."

"His current assignment is general monitoring. Commemoration residuals. The usual accumulation of sentiment that follows a public anniversary." She straightened the frequency analysis report by a fraction of a degree. "Redirect him. The specific source of the pre-Charter signature is the priority. He is to locate it, characterize it, and report before he acts."

"Before he acts," Tenne repeated, noting it.

"The characterization matters. Pre-Charter glass from the secondary anchor zone could be several things. It could be salvage residue — fragments sitting in the silt for five years, disturbed by the river's seasonal movement. It could be a grey-market retrieval, someone working the debris field without a license, who has no idea what they've found and will try to sell it through Pell's market in the next forty-eight hours." She paused. "Or it could be something that was placed there. Something that was waiting."

The room absorbed this.

"If it was placed," one of the senior Wardens said — the one on the left, whose name she retained because retaining names was useful — "the placement required someone with knowledge of the secondary anchor zone's pre-Charter encoding stratum."

"Yes."

"That narrows the field considerably."

"It does." She turned to face them fully. "The field is narrow enough that I have a working hypothesis. The surveillance redirection will either confirm it or rule it out. Davan is not to engage the source until I have his characterization report. If the source is salvage residue or a grey-market retrieval, we handle it through standard channels. If it is something else —" She let the sentence find its own ending. "Then we move to the second stage."

"Administrative containment," the Warden said.

"Administrative containment," she confirmed. "Covert first. We do not create attention around the source by moving against it visibly. Visible action produces documentation. Documentation produces questions. The second stage proceeds quietly, through the appropriate classification channels, without documentation that produced questions."

The Warden nodded. He had been doing this long enough to understand that *administrative containment* carried a specific operational meaning that required no elaboration. She appreciated this about him.

Tenne had already moved to the secondary table, where the next document waited. She knew what it was before he brought it to her — she had reviewed the lower-tier review queue herself, three days ago, and had flagged this file for this session. The elderly bridge worker. Thirty years of discrepancy reports, filed in the lower ward registry, accumulating in the review queue — one page after another, year after year, regular as a man checking his tools before a shift.

She read the file with full attention. She always read files with full attention. Processing them without reading them — signing orders for things she had not verified — was not a practice she permitted herself. It was important to know what she was signing. It was important to know exactly what the file contained, what the discrepancy reports said, what pattern they formed when read in sequence rather than in isolation.

The pattern was not resistance. She was clear about this. The man was not a resister — he had no network, no ideology, no relationship to the organized counter-archive activity she monitored. He was a man who had been a load-distribution surveyor for thirty years, who had been writing down discrepancies between the official post-collapse structural record and what he remembered observing before the collapse, because that was what his professional formation had trained him to do. He had filed these reports through legitimate channels. He had received no response. He had continued filing them.

Thirty years of professional habit, producing thirty years of discrepancy documentation, accumulating in a review queue that the lower-tier registry had been flagging for escalation for the past eighteen months.

The issue was not the reports themselves. The lower-tier registry's readers lacked the reference library to understand what the discrepancies documented — the same gap that had caused the monitoring desk to file the pre-Charter frequency signature as acceptable noise. The issue was that the reports existed in the queue, and the queue was a document, and documents could be cross-referenced, and cross-referencing was the specific activity she had most reason to prevent.

The memory trial was a public health matter. This was accurate. A man of his age, exhibiting this pattern of sustained discrepancy reporting against official record, was exhibiting a clinical profile consistent with the memory irregularities the Council's public health framework was designed to identify and address. The re-calibration would be a mercy. This was also accurate. She had reviewed the clinical literature. The literature was clear on sustained memory-record divergence in elderly patients — the divergence itself was a source of distress, and its resolution through re-calibration produced measurable improvement in patient wellbeing.

She signed the order.

The pen moved in the specific way she had trained it to move over the years — full attention, no hesitation, the signature even and unhurried, the same mark she had made on a thousand documents before this one. She did not linger over it.

Tenne took the order and placed it in the processing sleeve.

She did not know the man's name. This was accurate — the file contained his worker registration number and his ward, his years of service, his filing frequency. Not his name. She had not looked for it.

"The memory trial will be scheduled through the lower ward public health registry," she said. "Standard processing time. No reason to accelerate it."

"Understood."

"The frequency redirection to Davan goes through standard channels. His assignment update will read as routine redistribution of monitoring priorities. No notation connecting it to this session."

"Understood," Tenne said again.

The Wardens moved toward the door. She watched them go with the specific quality of attention she maintained in rooms she was leaving — noting what remained, what had been touched, what position each document occupied relative to the table's edge. The frequency analysis report was still at the edge, where she had placed it. The memory trial order was in the processing sleeve. The secondary frequency report was closed.

The documents were where they should be. In this room, they were always where they should be.

Tenne remained, gathering the documents with his particular efficiency. She watched him for a moment without appearing to watch him — the way she watched everything in a room, registering the order in which he lifted each folder, which he set squarely and which he tucked loose beneath the others.

"The pre-Charter glass," she said. He looked up. "When Davan's report comes in, I want it routed directly to me. Not through the standard distribution."

"Of course."

She nodded once. Then she crossed to the window.

The Spire's polished limestone exterior was always visibly dry — even now, with the city's usual damp sitting in the lower districts like something the stone had refused to absorb. From the upper floors, the gorge was clear on mornings like this one: the rope bridge a thin line across the gap, the ruins at the southern end, the debris field below the former anchor positions. At this distance it was reduced to shapes, the broken material settled into the riverbed silt the way things settled when nothing had moved them in five years.

She could see the riverbed.

On clear mornings, the stormglass embedded in the Sorrow's silt caught whatever light reached the water and held it — not reflecting, not transmitting, but retaining, the light sitting in the crystal the way encoding sat in the secondary register, present without being legible from the outside. From this height the effect was a pale luminescence, the light shifting in the current. She had looked at it for five years. Every clear morning for five years, from this window, because this window faced south and south was where the structural event had produced its most significant residual signature. She stood three paces back from the glass, the same distance she had stood every clear morning for five years, close enough that the gorge held its full width in the frame.

Eighteen seconds.

The pre-Charter encoding had been active for eighteen seconds — not merely accessed, Tenne had said, which was a meaningful distinction. Passive access could be many things. Active playback meant someone had held the crystal and listened to what it contained. Held it, and listened. What it contained had been encoded in the secondary register in the years before the standardization program had made that encoding stratum invisible to current readers. Before the standardization program had made it unnecessary to know how to read it.

She stood at the window and did not think about what the encoding might contain, because she pressed her weight forward onto her front foot and fixed her eyes on the far bank, the limestone wall above the waterline, until the water itself left her focus. Davan's report would characterize the source. The characterization would determine the second stage. The second stage would be handled through the appropriate channels, quietly, without documentation that produced questions.

This was the correct sequence. She had been maintaining this sequence for five years, and the maintenance had been successful in the ways that maintenance of this kind could be called successful — the official record was coherent, the public account of the structural event was stable, the forty-one families had received what official accounts could give them: dates, names, a settled version of events that let people keep going, mark anniversaries, carry the weight in a manageable shape.

The riverbed caught the morning light.

Four seconds — she did not count them, but afterward she would have said four, and she would have been correct, because her sense of time was precise in the way that all her senses were precise, trained toward accuracy over decades of work that required it. Four seconds of looking at the pale luminescence in the Sorrow's water, at the pre-Charter glass sitting in the silt, holding what it held in the secondary register the way it had held it for five years.

She turned from the window and moved back to the table.

The next document was a routine frequency audit request from the lower Registry. She pulled it toward her and read it with full attention, the window at her back, the morning light moving across the table's pale stone surface in the way light moved through glass polished until the grain was gone — clean, even, without the specific quality of resistance that older surfaces produced. She read the audit request, noted its contents, and set her pen to the response in the specific way she prepared all responses: with attention, with accuracy, with the understanding that documents were evidence of what had been done.

Outside, the stormglass riverbed went on catching the light, holding it in the secondary register. She did not look at it again.

Chapter 5

For most of a day, she had not moved.

Not paralyzed — the distinction mattered. In the first hour alone she had checked the shelter's entry points twice, relocated the salvage kit beneath the floor plank nearest the back wall, eaten half her remaining food, and drunk water until the trembling in her hands settled into something manageable. The amber shard lay wrapped in oilcloth inside the kit's false bottom. She had not touched it since. There was no need. Stormglass worked that way — not impression, not the residue of having witnessed something, but the thing itself, complete, lodged behind her eyes with the precise weight of a crystal held too long. Eighteen seconds, exact.

Solen in the calibration chamber. The files spread open across the bench. Her mother's hands moving over the encoding surface — steady, unhurried, the movements of someone well past shock, past the moment when documentation stops feeling like a choice and becomes the only act entirely within your control. The chamber walls in the recording were pale stone, close-set, the kind of room that existed in the Registry's lower levels where stormglass conduits ran thick through the masonry and the air held a faint harmonic resonance that sank below conscious hearing after the first hour. Vael had worked in rooms like it. She had not known, standing in them, that her mother had stood in them too.

The calculations are clear. The —

There. The cut. Eighteen seconds and then nothing, and the nothing was not the absence of encoding — she knew that silence well enough from salvage work, the flat quiet of a crystal that had simply run out — this was different. This carried the specific quality of a recording that had been interrupted, or sealed, or ended by something other than the session's natural close. Not the gradual consonant-fade of degradation. A wall. The kind built deliberately, which meant someone had known what followed and had decided it would not.

She sat with this for a long time. A strip of grey morning light entered through the shelter's single window and moved across the floor plank as the hours turned. She watched it move. Then she made her assessments.

The shelter was known. Not compromised — the three small tells she kept at the door showed no sign of disturbance, no evidence of entry — but known in the sense that the commemoration had placed her face in the warden rotation queue, and a face in the rotation queue eventually resolved into a location, and a location eventually resolved into a visit. The amber shard's activation had produced a frequency signature detectable by Council sensors. Whether they had traced it to this specific shelter, she could not say. What she could say was that assuming they hadn't would be a mistake she could not afford.

She packed quickly. Not in panic — the difference showed in what she took. Panic took everything. She took only what could not be replaced and left the rest. The salvage kit with the false bottom. Her notation folio, kept in the inner lining of her coat — four years of work built as a variation on Solen's frequency shorthand, the markers shifted just enough that the system belonged to no one but her. Her tools. The Council-origin fragment was already beneath the flagstone near the door, and she left it there; a fragment under a flagstone read as salvage income, not evidence, and she needed it to read that way if the shelter was searched.

Before sealing the kit, she opened the folio and made a brief record. The date. The bearing and depth of the shard's retrieval. The encoding duration: 18 sec. Then the content, compressed into her own shorthand — her mother's structural grammar with the specific frequency markers for the suppression order subtracted, leaving only the structural fact of what Solen had found: the altered load figures, the suppressed flagging, the authorization signature that was absent. She wrote it the way she had trained herself to write in registered spaces — in fragments, connective tissue removed, subject unnamed. A record that would mean nothing to whoever found it. Everything to her when she needed to return.

She folded the folio back into her coat lining. The oilcloth parcel sat in the kit's false bottom without warmth. She pressed the panel closed with the flat of her palm and held it there — the wood cool, the grain faintly rough, the amber shard somewhere beneath both, silent.

She left the shelter without looking back. Looking back was the kind of thing she had trained herself not to do, and her left hand had already checked the latch twice before she cleared the threshold.

The Silt Markets ran along the Ven's eastern bank from the lower bridge approach down to where the river bent south and the stone embankment dissolved into mud. Canvas stalls on timber frames, some permanent enough to carry names — painted on boards, chalked on support posts — and most of them operating in the specific gap between the certified vendor marks the Council painted on corner posts and the actual contents of the cloth-lined trays beneath the awnings. Unlicensed stormglass. Chipped crystal shards with no frequency certification, no origin documentation, no Registry mark. Glass that moved from a salvager's kit to a handler's tray to a buyer's pocket without ever touching the system designed to track it.

Three years Vael had been running this market. She knew its rhythms — which stalls moved in the early morning before the Registry presence arrived, which ones stayed open through the afternoon because their operators had an arrangement with the clerk who covered this stretch, which ones shuttered without warning when someone upstream had flagged an audit. She knew which vendors nodded to her and which ones looked through her, and she knew the difference was not personal. It was operational. She was a reliable source of mid-grade salvage crystal, she paid in coin, and she did not ask about provenance. That was the entire content of her relationships here, and it had been sufficient.

The smell reached her before the stalls did — river silt and wet timber, and underneath both the sharp mineral bite of the solvent vendors used to clean their trays. The stormglass in the trays caught the low morning light and fractured it into small refractions that moved across the canvas awnings as wind came off the water. It was the kind of light that made things look like evidence without being evidence. She had learned, early, not to trust it.

Pell's stall sat near the midpoint of the vendor row, wedged between a woman who sold river-smoothed decorative glass with no frequency content and a man who moved certified low-grade recording crystal from a conspicuously stamped tray. The positioning was deliberate — Pell had explained it once, briefly, not waiting to be asked, the way a man explains a thing he has already decided you need to know. The certified vendor on one side made his stall look like the legitimate end of a legitimate operation. The decorative glass on the other gave him something to gesture toward if a conversation required a pivot. Between them, his unlicensed frequency glass sat in a canvas-lined tray that looked, at a distance, like the decorative glass next door.

She did not go directly to his stall.

Through the vendor row she moved the way she always moved through it — stopping at two stalls she had no business at, handling glass she had no intention of buying, letting her eyes do the work her body was not permitted to do openly. Near the river-bend end of the row, a man in a plain coat was working through the stalls with the particular quality of someone who was not shopping. No uniform, no Registry insignia, nothing that would read as official presence to someone not paying attention. But he moved with the efficiency of someone working a grid, and he noted each stall with the small, precise quality of attention that was not interest but assessment.

She marked him. His position, his direction, the pace at which he was covering the row. At his current rate he would reach Pell's stall in approximately twelve minutes. She had been standing at the decorative glass stall for forty seconds. She moved.

Pell was behind his tray when she arrived, which meant he had seen her coming and decided she was not a problem. That was itself information. He was a short man, heavyset, with hands that were careful in the specific way of someone who handled fragile things professionally — not precious, not delicate, just careful, the way a butcher is careful with a blade. He did not look up when she reached his tray.

"Frequency salvage," she said. It was not a question.

"Always." He turned a piece of amber-tinted glass with two fingers, examining its edge. "What range."

"Pre-Charter amber. Secondary register." She kept her voice at the level of ordinary commerce. Around them the market noise continued — flatbread from the vendor three stalls down, the river, two men arguing at the certified crystal stall about a certification mark one of them claimed was forged. "I'm not buying. I'm asking whether there's been movement in that range. Recent movement. In the last month."

Pell set the glass down. He picked up another piece — clearer, cooler in color, nothing like what she had described — and turned it in his fingers without looking at it. "Pre-Charter amber doesn't move," he said. "Hasn't for years. Council pulled it from circulation before most of my buyers were born. Anyone who has it is sitting on it." He paused. "Or hiding it."

"Or looking for it."

The glass stopped moving in his hands. Not dramatically — a small stillness, the kind invisible to anyone not watching for it. He set it down on the tray with the same care he'd used for the first piece.

"Someone's been asking," he said. "Not purchasing. Asking. Same question you're asking, more or less — whether there's been movement, whether anyone's seen pre-Charter amber come through the market. Three times in the last four months." He picked up a third piece, this one opaque, and ran his thumb along its edge. "Not a salvager. Knows the terminology, knows the market, but the hands are wrong. Archivist hands. Someone who handles glass professionally but not from the ground up."

Vael's hands were flat on the edge of his tray. The wood was rough under her palms — old timber, river-weathered, the grain raised by years of damp. She counted the grain without counting it, the way she counted things when she needed to keep the rest of herself still.

"Name," she said.

Pell turned the opaque glass over once more. "Nava," he said. "No family name offered. Didn't press for one."

Nava. Not a name she knew.

Not her mother's name — in the half-second before he answered her hands pressed harder against the tray's edge, the grain rough under her palms. That cost did not arrive. What arrived instead was the description — careful, specific, professional, not wanting to say it aloud — and it landed in a different place entirely, because that was not the description of someone searching for evidence. That was the description of someone who already knew what they were looking for and had decided, for their own reasons, not to name it in a market where names were evidence.

The river smell moved through the stall. The two men at the certified crystal stall had stopped arguing.

"Where," she said.

Pell was quiet for the length of time it took him to set the opaque glass down and align it with the tray's edge. Then: "Lower Registry annex. Overflow storage. Third level below the main reading room." He said it with the manner of a man who had just surrendered something he had not intended to and was deciding whether to be troubled by it. "She works there. Or she uses the space for work. I don't ask."

Vael took a coin from her coat pocket and placed it on the tray beside the opaque glass. Not payment for information — payment for a transaction that had not occurred, which was a different thing and which both of them understood. It meant: you sold me decorative glass and I paid for it and we are done.

"The man in the plain coat," she said. "Working the row from the south end. He'll reach you in about eight minutes."

Pell did not look toward the south end of the row. "I know him," he said. "He comes through twice a month. He's not interested in me."

"He wasn't," she said, and left it there, because the rest of it — none of it was information she was going to leave in a market where names were evidence — all of that was information she was not going to leave in a market where names were evidence.

She moved back into the vendor row without changing her pace.

The man in the plain coat was six stalls away, working north. He did not look at her. She did not look at him. She stopped at the certified crystal stall and spent ninety seconds examining a tray of low-grade recording glass with the bearing of someone mildly considering a purchase, and when she moved on he was four stalls away and still not looking at her, and she turned at the end of the row and walked back toward the embankment without stopping.

The cold came off the river hard at the embankment steps — the Ven at low water carried a rawness that was mostly clay and iron, and when the wind shifted you caught the residue of the cleaning solvent from the stalls above, sharp underneath the rest. The market noise fell away behind her. She did not look back.

A name. A location — the lower Registry annex, overflow storage, not where you would expect to find someone operating outside the Council's apparatus, which was probably the point. Pell had given it to her with the look of a man who had just made himself a thread and was hoping she would forget where she'd pulled it.

She would not forget. She pocketed the location alongside the name alongside the description — careful, specific, professional, archivist hands, not wanting to say it aloud — and walked back into the market noise.

The shard was in her kit. She had not slept. The plain-coated clerk was still working his grid.

None of this was stopping her.

The lower Registry annex sat at the end of a service corridor that the main building's plans listed as a ventilation access route — either a filing error from the original construction survey or the specific kind of mislabeling that persisted because no one with authority had found a reason to correct it. The entrance was a door with no Registry insignia, set into stone that had been damp long enough to leave a tide-line of mineral deposit at knee height. The air in the stairwell below was cold in the way of rooms that had been sealed and reopened many times — not fresh cold, not outdoor cold, but a settled underground cold, the kind that stone holds after years sealed from sun and wind and gives back only in degrees.

The third level was storage. Raw timber shelving, floor to ceiling, packed with archival overflow that the main reading room produced when its classification system could not decide what something was — not active enough for a primary index position, not dormant enough for suppression, sitting in the institutional limbo where materials landed when someone had once considered them important and no one had gotten around to reconsidering. Crystal trays stacked in cloth sleeves. Folio boxes with handwritten labels that matched no classification system she recognized. The stormglass conduit running along the upper wall was older than the annex — older than the current Registry building, possibly — and it hummed at a frequency she felt in her back teeth before she heard it with her ears.

At the far end of the room, Nava sat at a table pushed against the shelving to make space for the materials spread across it. She did not look up when Vael came down the stairs. She was a small woman, perhaps sixty, with the particular stillness of someone who had learned to make themselves inconspicuous in institutional spaces — her hands rested on a folio box without fidgeting, without adjustment, settled into a position they had occupied so many times they required no thought. Archivist hands, as Pell had said: the slight callus on the right index finger from years of turning crystal trays, the deliberate placement of each finger when she moved something fragile.

Vael stopped at the foot of the stairs.

"You've been asking about pre-Charter amber," she said.

Nava's hands did not stop moving. She turned the folio box to its side and read the label on its spine. "I've been asking about a lot of things," she said. "For a long time." She set the box down and looked up. Her eyes were the grey of river clay, and they moved over Vael with the same precise, unhurried quality as her hands on the archive materials — not assessing threat, assessing something else. Whether the thing in front of her was what she had been waiting for, or something that only looked like it. "You found Pell."

"He found you first."

"He found me because I let him." She gestured at the chair on the near side of the table — an invitation and a test in the same motion, because sitting meant committing to the conversation, and she wanted to see whether Vael would commit. "Sit down. I want to see what you have."

Vael sat. She did not take the shard from the kit. Not yet.

"Show me yours first," she said.

Nava looked at her for a moment. Then something in her expression shifted — not softening, not warming, but settling, a slow release of tension held too long, the way a timber beam sounds when the weight it has been resisting finally transfers. She reached beneath the table and brought up a folio box that was different from the others on the shelving — older, its corners reinforced with a strip of oilcloth applied by hand, its label written in a shorthand Vael did not recognize at first and then did, in the way she recognized things in salvage work: not all at once, but in layers, structure becoming legible before content.

Not Solen's shorthand. But built from the same grammar. The same structural markers, the same frequency notation, the same way of compressing a suppression order into a symbol that looked, to anyone trained on the current Registry system, like a routine filing date.

Vael kept her hands flat on the table.

Nava opened the box. Inside were folios, dozens of them, each labeled in the same compressed shorthand, each dated. The earliest she could read was seventeen years ago. The most recent was six weeks back.

"I started keeping a separate record in the third year after the Bridge collapse," Nava said. "When I understood that the discrepancies I was finding in the primary archive were not errors." She lifted one of the folios and set it on the table between them, open to a page dense with notation. "There are four hundred and twelve of them. Discrepancies between what the primary index records and what the secondary frequency band contains. Alterations. Suppressions. Reclassifications with no authorization signature." She touched the edge of the folio page with one finger — not pointing at anything specific, just touching it, the way you touched something you had carried a long time and were not yet ready to put down. "Materials filed under maintenance logs. Under fiscal reviews. Under infrastructure assessments that no one was ever going to read twice."

Four hundred and twelve. The number sat in the cold air of the room without moving.

"You've been building this across seventeen years," Vael said.

"I've been building it since I understood what it was." Nava's voice was flat and even, stripped of anything that might be called performance — the voice of someone who had said the next part to herself so many times that saying it aloud to another person required no particular preparation. "The catalogue is complete. The discrepancy record is complete. What it has never had is the primary source material to anchor it — the original encoding, the source crystal, something that predates the first re-indexing and can prove that the alterations were made to something that already existed."

She looked at Vael's kit.

"Pre-Charter amber," she said. "Secondary register. Eighteen seconds."

The conduit in the upper wall hummed. Vael's back teeth registered it before the rest of her did.

"You knew about the shard," Vael said.

"I knew there was a shard. I didn't know who had it." Nava closed the folio and returned it to the box with the same careful economy she brought to everything. "I knew Solen had encoded something in the secondary band before the first re-indexing. I knew the primary archive had been altered to make it unfindable. I knew that if the shard still existed, it would be in salvage circulation — because the Council's archivists don't know to look in the secondary band, which means they wouldn't have known to pull it from the salvage pool." She paused. "Solen knew that too. I think that was the point."

Vael did not move for a moment. The room's cold pressed against the back of her neck, the damp chill of old stone giving nothing back. She thought about her mother's hands in the recording, moving across the encoding surface — steady, past surprise, past the moment when the work becomes grief and you encode anyway. The cut at eighteen seconds. The wall that was not natural degradation.

She opened the kit, took out the oilcloth parcel, and set it on the table between them.

Nava did not reach for it immediately. She looked at it the way you looked at something you had been waiting for long enough that the waiting had become its own kind of presence, and its arrival required a moment of adjustment.

Then she unwrapped it with both hands, careful, the oilcloth folded back in sections rather than pulled away, and the amber shard lay between them on the table, warm from the kit's interior, the frequency signature in its core a faint amber pulse just visible in the cold grey light of the storage room.

"There are things in the catalogue I cannot release," Nava said, not looking up from the shard. "Not yet. Not without the authorization chain being intact, and the authorization chain requires materials still classified at a level I cannot access without triggering a review that would end this before it started." She turned the shard once, slowly, with two fingers. "What I can give you is the discrepancy record. The four hundred and twelve. With the primary source material in the shard as anchor, the discrepancy record becomes a provable pattern rather than an archivist's private notation." She set the shard down. "That is what I have been waiting to be able to say seventeen years."

Vael looked at the catalogue box. Seventeen years of notation in a shorthand built from the same grammar as her mother's system — not coincidence, and not something she was going to ask about directly, because asking directly was not how you learned things in this room.

"The authorization chain," she said. "What's missing from it."

"The suppression order signature." Nava's voice did not change register. "The original filing. The one that initiated the first re-indexing. Filed without an authorization signature, which means it was filed by someone who knew it would not be questioned —

someone with enough institutional standing that the absence of a signature was itself a kind of signature." She looked at Vael. "You know whose seal is on the corner."

Vael knew. She had known since the eighteen seconds ended and she sat in the shelter counting the grain of the floor plank. She did not say it aloud. Neither did Nava.

The conduit hummed. The shard sat between them, warm.

She had a name. A location — the lower Registry annex, overflow storage, not where you would expect to find someone operating outside the Council's apparatus, which was probably the point. And now she had four hundred and twelve discrepancies in a folio box that smelled of seventeen years of cold stone, and a woman who had been building the case in the dark for longer than Vael had been looking for it.

"You could bring this out," Vael said. "With the shard as anchor, you have enough to —"

"I'm not leaving." Nava said it the way she said everything — flat, carrying, without performance. She was refolding the oilcloth around the shard, her hands moving with the same economy as before. "That's not what I'm offering you. I stay in the annex. I stay in the institution. I continue to be the archivist who files things correctly and maintains the overflow catalogue and gives no one a reason to look at me." She set the wrapped shard back on the table and pushed it toward Vael. "That is not timidity. That is the work. The moment I leave, the access closes. The moment I become visible, the catalogue becomes a target rather than a record." She looked at Vael directly. "You need someone inside. I am inside. That is what I have to offer you, and it is not negotiable."

Vael did not reach for the shard immediately. She looked at the folio box, at the seventeen years of notation in the cold grey light, at Nava's hands folded on the table with the stillness of someone who had already made every decision that mattered and was now simply waiting to see whether the person across from her would understand them.

She thought about what it cost to stay. Not to leave — she knew the cost of leaving, had been paying it for four years in shelters and salvage markets and a notation folio kept in her coat lining. Leaving was a cost she understood. Staying was a different arithmetic: staying meant being seen and not being seen, meant being useful to an institution you were quietly dismantling, meant filing things correctly for seventeen years while the thing you were actually doing lived in a folio box beneath the table. Staying meant trusting that the archive you were building in the dark would eventually find the hands it needed.

It had found them. She picked up the shard.

"The authorization chain," she said. "If I find the original suppression order — the filing, not the copy —"

"Bring it here." Nava's hands unfolded and refolded on the table. "Don't bring it anywhere else first. Don't encode a copy until we've established the anchor sequence. The shard's frequency signature has to be the first link in the chain or the whole record reads as reconstructed rather than original." She paused. "You understand the difference."

Vael understood the difference. The difference was the gap between a provable pattern and a document that merely looked like one. The difference was everything.

"I'll come back," she said.

Nava nodded once. She did not say: I'll be here. She did not say: I've been waiting. She reached under the table and returned the folio box to its place on the shelf, and by the time Vael reached the bottom of the stairs she was already bent over the table again, her hands moving across a new set of materials with the steadiness of someone returned to the only work that had ever mattered.

The stairwell was cold. The mineral tide-line at knee height caught the light from the upper corridor in a thin white line. Vael climbed the stairs, passed through the unmarked door, and stepped back into the service corridor — the shard warm in her kit, the folio box's contents sitting in her mind with the solid mass of four hundred and twelve things she had not known this morning she would be carrying.

She did not look back at the door.

Chapter 6

The shelter still held her shape.

Before anything else registered, Davan clocked the specific depression pressed into the pallet's straw — the faint body-warmth not yet fully surrendered to the cold stone around it. Three seconds in the doorway without moving. Not hesitation. Orientation. He kept his hands at his sides.

The clay jar was gone. The oilcloth wrapper from the salvage kit — noted in the preliminary profile, filed then as incidental — absent from the hook near the door. A single cup remained on the shelf, positioned at its far left edge the way objects end up when something beside them has been removed and nothing moved back to fill the gap. She had packed in stages, not in panic. One pass for essentials, a second for whatever she had decided she could not leave behind. The cup was what the two passes had left unclaimed.

He moved into the room and kept his hands to himself.

The hearth gave him the first confirmation. Crouching beside it, he held his palm two inches above the ash — not touching, just reading the differential. Faint. Within the hour, possibly two. A fire left to burn down to nothing on its own meant she had not fled. She had departed. The distinction mattered.

From that crouch, he read the rest of the room.

The floor planks near the door were worn in a path running between the entrance and the shelf — not toward the pallet, not toward the hearth, but the shelf, which told him she had spent her time here working rather than resting. Four anchor points marked the shelf's surface where objects had sat long enough to leave slight impressions in the wood. Four objects, regularly accessed, now gone. The cup was not among the four. The cup had been placed, not habituated.

He stood and turned toward the wall beside the pallet.

At approximately chest height, there was a mark on the plaster — a faint darkening, the kind left by a forehead or a shoulder returning to the same spot over weeks until the surface showed it. He had seen this before, in rooms where people had been waiting a long time. It was different from a hiding room. Hiding rooms carried a compressed pressure, everything directed toward exits. This room had been a place where someone had stopped expecting to leave — and then, at some point recently, had left anyway.

The notation on the floor nearly escaped him. A single line of what looked like freight shorthand, chalked faintly near the pallet's edge, partially smeared by a boot heel. Not hers. The smear was too deliberate — she would not have obscured her own notation. Someone else had been here before him, recently enough that the chalk still showed pale rather than ground to dust. He committed it to memory without moving his eyes too quickly, the way he had been trained, and continued his circuit of the room.

The loose flagstone near the door was the last thing.

He had almost walked past it. The edge sat slightly proud of its neighbors — not much, three or four millimeters — and the surrounding stones showed faint scored marks where something had been slid across them recently, the grit disturbed in a direction that meant the flagstone had been lifted and replaced in haste. Not sealed. Just set back in place and abandoned.

He looked at it for a moment.

Then he knelt and lifted it.

The fragment was smaller than he had expected. Not the amber shard — he had been briefed on the amber shard's dimensions, and this was not it. A secondary piece, darker, Council-origin glass by the density and the particular grey cast of its surface, the kind pulled from standardized production rather than salvaged from pre-Charter sources. It rested in a shallow depression lined with a scrap of oilcloth, and the oilcloth was clean, which meant the fragment had been stored here deliberately rather than dropped in haste.

She had not meant to leave it. The amber shard was gone, the notation folio was gone, the four regularly accessed objects from the shelf were gone. This fragment was what the second pass had missed when she was moving fast and the first pass had already claimed everything she knew she needed.

He should have set it down.

Instead his hand closed around it — the weight settling into his palm, the decision trailing behind the motion like a shadow that arrives late.

Four seconds.

The calibration chamber arrived with the specific clarity of something that had been waiting to be seen: pale stone walls, the particular quality of light coming through narrow windows set high in a Registry subfloor, a table with frequency equipment laid out in close, practiced order — each instrument within reach of the next, nothing wasted. A woman's hands — not young, not old, moving with a sureness that had come from long habit — working across the surface of a crystal he recognized as pre-Charter secondary register.

She was saying something. He caught the shape of it but not the words — the consonants eaten by whatever had degraded the recording, leaving only the stress and the rise of her voice, the urgency in the vowels. She was not frightened. She was documenting. The recording knew the difference, and the difference lived in every aspect of how she held herself at the table — spine straight, one hand steadying the crystal while the other moved, the body of someone who had made her decision before she sat down and was now carrying it through.

The shard sealed against him.

Not gradually. Between one heartbeat and the next, the warmth in his palm simply stopped. The crystal went cold and closed, and he was back in the empty shelter with the flagstone lifted and the ash cooling in the hearth and the cup on the shelf and nothing else.

He stayed kneeling for a long time, the flagstone's cold edge pressing through his trousers, the weight of the fragment still in his closed hand.

The fragment was Council-origin glass. Eleven years of service had given him the density, the weight, the specific thermal behavior of standardized archival crystal in his hands. This was that. This was the glass the Council produced and distributed and tracked through its own systems, sitting in a hidden space beneath a flagstone in a shelter belonging to a woman the Council had classified as inactive — deliberately hidden, and it had played four seconds of something that was not standard archival content before sealing against him as though it had decided he was not the intended audience. The outer layer of any pre-Charter encoding carried a threshold: enough to register that something had been recorded, not enough to reach what the recording held. Four seconds was not an opening. It was a boundary.

The woman's hands at the table. The frequency equipment. The particular quality of her stillness.

Council glass did not encode testimony. Council glass was for institutional records —
structural assessments, frequency logs, administrative documentation. What he had just
held was someone in a calibration chamber doing something the Council's own glass was
not supposed to be used for, and the glass had been here, hidden, and she had not taken it
with her, and the assignment he had been given was to locate a woman named Vael who
had been classified as inactive and file a full location report including the twelfth field.

He put the fragment in his coat pocket.

He replaced the flagstone.

One more look at the room — the cup, the hearth, the worn path between door and
shelf, the mark on the wall at chest height — and then he left, pulling the timber door
shut behind him.

His rented room above the cartographer's workshop was cold when he arrived. He had left
no fire, which was his habit on surveillance assignments — a cold room was a room that
had not been waited in, and he had learned early that the quality of waiting was legible in
the air of a place if you knew what to look for.

He lit the candle stub on the table and sat down.

The reporting form was in the document sleeve where he had left it: eleven fields
completed, the twelfth still blank. Three days he had carried it that way — the twelfth
field empty, which was a technical omission and not yet a formal violation, and he had
kept those two things separate in his mind without once sitting down to examine the
difference.

He took the form out of the sleeve and set it on the table.

Field twelve: location. The shelter above the basement brewer, Underbrim, alley entrance, timber door with the gap at the bottom. He knew the address. He had been

standing in that room twenty minutes ago. He could write it in the time it took to uncap the ink.

The Council-origin glass sat in his coat pocket. He could feel its weight against his ribs — cold, sealed, carrying four seconds of something that was not administrative documentation. He had been given an assignment. The assignment had a form, and the form had twelve fields, and he had completed eleven of them, and the twelfth waited.

The woman at the table in the calibration chamber had been documenting something. He did not know what. Four seconds of vowel-shape without consonants, a rhythm that told him she was not frightened, and the image of hands moving across pre-Charter glass with a steadiness born of long practice — someone who knew exactly what she was doing and had chosen to do it anyway.

He picked up the form.

He held it over the candle flame.

The paper caught at the corner first, the way paper always did, the flame moving inward in no hurry at all. He held it until the heat reached his fingers, then set the burning edge down on the stone floor beside the table and watched it finish. The ash came out grey and complete. He moved it apart with the toe of his boot so it would not hold its shape.

The negative-result form was in the second sleeve — standard language, pre-printed, requiring only a date and a signature and a brief notation of search parameters. Subject location not established. Shelter identified at preliminary coordinates vacated prior to arrival. No secondary materials recovered. He wrote this in the same hand he used for every form, the same pressure, the same spacing, signed it, dated it, and put it in the reporting sleeve.

The candle had burned down past the hour mark.

He sat at the table with both hands flat on the surface. The Council-origin glass was in his pocket. The negative-result report was in the sleeve. The ash of the location form lay distributed across the floor beside his chair. Three Charter statutes violated, and he was still naming what he had done as a sequence of separate actions — each one small, each one already behind him before he had fully weighed it.

He did not know where she was. He did not know what lived inside four seconds of a calibration chamber. What he knew was that the glass was Council-origin, had been hidden, had encoded something it was not designed to encode — and that whoever had commissioned his assignment had known the glass existed before she found it. The preliminary briefing had specified the secondary hiding location, had noted the flagstone specifically, which meant the briefing had been constructed from prior surveillance, which meant someone had been in that room before him and had left the glass in place rather than recovering it. That was a choice. Choices had reasons. No reason had been given to him.

The assignment was not what he had been told it was.

He had destroyed the form that would have told them where she went.

Below, the cartographer's workshop had been dark for hours. Outside, the Plateau's lower residential tier had gone quiet in the way of a place where the night watch made their rounds on a schedule — not true stillness, but a held-breath version of it, the street sounds dropping off at intervals and starting again, movement managed rather than absent.

His hands did not leave the table.

Chapter 7

He had left the timber door exactly as he found it.

That was what Davan noticed first when he came back — not a compulsion, not anything he would have named that way, but the room was cold and the ash was distributed and the negative-result form sat in the sleeve and none of it resolved into a category he recognized. He stood at the table in his rented room above the cartographer's workshop, hands flat on the surface, the candle burned to nothing, and he moved back through the shelter the way he moved through any room: the cup, the hearth, the worn path between door and shelf, the mark on the wall at chest height where someone had pressed a palm for years, the loose flagstone sitting slightly proud of the floor. The shelter had given off cold ash when he first stepped in, and under it something older — not food, not recently, but the residue of habitation pressed into stone across a long span of time, the walls and floor holding what bodies leave behind when they have nowhere else to go.

The briefing had specified the flagstone.

He had been turning this over since he left. Not the glass — the glass was in his coat pocket, cold now, sealed, and he had already understood what it meant, or understood enough that the rest was a question of time. What he kept returning to was the briefing. The flagstone had appeared in the preliminary notes. Secondary hiding location, notated with enough detail — dimensions, depth, the precise offset from the south wall — that whoever wrote it had been standing on that stone when they did it. They had assessed the flagstone's contents and chosen to leave them there. Not missed. Not overlooked. Left.

Someone had been in that room before him. Someone had read the glass, or known what it contained without reading it, and had decided that Davan should find it in place rather than find an empty flagstone and an assignment that made clean procedural sense.

He had been given an assignment. The assignment had been built around information that required prior surveillance. The prior surveillance had produced knowledge of the glass, and the glass had been left, and he had been sent.

He sat down.

The Council-origin glass was in his coat pocket. The negative-result form was in the sleeve. The ash of the location form lay distributed across the floor beside his chair, grey and fine, already beginning to disperse in the draft from the ill-fitting window frame. He was in violation of three Charter statutes and had not yet begun to name what he was doing as anything other than a series of individual actions, each of which had arrived before he had fully decided to take it.

The glass pressed warm against his ribs.

He pushed his thumb against it through the coat fabric. Cold. Sealed. Carrying four seconds of a woman in a calibration chamber doing something the Council's own glass was not supposed to be used for.

Four seconds of something that was not administrative documentation — her hands moving across pre-Charter crystal, each adjustment small and unhesitating, the kind of movement that no longer requires thought. The glass had sealed against him after four seconds as though it had decided he was not the intended audience. He was not the intended audience. The intended audience was a woman named Vael — classified inactive, somewhere in Bridgefall tonight that was not the shelter above the basement brewer in Underbrim.

He did not know where she was. He knew the assignment was not what he had been told it was. He had destroyed the form that would have told them where she went.

The room was very quiet. The cartographer's workshop below had been dark for hours. Outside, Bridgefall's lower residential tier made its nighttime sounds — the cooling stone of the Plateau's lower tier ticking and settling as the temperature dropped, the occasional footfall of someone cutting through the lane below, the kind of quiet that had edges to it. His hands did not move from the table. The wood beneath his palms was grained and slightly uneven, roughened from years of use, taking no impression from his weight.

There was a chalk notation he had found near the pallet. Partially smeared by a boot heel, freight shorthand style. Not her writing — the pressure was wrong, the angle different from the notations in her folio. Someone else had been in that room. Someone who used freight shorthand and had smeared their own notation before leaving, which meant they had realized they'd left it and had tried to remove it and had not fully succeeded, which meant they had noticed it on the way out.

Two visitors before him. One who had assessed the flagstone and left the glass in place. One who had left a chalk notation and tried to erase it.

He was not the first person the assignment had sent to that room. He was the one the glass had been left for — or not for, specifically, but left available to.

He thought about the teacup.

Not this room's cup — the cup in the shelter, sitting on the shelf, the single cup in a room where someone had been living alone for longer than she'd planned. He had noticed it the way he noticed everything in a room: involuntarily, before he had language for it. The rim was worn thin where it met the mouth, the glaze gone dull there, rubbed back to something closer to clay. She had been in that room for a long time. She had stopped expecting to leave. He had stood in front of that shelf for perhaps three seconds longer than the inventory required, noted it, moved on, and had been unable to stop returning to it since.

He thought about a different cup, in a different room, three years into his tenure. A woman in the lower wards who had already set it on the table when he arrived, the ceramic still faintly steaming, the gesture so habitual it had preceded any assessment of whether he was someone worth the courtesy. He had said no thank you. He had filed the report accurately and completely.

Fourteen days later her name had appeared in the re-calibration processing log he received as routine administrative correspondence. He had noted it. He had continued.

What his memory kept was not her face. It was the specific weight of the teacup she had already set out — the cup set at the near edge of the table, within reach of the chair, still holding the faint warmth of recent water.

The candle had been dead for an hour. He sat in the dark with his hands flat on the table and the glass cold in his pocket and the ash of the location form distributed at his feet, grey against the floorboards. He did not move. Outside, the city held its nighttime quiet. He was in violation of three Charter statutes and had not yet begun to name what he was doing as anything other than a series of individual actions.

But the series had a direction.

He had not filled in field twelve. He had burned the form. He had filed the negative-result documentation. He had kept the glass. The assignment was not what he had been told it was. The glass had been left for someone who was not him. The briefing had been constructed from prior surveillance, and the prior surveillance had produced knowledge of the glass, and the glass had been left in place — which meant someone with access to the briefing materials had decided that Davan should find it rather than find nothing.

Someone had wanted him to hold four seconds of a woman in a calibration chamber.

He did not know why. He did not know what the four seconds meant. What he had was a rhythm that told him she was not frightened, and hands moving across pre-Charter crystal without pause or correction, and a voice stripped of its consonants by degradation so that what arrived was vowel-structure without attribution — careful and deliberate and doing something the Council's glass was not designed to do.

The glass had sealed against him.

It was encoded for someone else.

He sat with that for a long time. The cold from the window frame had moved into the room properly now, settling against the back of his neck, finding the gap between collar and skin. He registered it the way he registered the ash at his feet and the sealed crystal in his pocket — each one a thing that had already happened, already fixed, past any undoing.

Then he stood, left the candle unlit, and crossed to the window. Below, the Plateau's lower tier lay dark and quiet, the archive annex wall catching a pale wash of quarter-moon across the stormglass, grey and flat. The glass was cold in his pocket. The series of individual actions had a direction, and the ash at his feet had already begun to settle into the cracks between the floorboards.

Field twelve: location. He had known the address. He could have written it in the time it took to uncap the ink.

He had burned the form instead.

He stayed at the window without moving for a long time, and the city below held its quiet, and the sealed crystal held its secret, and the ash lay undisturbed on the floor.

Chapter 8

The briefing form arrived through standard routing, and that was the first thing wrong with it. Davan's name sat in the assignment field, Brek's in the co-investigator field. He filed the confirmation in his sleeve without lifting his eyes from the table. The ink on his negative-result documentation had barely dried. Someone had moved fast.

The operational briefing room occupied a narrow corridor off the Spire's third tier — not a room anyone was assigned to, more a room that existed between assignments, its walls lined with a single row of document cradles and a table long enough for four people who preferred distance. Davan arrived first. The gas lamp above the table was already burning, which meant someone had been there before him and left it lit, which meant the room had been prepared rather than incidentally occupied. He positioned himself at the far end and remained standing.

Brek entered two minutes after the fourth bell, exactly when the form had specified. He carried a leather case, the clasp already undone — the top flap loose, the contents ordered and waiting. Which was wrong, because the assignment had been issued that morning. Either Brek had received earlier notice, or Brek kept a case that was always packed.

"I was hoping it would be you," Brek said. He set the case on the table and opened it in one motion, the lid back before the latch had stopped swinging. Inside: two sets of documentation forms in separate sleeves, a frequency reader no larger than a thumb joint, two field report blanks, and a small glass vial of the amber sealing compound used to close completed stormglass after audit. "The Vael case has been sitting in general monitoring for three days. I told them it needed a second set of eyes."

Davan looked at the vial. Not at the documentation forms — he already knew what they contained. Not at the frequency reader — that was equipment used to verify whether a subject had been carrying active stormglass. He looked at the vial.

"Whose idea was the pairing?" he said.

"Mine, technically." Brek closed the case. "Though I imagine someone above agreed. You've been running general monitoring in the lower district for three weeks. I've been running the secondary surveillance review. It made sense to consolidate."

It made sense. Davan turned this over. It made sense. Davan looked at the case on the table — clasp already loose, for an assignment issued that morning. Brek's secondary surveillance review would contain everything Davan had filed — his negative-result form, the accurate and complete negative-result form that stated, in field four, that the subject's shelter had been vacated prior to arrival, and that, in field twelve, contained nothing, because field twelve was location, and field twelve had been left blank, and then the form had been burned and a second form filed in its place, accurate in every field except the one that mattered.

"What's your read on the case?" Davan said.

Brek sat. He had the ease of a man for whom briefing rooms had long since become unremarkable — the table, the lamp, the document cradles just the furniture of the work, not its occasion. "Pre-Charter glass in the lower district, active frequency signature, duration eighteen seconds. Someone in the salvage market with archival training. Your negative result on the shelter is consistent with a subject who moves frequently." He looked at Davan steadily, his attention even and without suspicion, taking in the room the way a man does when he already knows what he expects to find. "I want to run the re-calibration assessment on the lower-ward family we flagged last week. Before we pursue the primary subject. It's been sitting in the queue."

"The pamphlet reader."

"The pamphlet reader. Her daughter, specifically. The reading material was resistance-adjacent — nothing that would hold under formal review, but enough to warrant a preliminary assessment." Brek's tone carried the specific quality of someone discussing a maintenance task: not unkind, not indifferent, simply accurate. "I'd like you to observe. Given that we're working the same district, it makes sense to have consistent documentation."

Davan looked at the wall behind Brek's head. The plaster had been painted over twice in recent years; the seams showed where the layers had cracked and separated, the older color bleeding through at the edges.

"All right," he said.

The family lived in the Warrens, in a building constructed against the gorge wall and then partially into it, so that the back room's far wall was the gorge's raw stone. The cold that came off it in winter was a different quality of cold than the cold in the street — stiller, older, the kind that pressed against the skin from within the rock itself rather than from wind and weather. Three rooms. The main room smelled of cooked grain and tallow, and underneath those, the wet mineral smell of old stone. The gorge base held moisture the way it held cold: permanently, regardless of season.

The father was standing when they arrived. He had placed himself between the door and the table in the manner of someone who had been standing there for some time before they knocked, who had decided in advance where he would be. His hands were at his sides. The mother sat at the table — she had sat down recently; Davan could see it in the specific quality of her stillness, the way a person goes still when they have made themselves sit rather than stand because standing would have communicated something they did not want to communicate. Two children were in the back room. Davan could hear them not moving, which was the particular sound of children who had been told to stay and were staying with the total focused attention that children brought to instructions issued in a voice they recognized as serious.

Brek set his case on the table beside the mother's hands without asking. He opened it and removed the frequency reader first, then set it aside — a deliberate ordering, unhurried, each piece placed where he could reach it — and the first thing he actually used was not the reader but a folded form, which he placed on the table in front of the father.

"This is a preliminary assessment notice," Brek said. "It explains the process. I'd like you to read it before we begin." He paused. "There's no urgency. Take the time you need."

The father read it. Davan watched the specific way the man's hands did not move from his sides while he read, the way he had decided not to pick the form up, so that reading it required him to lean forward slightly over the table — a small act of refusal that Brek either did not notice or chose not to acknowledge.

The mother looked at Davan. He met her eyes and then looked at the wall.

"The assessment is for our daughter," the father said. He had not asked it as a question.

"The materials recovered from your residence indicated that your daughter had been in contact with frequency-adjacent content outside the standard archival register," Brek said. He said it the way a physician might describe a symptom: accurately, without alarm, his voice level in the way of a man who had learned that level voices settled frightened rooms. "The assessment is a precaution. It addresses only the affected frequency range. She will not experience discomfort."

The mother said: "What does it do to her?"

Brek looked at her. His expression was the expression of someone who had been asked this question before and had a genuine answer prepared, an answer he believed. "The re-calibration process works on the frequency register the way a lens works on light — it adjusts how certain inputs are processed. Your daughter will not lose her memories. She will simply find that certain materials, certain frequencies, no longer produce the same kind of engagement. It's a very narrow adjustment."

Davan looked at the floor. The floorboards were worn in a path between the door and the far wall, wood gone soft and pale where feet had crossed it daily for years. He looked at it the way he looked at everything in a room: before he had language for it, as information that arrived before the question that would have prompted him to look.

The daughter was brought out from the back room. She was perhaps eleven, with the watchful quality of a child who had learned to read adult rooms accurately and was reading this one. She looked at Brek's case first, then at Brek, then at her father's hands. She sat in the chair her mother had vacated.

Brek worked carefully, explaining each step before he performed it. He told the girl what the frequency reader would feel like against her temple — cool, he said, like a glass left in a window — and he was right, or he had been told he was right by someone who had felt it. He told her the process would take approximately four minutes. He told her she could ask him to stop at any time.

She did not ask him to stop.

Davan stood at the edge of the room and watched. The frequency reader produced no sound. The girl sat in the chair with the stillness of someone who had decided to endure rather than resist, which was a different quality of stillness than her father's. Her hands rested in her lap. At some point during the four minutes, her expression shifted in a way that was not pain and was not sleep but was something between them — a quality of absence, brief and complete, like the moment after a stormglass encoding fades and the crystal returns to neutral.

Brek removed the reader. He made a notation on his form. He looked at the girl closely, confirming whatever he needed to confirm.

"That's everything," he said. He was speaking to the girl, not to her parents. "You did very well."

The girl nodded. She looked at her hands.

The mother, who had been standing against the far wall for the duration of the four minutes, came to her daughter and placed her hands on the girl's shoulders. She looked at Brek. "Is she — will she remember —"

"She'll remember the morning," Brek said. He was already closing his case. "She'll remember this room, this conversation. The adjustment is to the frequency register, not to event memory." He looked at the mother directly. "She'll be fine. I want you to know that I understand this is difficult. The assessment is a precaution, not a judgment."

The mother said: "Thank you. For explaining it."

She meant it. Davan could hear that she meant it — something Davan had not expected: she looked at Brek directly, not at the floor, and her hands, which had been pressed flat against the wall behind her, opened at her sides. She was thanking Brek for the explanation, for the patience, for the fact that he had told her daughter she could ask him to stop.

Brek said: "Of course."

They left. On the walkway outside, Davan completed the accompanying documentation, his handwriting steady in the cold gorge air, the form accurate and complete in every field. He filed it because the form was accurate.

Brek walked beside him toward the Shelf stairs. "She'll be all right," he said. Not to Davan specifically — to the air, the way a person said something they needed to hear said aloud. "The adjustment is genuinely narrow. I've seen cases where it wasn't — where the calibration ran wider than intended. This one was clean."

Davan said nothing.

"It's harder when they're young," Brek said. "But it's also cleaner. The frequency register is less established. Less to work against." He glanced at Davan. "You look like you need a drink."

The tavern sat in the market district on a street running between a cooperage and a cloth merchant — the kind of street that existed to connect two other streets rather than to be a destination itself. Inside, the air smelled of sawdust and barley wine gone sharp from long use. Brek bought the drinks without asking what Davan wanted, which meant he already knew, which meant they had accumulated habits without naming them.

Davan held the cup. He did not drink from it immediately.

"The Vael case," Brek said. He was looking at the surface of the table. It was a different table than the one in the briefing room — older, more marked, the kind of surface that had absorbed years of other people's work and held none of it. "I've been looking at the frequency signature. Pre-Charter secondary register, eighteen seconds active duration. That's not salvage. That's a deliberate encoding." He turned the cup in his hands. "Someone's been building something."

"The negative result on the shelter is consistent with a subject who moves frequently," Davan said. His own words from the briefing room, returned.

"Consistent with," Brek agreed. "But the signature duration is too controlled for incidental activation. Eighteen seconds is a specific choice. Long enough to encode a substantial fragment. Short enough to read as ambient noise on a standard sweep." He looked at Davan. "Your read?"

Davan thought about the glass in his pocket. The glass that had been warm when he found it. The glass that had given him four seconds of a woman in a calibration chamber before it sealed itself against him — before it decided, or was decided, that he was not the person it had been left for.

"Someone with archival training," he said. "Pre-Charter familiarity. Probably operating alone."

"That's my read too." Brek drank. He set the cup down and leaned back the way a man does when he has run every thread he can think to pull and found them all consistent. "The resistance networks have been quiet since the commemoration. This doesn't read like a network operation. It reads like a private investigation." He set the cup down. "Which is more concerning, in some ways. A network has structure. A single operator with pre-Charter glass and archival training is harder to anticipate."

Harder to anticipate. Davan turned this over. She was harder to anticipate because she had been moving for longer than anyone had been watching, because she had built something in the secondary frequency band where the Council's archivists did not know to look, because the glass she carried had been encoded for her specifically and would not open for anyone else.

"You look tired," Brek said. He was watching Davan the way he had watched the girl in the chair, the way he had watched the mother when she asked her question — the same attention, turned without calculation toward whatever was in front of him. It was not performed. Davan had known Brek for a decade and had never once caught him performing concern he did not feel.

"I'm fine," Davan said.

"You're not," Brek said, without judgment. "But you will be. You always are."

Davan looked at his cup. The rim was worn in the way of something used daily and washed without care, the glaze thinning at the edge. He thought about a different cup, on a different table, set out before he arrived. He thought about the weight of hospitality offered in a room that was about to stop being someone's room.

He drank.

His rented room above the cartographer's workshop was dark when he returned. He left the candle unlit. He sat at the table in the dark of a room that had been empty for hours, cold from the ill-fitting window frame settled into the corners. Across the street, the stormglass on the archive annex held what was left of the evening light and broke it into pieces against the opposite wall.

He took the glass from his pocket and set it on the table.

It was warm. Not the warmth of his own body heat — he had carried it in his pocket for hours and knew the difference between glass warmed by proximity and glass warmed by use. This was the latter. Someone had accessed it recently. Not in the last hour, perhaps, but in the last several. She was alive and moving and had been at the shelter, or near it, or had accessed the archive the glass connected to, and the glass had warmed the way stormglass warmed when touched by the person it was encoded for.

He pressed his thumb against the edge of it. Not the flat face — the edge, where the crystal had been cut, where the facet was sharpest. He pressed until it cut.

Nothing activated.

The cut was small. He held his thumb against the glass and watched the blood gather at the edge of the wound, slow and dark, closing at its own pace. The glass sat on the table and did not hum and did not warm further and did not give him anything — not four seconds, not one second, nothing. He was not the person it had been encoded for. He had known this since the shelter, had known it when the glass sealed itself after four seconds as though a door had been closed quietly and with finality. Knowing it had not changed anything. Pressing his thumb against the edge had not changed anything either.

He was not angry. There was nothing to be.

He sat with it. He had understood something about his situation and had no use for what he understood — no action it unlocked, no category it fit, no next step it illuminated.

He could not access what she had built. He could not verify what he had glimpsed in four seconds — the hands moving across pre-Charter crystal, the way of deliberate attention, the voice stripped of its consonants by degradation so that what arrived was intention without attribution. He could not do anything except maintain the fiction of the investigation, file accurate forms, stand in a room while Brek worked and say nothing, and wait.

Brek was probably at his own table now, filing his own forms, reviewing the secondary frequency cross-reference with the settled attention of a man whose findings had come back consistent, whose process had held. Not troubled by the girl in the chair — or troubled in the way that had a category: anomalous result, within acceptable parameters. The category held. The holding was not performance and was not corruption; it was simply what happened when the categories available to you were adequate for the work you were doing.

Davan's categories had stopped being adequate in a shelter in the Underbrim, in the dark, with his palms flat on a table that had absorbed years of other people's work and held none of it.

He looked at the cut on his thumb. The blood had already begun to clot, the edges of the wound drawing together in the quiet way of a small injury completing itself.

The glass sat on the table, still warm. Somewhere in Bridgefall, she was moving — carrying the archive his four seconds had shown him the edge of, carrying whatever she had built in the secondary frequency band where no one had known to look, carrying the eighteen seconds that had triggered a Council detection and a briefing and a co-investigator assignment and a morning in a lower-ward apartment where a girl had sat in a chair with her hands in her lap.

He thought about Brek's genuine concern on the walkway. He thought about the mother's genuine gratitude for an explanation. He thought about the specific quality of sincerity that did not require examination because the categories held, and about the specific quality of sincerity that did require examination because the categories had broken, and about the fact that he could not locate, even now, a principle that explained the difference between the two — except the glass, except the four seconds, except the accident of which hands the glass had opened for.

He put the glass back in his pocket. He reached for the candle he had never lit, made the gesture of blowing it out, and the room remained the same dark it had always been. Outside, the archive annex stormglass went on breaking the quarter-moon into pieces. The glass was warm against his hip and would not open for him. Somewhere in the city she was still moving, and he did not know toward what.

Chapter 9

The resonance reached her through the soles of her boots before it became anything she could name.

Not sound — not yet. A faint differential in the way the temple quarter's paving transmitted weight, as though the ground here kept a different relationship with whatever lay beneath it. Twenty minutes of walking had brought Vael through streets that grew quieter by degrees, less lit, the stormglass conduits overhead dark or simply absent, the buildings withdrawn from their own facades in the particular way of structures emptied of purpose and not yet assigned another. Three blocks out, the Remembrance Hall's collapsed eastern wing announced itself: a raw seam of rubble where the foundation had surrendered, the upper stories tilted at an angle that should have been corrected years ago, the whole face of it held in the stillness of a structure the city had simply stopped looking at — no scaffolding, no posted notice, nothing.

She stopped at the corner, hands loose at her sides, and let the resonance come to her.

This was not the older stratum's pressure. She had learned that distinction in the past week — the specific heat of that other signal, directional and sourceless, pressing from outside the frequency rather than rising within it. What moved beneath her now was different. It came from below the stone, from a depth she associated with old foundations, old water channels, old construction that predated the Council's standardization of what went underground. The frequency had no notation she could immediately reach for. She stood with it and catalogued what her feet were telling her: the temperature differential was minimal, the vibration low and steady, and the pull came from ahead rather than from below — drawing her forward rather than warning her back. That distinction mattered.

Something was drawing her toward it. Not warning her away.

The entrance was not where she had expected. She had anticipated a maintenance hatch, a cellar door, something that read as infrastructure. What she found instead was a woman seated on the rubble at the base of the collapsed wing's eastern edge, sorting through fragments of old stormglass with the unhurried attention of someone whose work carries no deadline. Perhaps fifty, her hands thick-knuckled and deliberate, her coat the color of the stone she sat against. She did not look up when Vael stopped three feet away.

"The hall's been closed since the foundation went," the woman said. "Nothing to see."

"I'm looking for someone."

"Most people who come here are."

Vael waited. The woman turned a fragment of glass over in her palm — pale grey, the kind of piece that had been in rubble long enough to lose its surface finish, its encoding stratum worn to ambient — and set it in a pile to her left. Started on another. The resonance was stronger here, rising through the soles of Vael's boots with a clarity that was almost readable, though she still lacked the notation for it.

"The name is Tace," Vael said.

The woman set down the fragment she was holding. Not quickly.

"Second gap in the rubble line," she said. "Mind the threshold. The stone's uneven."

She did not look up.

Vael found the gap: a space between two fallen sections of foundation wall, wide enough to enter sideways, the stone above it stable in the way of stone that has settled into its new configuration and stopped moving. Beyond it, a descent — three rough-cut steps into the dark, then a passageway that had been cleared of debris with evident care, the rubble moved to the sides and stacked, the floor swept clean. The resonance intensified as she descended. Not unpleasantly. Like a frequency she had been hearing at the edge of perception finally becoming audible.

The passageway opened into a junction chamber.

Four people occupied it, none of them looking at her directly. An older man sorted documents beside a clay lamp, his handwriting small and regular. Two younger ones — a woman and someone who might have been her brother — sat against the far wall with their eyes on their hands. A child of perhaps nine lay curled on a folded blanket in the corner, asleep, her face smooth with the specific blankness of deep sleep in a cold room. The man with the documents glanced at Vael once, registered her presence, returned to his work.

No one spoke.

Vael recognized this. She had been inside resistance spaces before — the lower Registry annex, Nava's overflow room — and she understood that the silence was not hostility but discipline — no one offered a name, no one looked at her long enough to require acknowledgment. She did not offer her name. She waited.

A woman appeared from a passage to the left — middle-aged, moving with the slightly deliberate quality of someone whose joints have opinions about stone floors — and studied Vael with an attention that had nothing to do with welcome and everything to do with risk calculation.

"Tace's chamber is the second on the right," she said. "She's expecting you. Leave the bag at the junction."

Vael looked at the bag. The amber shard was inside it, wrapped in oilcloth, nested in the false bottom of the salvage kit. She had not left it anywhere since the shelter. The woman's expression did not shift.

"The bag stays here," the woman said. "You go through."

Vael set the bag against the wall beside the document-sorting man. He did not acknowledge it. She went through.

The second chamber on the right had a low ceiling — four feet of clearance at the center, less at the edges where the original vaulting had partially collapsed and been shored with timber — and the walls were covered in carved notation. Not recent carving. The cuts were old, the stone soft-edged where centuries of damp had worked at them, the notation style belonging to the memorial rites of the pre-Charter period: a system of frequency marks used to encode the names and voices of the dead into ritual stormglass, so that the glass could be consulted during remembrance ceremonies. Vael had seen this notation style in the Registry's historical archive, filed under decommissioned practice, dated to approximately three hundred years prior. She had not expected to find it here — on walls that had been lived against for some time, that carried the specific wear of habitation rather than preservation.

The chamber held the smell of cold stone and tallow and, beneath both, stormglass solvent — the kind used to clean crystal that had been in contact with degraded encoding, its sharpness still faintly present in the air.

Tace sat at the small table.

Seventy-one years old. Vael had known this before arriving, had assembled it from Nava's notes and from the Registry records Nava had been maintaining those seventeen years, but the number had not prepared her for the woman's stillness. Not age-stillness — not the careful immobility of someone managing pain or fatigue. Her hands rested flat on the table, unmoving but not clenched, the way an engineer's hands rest when they are not working — at ease but available. She had made some accommodation with the waiting; she had not made one with the reason for it. Her hair was white and cut close. Her eyes, when they found Vael's, carried the particular clear grey of someone who has not stopped paying attention.

"Sit," she said. Not unkindly. As if sitting were simply the next logical step.

Vael sat. The stool was wooden, three-legged, its seat hollowed slightly by long use, the grain raised where the finish had gone. On the shelf behind Tace, a row of glass cylinders stood arranged with the precision of someone who had been an engineer before she was anything else. Eight of them, identical in size, differentiated by small notations scratched into the bases. A clay lamp positioned between the cylinders and the table threw the light unevenly, leaving the upper carving on the walls in shadow.

"You're Solen's daughter," Tace said. Not a question.

"Yes."

"You have the amber shard."

"It's in my bag. They asked me to leave it at the junction."

Tace's mouth moved in something that was not quite a smile. "Mira's careful. She's right to be." She studied Vael for a moment with the assessing quality Vael was beginning to recognize as the default register of people who have been living underground — not suspicion, something more precise than suspicion, closer to the attention of someone reading a document for the second time to confirm what they found on the first. "You're smaller than I expected. Solen was tall."

"I know."

"The readings started four years before the collapse," Tace said. Not a transition — or rather, the transition was the same as no transition, the way a person begins a sentence they have been composing for a long time. "I was the lead calibration engineer on the Glass Bridge's stormglass installation. We had a team of seven. The installation took fourteen months. I logged the first anomalous reading in the third month."

Vael did not move. The resonance from below had become a constant presence, low and consistent, something she had stopped actively noticing and begun simply receiving.

"What kind of anomaly."

"Frequency variance in the load-distribution nodes. The bridge's stormglass wasn't decorative — you know this. It was structural monitoring. Each node was calibrated to a specific load-bearing frequency, and when the load approached tolerance thresholds, the frequency shifted and the monitoring system flagged it. Standard engineering. The variance I found in the third month was in the calibration itself, not in the load readings. The nodes were reading correctly. They were reading correctly because they had been calibrated to read correctly regardless of what the actual load was."

She delivered this with the flat precision of someone who has held a technical conclusion for a long time and learned to present it without the emotional register that originally accompanied it.

"The calibration was wrong by design," Vael said.

"The calibration was wrong by design." Tace's hands shifted slightly on the table — not a gesture, an adjustment. "I logged it. I filed the anomaly report through the standard channel — the Registry's engineering review queue. A response came within two weeks. It said the variance was within acceptable parameters for the installation environment and that no further action was required. It was signed by a senior Registry official whose name I did not recognize. I had been working in Registry engineering for twenty-two years at that point. I knew every senior official in my division. I did not know this name."

"Was the name in the Registry records?"

"I checked. The signature corresponded to a valid Registry employee identification number. The employee had been registered for six years. There was no other record of that employee in any engineering review queue I had access to. No other filings. No other correspondence. A name that existed in the system for the purpose of signing one document."

The clay lamp threw its light sideways across the carved notation on the wall nearest to Vael. She could read some of it — the memorial frequency marks, the encoding syntax for the names of the dead. The rest was in a variation she didn't have.

"You filed again," Vael said.

"Three times. The second response was identical to the first. The third response did not come. Instead, the anomaly reports I had filed disappeared from the engineering review queue. Not sealed — absent. As though they had never been submitted. I had kept copies. I always kept copies." A pause, brief and specific, the pause of someone confirming the accuracy of what they are about to say. "The copies were in my office at the installation site. When I went to retrieve them the following morning, my access had been revoked. A letter arrived that afternoon informing me that my position on the calibration team had been terminated for performance reasons, effective immediately."

Vael's hands lay flat on her thighs. The stillness that preceded a frequency read — her body moving to its working register before she had made a decision to work.

"The bridge was completed without you."

"The bridge was completed without me. The installation team finished the work. The bridge opened. The bridge stood across eleven years." Tace's voice had not changed in register, but something in its rhythm had shifted — a slight compression, the words coming faster and then stopping. "During those eleven years, the anomalous calibration I had identified meant that the load-distribution nodes were reporting false readings. The bridge could tolerate a certain load, and the monitoring system said it could tolerate more. The margin between those two numbers was the architecture of the collapse. Someone built that margin into the bridge deliberately."

"You said someone. Not the installation team."

"The installation team calibrated the nodes according to specifications provided by the Registry's engineering standards division. The specifications themselves were wrong. The team did what they were given. They didn't know." She said this with the flat clarity of someone who has been asked the question before and arrived at an answer they can give without flinching. "The specifications came from above the installation team. They required senior Registry access to alter. The altered specifications would have been reviewed and approved before they were issued."

"Reviewed by whom."

"That's the question Solen was working on."

The name arrived in the chamber without preparation, and the chamber received it in the way of small spaces that have been lived in long enough to absorb what is said inside them. Vael did not move.

"She came here four years before the collapse," Tace said. "She had found the anomaly in the secondary frequency band — she was working the Registry archive's engineering files, and she found the original specifications and the altered specifications filed in the same record. Someone had re-indexed the original specifications as a draft version and promoted the altered specifications as the final. Standard re-indexing. If you didn't know to compare the two, you would simply see the final version and accept it."

"She knew to compare them."

"She had been in the Registry archive for nineteen years. She knew the filing structure the way you know the rooms of a house you grew up in. She found the draft. She found the final. She saw the difference." Tace's gaze moved briefly to the shelf behind her — the row of glass cylinders — and returned. "She came to me because I was the engineer who had originally flagged the anomaly. She found my name in the engineering review queue through the secondary frequency band. My reports were gone from the primary record. They were still in the secondary band. No one had cleared them from there because no one knew to look."

Vael's hands had not moved. Beneath the stone floor, the resonance continued its low, consistent pull.

"She was investigating a murder weapon," Vael said.

Tace looked at her for a moment. Not confirming, not denying — something more precise than either. Receiving the sentence and measuring it against what she knew.

"Yes," she said. "That's the accurate word for it."

The accurate word. Its weight was not in the word itself but in what the word displaced — malfunction, accident, tragedy, negligence, all the words the official record had used, all the words that assumed a gap between intention and outcome that the evidence did not support. Someone had built a structural vulnerability into the bridge's frequency architecture. The collapse had been the execution of a design. Forty-one people.

Vael thought of Solen's recording in the amber shard. The calibration chamber, the pale stone walls, the voice moving through the evidence with the systematic attention of someone who has already understood the worst and is now documenting it for the record. She had believed her mother was investigating a malfunction. She had believed the cover-up was about institutional failure, about the Council's unwillingness to admit that their infrastructure had been inadequate. She had been building toward a story about negligence hidden and maintained.

This was different. Vael's hands did not move. The same material, she thought — reorganized at the load-bearing level.

"The three names," Vael said.

"Solen narrowed the list to three. She did not tell me who they were."

"She encoded them."

"She used her own notation system. I recognized it as a deliberate encoding — she had a frequency grammar she'd developed over years of working in the secondary band, and when she was writing in it, the notation looked like standard archival shorthand to anyone who hadn't been trained in it specifically. She wrote the three names in that system. She showed me the document. I could see the names were there. I could not read them." A pause. "She told me afterward that she had done it deliberately. That she was protecting me from knowing."

"Protecting you."

"If I knew the names," Tace said, "I would be someone who knew the names. The people who hold that knowledge have a specific relationship to the people who want it suppressed. Solen had already lost her position at the Registry by that point — she had been removed from engineering archive access two months after she came to me. They knew she had found something. They didn't know yet what she had found or how much she could prove. She was trying to limit who else became a liability."

Vael looked at the wall with its carved memorial notation, the frequency marks for the names of the dead. She thought about Nava, who had known for seventeen years that the suppression order existed and had not known whose authorization had filed it. The same logic. The same protection, offered at the same cost: a kind of mercy that left the recipient unable to defend themselves with information they had been denied for their own safety.

Solen had been precise about terrible things. She had been precise about this.

"She came back twice after that," Tace said. "Once to tell me she had found a way to encode the evidence in the secondary frequency band in a form that couldn't be re-indexed or suppressed — that the encoding key was tied to a specific frequency signature that the Council's archivists wouldn't know to look for. Once more, approximately eight months before the collapse, to tell me she had finished. That it was there. That it would hold until someone came for it." She looked at her hands on the table. "I asked her what she was going to do. She said she was going to stay in her position and continue filing through legitimate channels for as long as they let her, because every accurate report she filed created a record that the Council would eventually have to account for. She said she thought she had another year before they removed her entirely. She was wrong about the year."

The clay lamp guttered slightly — a draft from somewhere in the passage system, moving through the junction chamber and finding this room. The light steadied.

"She didn't survive the collapse," Vael said. Not a question. A statement placed into the room to be received.

"No," Tace said. "She didn't."

What followed was not silence at the end of a conversation. It was the silence of two people who already knew the same hard fact — who had come to it separately, across different years, and had nothing left to establish between them. The knowing simply sat in the room.

"I came here four years ago," Tace said. "After the collapse. After the investigation — the official investigation, which found structural failure due to maintenance inadequacy, which named no design flaw, which filed no anomaly reports, which did not look in the secondary frequency band because the Council's archivists don't know the secondary band exists." She said this without heat. The heat had been present once, Vael understood. It had been present for a long time. What remained was something else — not cold, not resigned, but banked down and still usable, the way coals hold through a night without flame. "I came here because there was nowhere else to go that was not inside their record of what had happened. And because I had something that belonged to the person who was going to come."

Without looking, Tace reached behind her — the specific reach of someone who knows a shelf the way they know their own hands — and brought the cylinder forward and set it on the stone between them.

Finger-joint sized. The color of amber, the deep warm gold of pre-Charter stormglass that had been working for a long time, its surface darkened at the grip to a deeper tone where handling had polished away the original finish. A calibration cylinder — the kind used in engineering documentation, smaller than archival glass, designed for single-operator use in field conditions. Vael had seen dozens of them in salvage work. She had never seen one this color. Pre-Charter amber of this quality had been out of circulation for thirty years.

"It's Solen's calibration signature," Tace said. "She left it with me before the collapse. She said it was the authentication anchor — that whatever she had encoded in the secondary band, this was the key that would confirm her authorship. That the frequency signature in this cylinder would match the encoding signature in the archive and prove they came from the same source." She looked at the cylinder on the stone. "She told me it would only open for her. And then she said — she said she thought it might open for someone else. Eventually."

Vael looked at the cylinder.

It caught the clay lamp's light and returned it differently than glass returned light — warmer, less reflective, as if the light was being absorbed into the amber's depth rather than bounced from its surface. It held a faint warmth even at this distance, the kind that comes from crystal carrying an active frequency rather than merely storing one. Four years in this chamber, and it had not gone cold.

"You've tried to open it," Vael said.

"Many times. In the first year, frequently. After that, less." Tace's voice was level. "It does not open for me. I am not the person it was encoded for." She held Vael's gaze with the clear grey attention that had not shifted since Vael sat down. "I did not know, when Solen left it with me, whether the person it was encoded for would come. I did not know if they would come in time. I kept it." She said this plainly, without ornament. The keeping had been its own long work and she did not dress it otherwise.

Vael had not yet extended her hand.

She sat with the stillness of someone who has arrived. Four days of moving — since the shelter, since the Silt Markets, since Nava's overflow room with its seventeen years of unwitnessed work — and now the thing she had been moving toward was three inches from her hand and she had not touched it. The cylinder sat on the stone. The lamp's light moved across its surface. The resonance from below held steady and low and present, as it had been since she descended into the Hollows, as it had been since she stood at the corner of the temple quarter and felt the ground shift beneath her feet.

Tace said nothing. She sat with her hands flat on the table and watched and did not move toward the cylinder or away from it. She had waited four years. She could wait another breath.

Vael reached out and picked it up.

The warmth arrived before anything else — not the ambient warmth of a room, not the warmth of her own body heat. Something that pressed against her palm directly, as though the crystal had been clenched shut for a long time and was only now releasing. It had been held very still for a very long time and was now, finally, not required to be still.

The cylinder hummed. Once. Low and clear, in a frequency she knew — had grown up knowing, had heard beneath every recording she had ever accessed that carried her mother's encoding signature, the specific resonant note of Solen's calibration key, present in every piece of glass Solen had ever worked.

Five years of silence, and now this.

The amber caught the light. It did not release it.

Chapter 10

The amber sat warm against her palm, and then it opened.

Not the way the shard had opened — not with a threshold, a moment of granted permission. This was a different quality entirely, the way a room opens when a door sealed for years finally tears free of its frame. Resistance, and then none, and then the particular sensation of air held motionless for a very long time pressing toward her — a pressure against the chest, something dense and directional, the way a held breath feels when it is finally someone else's and not your own.

The chamber did not dissolve. The clay lamp kept burning. Tace's stillness persisted at the edge of Vael's awareness, the way the resonance from beneath the stone persisted — low, steady, requiring nothing from her. What the cylinder delivered was not a vision. It was not a dream. It was Solen's working mind arriving whole, the way a frequency arrives before you have words for it — as pressure against the inside of her skull, as the unmistakable sense of another person's attention already in motion.

Her mother was inside a calibration chamber.

Pale stone walls. Light from a fixed gas lamp, not stormglass — older, steadier, the kind of light that left no record. Solen's hands moving across a frequency reader the way hands move when they know the instrument without consulting it. The reader was pre-Charter, smaller than current models, its casing worn at the corners, the metal there gone dull and slightly soft from years of grip. Solen's hands were her mother's hands. Vael had not seen them in five years. They were exactly as she remembered and nothing like she remembered at the same time, the way a specific thing always is when you have been holding a general version of it in your mind for too long.

Solen was working.

Not performing work — working. The distinction lived in the quality of her attention, which was the most complete attention Vael had ever received from her mother, and which was not directed at Vael at all. It was directed at the frequency reader, at the documents spread across the table beside it, at the specific problem she was in the process of solving. Vael was present the way a recorder is present — receiving, not received.

This was the specific quality of her mother's working mind. Vael had grown up inside it. She had spent years trying to replicate it and years trying to escape it, and she had not understood until this moment — palm pressed against amber in a chamber below the abandoned temple quarter — that what she had been doing for five years was trying to return to it.

Solen cross-referenced.

The documents spread across the table were Registry personnel logs — Vael could read the heading format, the column structure, the specific density of text that meant administrative record rather than technical documentation. Solen moved between the logs and the frequency reader the way someone moves when they have already run a sequence twice and are now running it again — not searching but checking, her hands finding the right page without looking, her eyes moving in the pattern Vael recognized: left margin first, then the secondary column, then the specific entry, then back to the reader.

She was narrowing.

Vael had done this work. She knew the specific quality of an investigation that has moved past accumulation and into elimination — when you are no longer asking what happened but who, and Solen had pulled one log from the stack and set the rest aside, her finger moving down a single name column, and you are cross-referencing names against dates against access records against the gap between what someone was authorized to do and what someone actually did. The work had a particular texture at this stage. A particular silence.

Solen's silence was this silence.

The personnel logs were from seven years before the collapse. Vael registered this without being told — the date format in the header, the specific Registry ID generation sequence that changed six years before the collapse when the Council standardized the system. These were old logs. Logs from the period when the Glass Bridge was being built.

Solen held a document up to the lamp.

It was handwritten — not a printed form, not a standard Registry document. A page from someone's notation system, the kind of dense shorthand archivists developed over years of field documentation to compress technical observation into portable form.

Solen's eyes moved across it without hesitation, without the small stops and starts of someone encountering unfamiliar marks. She had read this hand before. She knew its author.

Three names.

Written in frequency notation — Solen's own system, the one Vael had grown up watching her use, the one she had spent four years of salvage work adapting into her own variation. The names were not spoken. They were written in the specific notation Solen used for personnel markers, which Vael had decoded six months ago from the amber shard's eighteen seconds and had been carrying since as a framework she had not yet been able to populate.

The framework populated.

The first name resolved cleanly. Vael read it the way she read frequency notation — not word by word but as a whole, the pattern completing before she had consciously parsed the individual markers. A Registry administrative name. A senior position. Someone who had been in the Registry's upper structure during the Bridge's installation period, who had access to the calibration reports, who had the authorization level required to file an approval without flagging an anomaly in the readings.

Maerath.

Not the name she had feared most. Not a name she had been moving toward with the specific dread of a confirmed worst case. A name she knew the way everyone in the Underbrim knew it — the Registry director, the institutional face, the figure whose signature appeared on the public-facing documents that governed access and classification. A name that was everywhere and therefore, in the specific way of institutional ubiquity, somehow nowhere — present in every record without being attached to any single act.

Now it was attached.

Vael held the recognition carefully, the way you hold something heavier than you expected. The amber was warm against her palm. The clay lamp burned. Tace did not move.

Maerath's name appeared in Solen's notation not as architect but as approver. The distinction lived in the notation's grammar — Solen's system carried specific markers for originating authority versus authorizing authority versus implementing authority, a three-level structure Vael had decoded from the shard and had been trying to understand in the abstract. Now it was concrete. Maerath had not designed the miscalibration. Maerath had signed off on the installation specifications seven years before the collapse —

a routine authorization, one of hundreds filed in a fiscal quarter, an approval that required a technical review the records showed had been completed by someone two levels below Maerath's position.

Whether the technical review had actually been completed was the question the notation was asking.

The anomaly was in the readings. Tace had logged it in installation month three. Someone had dismissed it. The dismissal signature belonged to a Registry ID with no other filing history — a name that appeared once and nowhere else, which was either an administrative error or something that required more effort to create than an error would. Solen's notation placed Maerath's authorization date fourteen days after the dismissal. Whether Maerath had seen the anomaly report before signing. Whether the anomaly report had been filed before or after the dismissal. Whether the dismissal was the mechanism by which the anomaly report ceased to be something an authorizing official would encounter in a standard review.

Solen's face in the memory showed her asking these questions.

Vael had been watching her mother's hands. She looked now at her mother's face.

Solen was forty-three in this memory. Vael had been eighteen. She had not understood at eighteen what her mother's working face looked like from the outside — she had only ever experienced it as a quality of available attention, a shift in the room's temperature when Solen moved from presence to focus. Now she could see it as a face. The specific compression around the eyes. The way Solen's mouth was very slightly open, not for speech but for breath — the breath of someone holding a great deal very still while they think.

Her mother was not afraid.

She was — Vael did not have the word for it, and then she did. Her mother was precise. The fear was present — it lived in the quality of the stillness, in the way Solen's hands moved in tight, economical gestures, nothing wasted, nothing repeated — but it was not the dominant register. Solen was doing the most careful work she had ever done, in a room that was not safe, with the full attention of someone who understands that this may be the last time she is able to.

Vael's hands, in the chamber below the temple quarter, were flat against her thighs.

The second name was partially obscured.

Solen had shifted the document slightly — not deliberately, the small adjustment of someone who has been holding a page at lamp-height for too long and whose grip has corrected. The shift brought the first name into clearer light and moved the third into shadow, but the second name, which had been in the center of the page, was caught in the transition — partially lit, partially shadowed, its notation markers present but the connecting tissue between them interrupted by the fold in the paper where Solen's thumb pressed.

Vael could read the Registry prefix. She could read the authority level marker. She could read the first notation cluster, which told her the position was above Maerath's in the administrative hierarchy — not a technical position but a governance position, someone with institutional standing that predated the Council's current structure.

The rest was the fold.

The third name was clear. Vael read it and it meant nothing to her — a Registry name, a senior position, the specific notation markers indicating implementation authority rather than authorization authority. Someone who had executed rather than approved. Someone in the middle of the chain. A name that did not appear in the parts of the world she had been moving through.

Solen lowered the document.

Her hands moved to the frequency reader and she made three notations in quick succession — the specific shorthand of someone recording a conclusion, not developing one. The conclusion was already formed. The notation was the record of it, made with the care of someone who understands that the record is the point, that the work of the past several hours is only as durable as the encoding that carries it forward.

Solen looked up.

Not at Vael. The chamber was empty except for Solen. She looked up at the wall opposite — pale stone, unmarked, the specific blankness of a surface chosen for its blankness. She held that look for a moment Vael could not measure. It was not the look of someone who has finished. It was the look of someone who has arrived at a place they have been moving toward for a long time and is now standing in it, taking a moment to understand what it means to be here.

Then Solen reached for the calibration cylinder.

Vael recognized it. The amber. Pre-Charter, by the look of it. The grip worn to the wood. Solen held it for a moment — not operating it, not encoding into it, simply holding it — her hands careful and still around it, the way you carry something that is not yours and must reach someone else whole.

The memory ended.

Not gradually. Not with the degraded edges she associated with standard stormglass playback, the consonants softening, the frequency thinning. It ended with the clean finality of something that had reached its conclusion — four minutes and thirty-seven seconds of Solen's working mind, complete.

The amber was cold.

Vael sat in the ritual chamber below the abandoned temple quarter. The clay lamp burned. The frequency notation carved into the walls surrounded her — pre-Charter memorial script, older than the Registry's standardized forms, cut by hands that had worked in a different grammar entirely. Tace occupied her chair across the table, very still, watching.

Vael's face was wet.

She became aware of this the way you become aware of something that has been true for some time without registering — a specific coolness along her jaw, a weight beneath her eyes that was not the weight of her own attention. She had been crying. She did not know when it had started. She set the cylinder on the stone between them and folded her hands. Already drying. She did not move to address it.

She pressed her palms flat against her thighs until the pressure registered.

The cylinder lay dark on the stone between them.

"Maerath," she said.

A statement placed into the room. The way she had placed statements into rooms before, when she needed to hear them exist outside her own skull.

Tace's expression did not change. "Yes," she said.

The quality of that yes.

Not surprised. Not confirmed — confirmation implies something that was uncertain, and this was not uncertain. It was the yes of someone who has been carrying a piece of knowledge for a long time and is now in a room where it can be set down.

"You knew," Vael said.

"I knew the name that appeared in the authorization chain," Tace said. "I logged the anomaly in installation month three. The dismissal came fourteen days later. When I began tracing the authorization sequence — after the collapse, after the investigation that found nothing, after I came here — Maerath's name was in the approvals. It was not difficult to find. It was simply in a position where finding it required knowing to look."

She said this without heat. The heat had been present once, Vael thought — four years ago, when Tace had arrived in the Hollows with her evidence and her finding of structural failure due to maintenance inadequacy, which named no design flaw, which filed no anomaly reports. What remained now was not the heat. What remained was what was left after the heat had gone — a steadiness in the jaw, in the hands, in the level way she held her eyes on Vael across the table.

"It was not the authorization that tells you what he knew," Vael said. The words arrived from the notation, from the grammar of Solen's system, from the four minutes and thirty-seven seconds of her mother asking the same question with the same precision. "The authorization is a record of a signature. Whether he had seen the anomaly report before he signed — whether the report had been filed before or after the dismissal —"

"Whether the dismissal was the mechanism," Tace said.

"Yes."

Tace was quiet for a moment. The lamp shifted slightly — a draft from the passage system, finding the chamber the way it had found it before, the light steadying after.

"Your mother was asking that question," Tace said. "I know she was asking it. She came to me twice in the year before the collapse. She had the anomaly logs — my anomaly logs, the ones erased from the primary record. She had found them in the secondary frequency band. She was asking whether the dismissal had preceded the authorization or followed it, because the answer to that question is the difference between an official who signed without knowing and an official who signed in order to make the not-knowing official."

She held Vael's gaze with the clear grey attention that had not shifted since Vael sat down.

"Architect versus approver," Vael said.

"Yes."

"Solen's notation marks him as approver."

"I know what Solen's notation marks him as," Tace said. "I have been living with that distinction for four years. It is the question the memory does not answer."

Vael understood. The distinction was not a technicality. It was the central moral question — the one the archive had been built toward, the one Solen's face had been asking in that pale-stone room with the gas lamp and the personnel logs and the frequency reader worn at the corners. Whether Maerath had known. Whether the chain of approvals and dismissals and authorizations had been constructed around him or by him or simply in the specific way of institutional processes that do not require individual architects because the quarterly approval forms came pre-printed, their blank signature lines already bound into the Registry's standard filing before any hand reached them.

The archive would not resolve it. It was built to document.

Solen had understood this. Solen had encoded the question alongside the evidence because the question was part of the evidence — the specific shape of what remained unknown after everything knowable had been known.

Vael picked up the cylinder. Not to access it. She set it in her palm and held it the way Solen had held it in the memory — her hands careful around it, still.

"There were three names," she said. "I could read two of them clearly. The third was in the fold of the page."

Tace's expression shifted. Not surprise. Something more careful than surprise — the look of someone arriving at the part of the account they have been waiting for.

"The second name," Vael said. "Above Maerath in the administrative hierarchy. A governance position, not a technical one. Institutional standing that predated the Council's current structure." She paused. "I could read the Registry prefix. The authority level marker. The first notation cluster. The rest was obscured."

Tace was quiet for a long moment. The resonance from below the stone was steady. The lamp burned.

"I have been trying to find the third name for four years," Tace said. Her voice was level. She had been working this question for a long time, and she was not going to stop working it now — that much was plain in the way she held herself across the table, the way her hands lay flat and open. "I have not found it. I know the position. I know the authority level. I know the institutional standing the notation describes. What I do not know is the name attached to that position in the period when the Bridge specifications were approved."

She held Vael's gaze with the clear grey attention that had not shifted since Vael sat down.

"The personnel records from that period," Tace said, "were reclassified. Standard procedure for inactive investigations — their word, not mine. The reclassification removed them from any index a non-senior archivist could access. To find the name, you would need access to the classification tier above what Nava has been working with for seventeen years. You would need access to the level where the reclassification was authorized."

The clay lamp burned very steadily now. The draft had moved on.

Vael held the cylinder in her palm. The amber had a specific weight — heavier than its size suggested, the specific density of pre-Charter glass that had been working for a long time. She was thinking about the second name. She was thinking about the Registry prefix, the authority level marker, the first notation cluster. She was thinking about the specific position the notation described — a governance position, not a technical one, institutional standing that predated the Council's current structure — and she was thinking about who she knew who moved through the levels of Bridgefall's institutional architecture, who had spent eleven years developing the specific fluency required to navigate a system without being consumed by it, who had filed a negative-result form with a blank field twelve and was sitting above a cartographer's workshop in the lower residential tier with a sealed Council-origin glass fragment in his coat pocket.

She did not say his name.

She did not know yet that she was thinking of him.

Chapter 11

Cold ash and the smell of emptied rooms — tallow burned down to nothing, stone that had held warmth not long ago but had stopped holding sound. Brek registered this as he came through the outer passage, frequency reader already in hand, dial set to the secondary register where Vael's signature lived. He moved without urgency. He always moved without urgency. The sensor alert had come through Registry channels at the third bell, flagged low-priority by the duty archivist, and Brek had spent twenty minutes with the preliminary data before collecting his two assistants from the Plateau-side annex and walking down to the temple district. The walk had served its purpose. The data had served a greater one.

Seventeen years ago, the Remembrance Hall's collapse had been documented, its decommissioning filed under structural liability and processed by a clerk who had not, as far as Brek could determine, set foot on the site before or after. This was the kind of administrative gap he found worth examining — the decommissioning record pointed toward the unmonitored space, and the unmonitored space pointed toward the kind of entry that required no key, only the knowledge that a sealed door and a locked one were not the same thing.

Locating the entrance required no particular effort. Dust at the threshold had been disturbed in a pattern consistent with repeated recent use — not a single entry, but a community of entries, tracked in and out with the economy of people who lived in a space rather than visited it. Brek crouched at the threshold and studied the pattern without touching it. His assistants held position behind him.

"Document the entrance geometry," he said. "Full width. The scuff pattern on the left side is older than the right — two different traffic patterns, two different periods of use. Log them separately."

One assistant began sketching. The other activated a secondary reader and swept the passage walls for frequency residue.

Brek moved through.

The junction chamber was empty in the way of rooms that had been emptied deliberately rather than abandoned. The distinction always lived in small things: a hook on the wall where something had hung long enough to leave a shadow of its shape in the stone dust; a flagstone near the back wall with wear at its corners from regular foot traffic that stopped precisely at its edge, meaning something had occupied that spot for a long time; tallow and cold stone and the close, stale warmth that came from many people breathing in a low-ceilinged room over many months. Someone had lived here. Multiple someones. They had left in an organized fashion within the last several hours — the air still held the temperature of recent occupation, not warm but warmer than the passage outside, which was warmer than the gorge, which meant the heat was human and recent and deliberate.

He followed the passage deeper.

The chamber at its end was low-ceilinged and stone-floored, lit now only by the lamp one of his assistants carried. A clay lamp on the ledge had a recently snuffed wick — he held his hand above it without touching and felt the residual warmth, then brought his reader close. The instrument registered ambient temperature at the wick's position as three degrees above the passage air. Someone had been here within four hours. Possibly two.

The pallet in the corner still held the impression of a body. He did not need to touch it.

What stopped him was the shelf along the east wall.

It ran the full length of the wall, mounted with care that showed in the brackets — hand-forged, irregularly spaced, not from incompetence but from the geometry of a person who had added objects to the shelf over time and moved the brackets to fit them. The shelf itself was clean. Swept within the last day. On it sat twelve empty glass cylinders, arranged at intervals that suggested each had occupied its spot for a long while and been lifted and replaced many times, the stone beneath each one worn faintly pale. Whatever had stood here had been removed in the last several hours: the cylinders left behind were set with a tidiness that did not match the haste of everything else in the room — as if the person packing had paused over the shelf, handled each piece deliberately, taken what mattered, and set back what remained with the same habit of care they had always used.

Pre-Charter amber. He could identify it by the color alone, even empty — that specific warmth of glass manufactured before the Council standardized production density. He lifted one from the shelf without disturbing the others and turned it in the lamplight.

Worn at the grip points. Thirty years out of circulation, at minimum. Empty, but not inert — when he brought his frequency reader to it, the instrument registered a residual encoding signature, faint, the ghost of a frequency played many times. He checked the secondary register.

Solen's frequency range. Adjacent to it, at minimum — the same period, the same archival tradition. Laboratory analysis would be required for certainty, but the signature was consistent.

He set the cylinder back in its exact position.

Twelve rings in the stone where the cylinders had rested. He looked at them after he looked at the cylinders — the pale circles worn by weight and time, the record of years of handling in the surface itself. Whatever the cylinders had held, someone had opened and returned them many times. The stone remembered this whether or not the glass did.

"Catalogue each cylinder individually," he told his assistant. "Full provenance assessment, secondary register included. I want the residual signature documented before we remove anything."

The assistant moved to comply. Brek continued his examination of the chamber.

The floor near the shelf was stone, cold and even. Near the pallet, a depression had been worn by regular foot traffic — someone had stood in that specific spot often enough to leave a record in the stone. Near the passage entrance, the floor was clean. In the middle distance between the shelf and the pallet, the floor was also clean, recently swept, which told him the sweeping had been thorough but rushed — whoever swept had prioritized the areas closest to the shelf and the pallet, where evidence was most concentrated, and had not reached the floor near the passage wall.

That was where he found the notation fragment.

A small rectangle of paper — half a page, torn at the edge rather than cut, the tear running through what appeared to be a line of notation. It had fallen from somewhere; the fold in it was the fold of something that had been in a pocket or a folio, not the fold of something set down deliberately. The paper was not damp, which meant it had been dropped within the last several hours, after the space had shed the moisture that came from long habitation and stone cold.

Brek picked it up carefully, holding it at the edges.

The notation was small and precise. Not Registry grammar — he recognized the frequency markers, the general architecture of an archival notation system, but the grammar organizing them was not standard. The markers were placed in a non-Registry sequence, using frequency designations he recognized as valid but arranged in a logic he could not immediately parse. Not a corruption of the Registry system. A parallel system. A private grammar built on the same technical vocabulary but organized by a different set of rules.

He had encountered something adjacent to this before. In the shelter in Underbrim, Davan's preliminary notes had mentioned a folio with handwriting that showed the specific pressure and angle of someone trained in Registry archival notation who had subsequently developed their own system. Brek had read that line twice. He had filed it as a detail consistent with the subject's known archival background and continued. He was not continuing now.

He studied the fragment for a long time.

Within two minutes he was certain he could not read it — not because the notation was obscure, but because it was coherent in a way that made clear it was not meant to be read by someone who did not already know the rules. This was not encoded to conceal. It was encoded in the private grammar of a person who had spent years developing a notation system for their own use and had stopped translating it for outside consumption.

This was the subject's own system. He was almost certain.

He placed the fragment in a documentation sleeve and sealed it.

"Log this as an uncatalogued notation fragment, non-Registry grammar," he said. "Routing to cryptography for analysis. Flag it as priority secondary — not primary. I want the cylinder assessment completed first."

His assistant noted it without comment.

Brek stood in the center of the chamber and took it in as a whole. The empty shelf. The indented pallet. The snuffed lamp. The twelve pre-Charter cylinders arranged with care. The swept floor and the one unswept corner where the notation fragment had lain. The frequency residue in the secondary register, consistent with Solen's archival period.

Someone had been meeting here. Regularly, over an extended period. Someone with access to pre-Charter stormglass cylinders that should have been in Registry custody or decommissioned decades ago. Someone who had known the space well enough to evacuate it efficiently when the sensor alert triggered — or when they anticipated it would.

The subject had been here recently. The notation fragment belonged to her system, which meant she had been here within the last several hours, in contact with whoever occupied this space. The investigation had a depth that had not been visible from the shelter in Underbrim.

Brek found this genuinely interesting. It concerned him too.

He lifted his frequency reader and brought it close to the nearest cylinder a second time, then set it back on the shelf — not with alarm, but with the attention he gave to any system that had developed further than its last documented state.

"Recommend a full sweep of the temple quarter," he told his assistant. "Probable resistance staging area — secondary function, long-term occupation. The evacuation was organized, which means there's a network, which means there are other spaces. We document this one completely and flag the sector for a systematic assessment."

His assistant noted it.

Brek took one more look at the shelf of empty cylinders, each one sitting in the pale ring its own weight had worn into the stone. Then he turned and began documenting the chamber's dimensions, working methodically from the entrance wall to the far corner. There was no sense in standing still over what he did not yet understand. The measurements would tell him something. They always did.

The preliminary report arrived at Davan's secondary desk in the Council operational offices at the seventh bell, routed through standard channels with Brek's notation in the header field: temple quarter, decommissioned Remembrance Hall, probable resistance staging area, evacuation within four to six hours of Registry sensor alert. Davan read it the way he read all preliminary reports — once through at pace, then again at the detail level, marking nothing on the first pass and everything on the second.

The second pass took longer than usual.

He was sitting at a table in the operational annex, a narrow room off the main corridor with two desks and a gas lamp that ran cold in the afternoons. His own desk stood against the far wall. Brek's preliminary reports came to his secondary desk by convention — they had established the routing three assignments ago, on the grounds that Davan's secondary desk was closer to the filing cabinet for active investigations, and the convention had persisted because conventions in the operational annex persisted unless someone actively dismantled them, and neither of them had.

The report's main body was standard: chamber dimensions, occupancy evidence, evacuation timing, cylinder count and preliminary frequency assessment. Twelve pre-Charter amber cylinders, empty, residual signature consistent with Solen's archival period. The chamber had been occupied for an extended period by multiple individuals. Evacuation was organized. Recommendation: full sector sweep, systematic assessment of adjacent decommissioned spaces, resistance network classification.

Davan read that section twice and set it aside.

The notation fragment appeared in the supplementary documentation, item four of six. Brek had described it in the same economical way he described everything: small rectangle, torn edge, non-Registry grammar, frequency markers arranged in a private notation system consistent with the subject's known archival background. Unable to parse. Routing to cryptography for analysis. Flag: priority secondary.

Davan did not move for a moment.

He had encountered the notation system before. Not this specific fragment — but the system itself, or its predecessor, or something close enough that the description in Brek's report landed with the weight of something already known. The folio in the shelter had been written in a variation of Registry archival notation with a private grammar layered over it. He had documented this in his own preliminary notes from the Underbrim visit, and those notes were now inside Brek's secondary surveillance review. Brek had read them, connected the shelter notation to the temple quarter fragment, and was almost certainly correct that the fragment was the subject's.

Which meant she had been in the Hollows within the last several hours. Which meant she had been talking to someone there. Which meant she had moved further into the investigation than the shelter evidence had suggested — further than Davan had been operating on the assumption of, which was itself a problem, because his assumptions about her location and her progress had been shaping his secondary reports, and if his assumptions were wrong then his secondary reports were wrong in ways that would become visible when Brek's sweep produced more data.

He set the report down. His eyes went to the gas lamp.

The cryptography section's processing timeline for non-priority items was currently running at four to six days, depending on load. Priority secondary items moved faster —

two to three days, under normal circumstances. Brek had flagged the notation fragment as priority secondary, which meant it would be processed within two to three days, which meant the cryptography section would have a partial or complete reading of the subject's private notation system within the week, which meant whatever she had written on that fragment would be legible to the Registry within the week, available to Brek before Davan had found her.

He picked the report back up and read the routing information for the notation fragment.

A secondary processing pathway existed for items flagged as non-Registry grammar — a preliminary linguistic assessment that preceded the cryptography section's full analysis, conducted by the archival systems office to determine whether the notation required specialized decryption tools or could be processed with standard equipment. This assessment was logged separately from the main cryptography queue and ran on its own timeline, typically three to four days ahead of the full analysis.

Davan considered this. Then he opened the operational annex's secondary filing cabinet and removed a standard routing amendment form.

The form required a justification. He wrote: preliminary linguistic assessment to be completed by archival systems office before routing to cryptography; notation grammar requires contextual archival analysis to determine appropriate decryption pathway; recommend sequential processing to avoid misclassification of private archival notation as encrypted resistance communication.

This was accurate. It was also the kind of procedurally correct justification that would pass a review flag without triggering one — the kind of thing that happened when an investigator with archival background flagged a notation for appropriate handling. It was not the reason he was filing it.

The routing amendment would push the full analysis to eight to ten days rather than two to three. He had bought, at most, a week. Perhaps less if Brek noticed the amendment and questioned it. Brek noticed most things.

Davan filed the amendment in the routing sleeve alongside the notation fragment documentation and set it in the outgoing tray.

Then he sat with the report in his hands and looked at the section on the twelve empty cylinders.

Pre-Charter amber. Secondary register residue consistent with Solen's archival period. Someone had been using them — or someone had stored things in them, and the things had been removed before Brek arrived. Whatever had been in them was gone, which meant whoever had occupied the chamber had taken the contents when they evacuated, which meant the contents were still in circulation, somewhere in Bridgefall with the people who had carried them out.

He did not know what was in the cylinders. He did not know who had been in the chamber. He did not know where the subject had gone after the Hollows, or what she had found there, or what she was doing now. He did not know.

He knew that in eight to ten days — perhaps less — the cryptography section would have a reading of the notation fragment. He knew that Brek's sector sweep would begin within the next day and would produce additional evidence of the resistance network's structure and extent. He knew that the preliminary report in his hands would generate a follow-up action list requiring his co-signature, and that co-signing it would mean formally endorsing the sweep recommendation and the resistance network classification, and that endorsing those things would accelerate the investigation in directions he could not redirect.

He set the report in the active file.

The gas lamp in the annex had been running cold for the last hour. He had not noticed until now. Its light had gone the color of something nearly spent — flatter than the room's ordinary cold, and different again from the damp chill he remembered from the stone in the Underbrim shelter. He reached over and trimmed the wick without thinking, the way he had learned to read a room's small signals: what it was running out of, what had changed without announcement, what would be gone before long.

The notation fragment was in the outgoing tray.

The routing amendment was with it.

He had three days, perhaps four. He did not know where she was. He did not know what the cylinders had held. He did not know what she had found in the Hollows or what she was moving toward, and the amendment he had just filed would tell her nothing and tell Brek nothing and tell the cryptography section nothing except that an investigator with archival background had flagged an item for appropriate sequential processing — the kind of thing that happened, the kind of thing that left no trace.

The lamp dropped another degree colder.

Davan opened the active file and began reading the follow-up action list, because his co-signature was due by the eighth bell, and the eighth bell was forty minutes away. The cylinders, the notation, the amendment in the tray — he set none of it aside. He read what was in front of him, because that was what the next forty minutes required, and he had learned not to confuse what he had just done with permission to stop working.

Chapter 12

The reports came in at the seventh bell, the way they always did when Brek had a sweep running. Maerath read them in filing order — temple quarter assessment first, then the notation fragment routing confirmation — because filing sequence mirrored discovery sequence, and discovery sequence was the only arrangement that kept the investigation's actual shape intact. Her predecessor had taught her this. His predecessor had taught him. The practice had outlasted four administrations because it was right.

Brek's temple quarter report was thorough. His documentation was exact in the way she had come to rely on across the years — not brilliant, not interpretive, simply exact. Twelve pre-Charter amber cylinders, empty, residual frequency signatures consistent with the Solen archival period. A torn notation fragment in a private non-Registry grammar. Evacuation timing placed at four to six hours before arrival. The sweep recommendation matched what the evidence could support, no more and no less. She read it twice, confirmed the sweep authorization in the lower margin, and placed it to one side.

The notation fragment routing confirmation ran to a single page. Cryptography section, priority secondary queue. Estimated processing timeline: two to three days under current load. She read through the routing information and noted the amendment filed by the secondary investigator — Davan, the one with archival background, whose secondary reports had been running slightly oblique for the past several weeks in ways she had not yet formally flagged. The amendment's justification was procedurally sound. It was also exactly the kind of justification that someone with archival training would know how to construct so that it passed review without triggering it. She set the confirmation beside the sweep authorization and looked at both documents.

She had been managing situations of this kind for a long time. The particular texture of an investigator beginning to drift — reports accurate in every particular and slightly wrong in their orientation, procedural justifications that were correct and also something else — she recognized it the way she recognized cold glass under her fingers, or the Spire's stillness at this hour. There was no need to act on it immediately. She needed to note it and continue.

She confirmed the notation fragment routing as filed. The amendment would add three days to the processing timeline. That fell within acceptable parameters. If the cryptography section returned a partial reading within the week, the investigation would have what it needed regardless of any investigator's drift. Brek was methodical and would produce additional evidence through the sector sweep.

She signed both confirmations and placed them in the outgoing sleeve.

The Spire's ledger room was quiet at this hour. The stormglass panels had dropped to their overnight setting — not dark, but reduced to something that flattened the room's angles, made the shelving indistinct, turned the window into a rectangle of city-dark through which no specific shape could be read. The gas lamp on her table was the room's only directed light. Three hours of work behind her, two more before the night bell, and the work remained what it had always been.

She reached across the table and opened the personal ledger.

Smaller than the Registry files — narrower, its cover unmarked, its binding repaired twice in seventeen years with the same dark thread because replacing a functional object had never seemed necessary. She kept it in the lower left drawer of the ledger room's secondary desk, beneath two administrative manuals whose spines she had never cracked. No one had reason to look there. No one had looked there in seventeen years, as best she could determine, and she had a practiced eye for such things.

She turned to the section she had come to think of as the first weight.

The entry was dated to the month of the Glass Bridge's final installation inspection. She had written it the same night she signed the authorization — not from compulsion but from the specific discipline of a person who had decided, early in her career, to maintain an accurate record of her own decisions even when the Registry's record would not. The entry was brief. Six lines in her handwriting, which had been smaller then, more compressed.

Anomalous load-distribution readings from installation month three reviewed. Tace's anomaly report reviewed. Classification as equipment variance confirmed. Installation authorized.

Six lines. The date. The summary of what she had reviewed. The decision she had made.

What the entry did not record was the name that had appeared in the briefing document accompanying Tace's anomaly report — the name above hers in the authorization chain, the name that had been present in the room, in the document, in the specific pressure of the conversation that preceded her signature. She had not written that name anywhere. Not in the personal ledger, not in the Registry's files, not in any document that had ever existed in any archive she could access or had ever been asked to access. The name lived only in the place where she kept it, which was not a place that could be indexed.

She had known, reviewing Tace's anomaly report, that the readings were not equipment variance. The load-distribution nodes showed a deviation pattern consistent with altered specifications, not instrument drift — she had seen enough genuine equipment variance to know the difference, and this was not it. Tace had been correct. The anomaly was real.

She had classified it as equipment variance and signed the authorization.

The question she had been carrying for seventeen years was not whether she had known. She had known. The question was whether what she had understood about the alternative — about what declining to authorize would have produced, about what the name above hers in the authorization chain had communicated in the register of a person who did not make requests — constituted a justification. Whether *justification* was even the correct category for what she was examining when she examined this.

She had not been able to conclude that it was. She had also not been able to conclude that it was not.

This was the weight she had been carrying across seventeen years, and it had not grown lighter with time, and she had not expected it to. It had grown more precise — the shape of what she had done clearer now than it had been the night she wrote the entry, because seventeen years of examination had sharpened the image without settling it. She knew exactly what she had done and exactly why and exactly what had followed from it. She did not know whether the chain of causation ran from her signature to forty-one deaths in the way the counter-archive — if it existed in the form the investigation suggested — would claim it ran. The chain was probably more complex than that. Complexity, though, was not the same as absence.

She turned to the second weight.

This entry was dated eleven years after the first. Longer — twelve lines, her handwriting larger by then, less compressed. It recorded an administrative reassignment. A colleague in the Registry's senior analysis division, one of three people who had shared knowledge of the name Maerath kept only in her memory. The reassignment had moved through standard channels, authorized by a division director three levels below Maerath, filed correctly in all its particulars. Maerath had received the routing notification as routine administrative correspondence. She had noted it. She had continued.

The entry recorded the reassignment. It recorded the date. It recorded that she had received the routing notification.

It did not record that she had understood, upon receiving it, what the reassignment was. It did not record that she had held the notification for four hours before setting it in the outgoing tray. It did not record what she had been examining during those four hours, or what she had decided, or whether *decided* was the right word for what had occurred in the space between receiving the notification and filing it.

She had not written those things down because writing them would have required a grammar she did not possess. The notation she had was adequate for recording actions and inadequate for recording what it was to keep walking the correct corridor, holding the correct document, wearing the correct expression — to perform each piece of institutional routine with full knowledge that the document in her hands was a death notice for someone who had known the same name she knew, and that the death notice had been generated by the same apparatus she served, and that she was about to return it to that apparatus with her routing confirmation in the lower margin.

She had filed it. The reassignment had been processed. The colleague had not been heard from afterward in any capacity that left a record.

The entry read: *Administrative reassignment, senior analysis division. Routing notification received and confirmed. Standard procedure.*

Standard procedure. Written eleven years ago. She had not been able to determine, in the time since, whether those words constituted a record of what had happened or a record of what she had needed it to be. Both, probably. The ledger was an honest document — the document of a person who had learned to be honest within certain limits, and who had drawn those limits herself.

The third person who had shared knowledge of the name was still alive. She was the only one now. The name sat in the place where she kept it, and it had been there eleven years without a second holder, and she had been the sole custodian of its absence from the record since the administrative reassignment the entry described as standard procedure.

This was the second weight. It did not sit easy beside the first, and she had never expected it to. Two burdens of unequal origin but matching permanence — the first a signature, the second a silence — and she had stopped trying to weigh one against the other some years ago, because the scales did not balance and never would.

She closed the ledger.

Below the Spire, the streets had gone over to their night sounds — a cart somewhere on the lower avenue, the distant clang of the hour-bell in the Bridgefall merchant quarter, nothing else. The stormglass panels registered the ambient frequency at their dimmed setting: a low, even hum, nothing anomalous. She had been monitoring the frequency readings from this room for four years, since the first signs of instability in the older stratum had become legible to someone who knew how to read them. Tonight's readings fell within the range she had come to think of as managed. Not stable. Managed.

The subject — Solen's daughter, the girl, who was not a girl but whom Maerath continued to think of as such because it was easier than thinking of her as what she actually was, which was the specific instrument Solen had built for a specific purpose — had been in the Hollows. Had accessed the cylinders. Had, in all probability, received whatever Tace had been holding in trust for eleven years. The investigation had confirmed the cylinder residue. Brek's sweep would confirm the extent of the network. The notation fragment, once processed, would confirm the encoding system.

The surveillance had not been sufficient. She had known it would not be sufficient since the third bell last month, when the frequency reader in the Spire's lower monitoring room registered a secondary band activation consistent with pre-Charter amber in the temple quarter. She had noted it. She had authorized increased surveillance rather than immediate containment because immediate containment at that stage would have been — the word that arrived was *visible*, and visible was not the correct operational posture when the situation still had the shape of a manageable investigation.

The situation no longer had that shape.

She drew a sheet of correspondence paper from the desk's upper drawer. Plain paper — no Registry header, no seal — because what she was about to write was not a Registry document. It was a note. The distinction mattered to her the way the distinction between the personal ledger and the Registry files mattered: both were accurate records, but accurate about different things, and conflating them would produce a document accurate about nothing.

She wrote the note in the specific register she used for communications of this kind. Not the Registry's grammar — not *situations* and *variables* and *factors* — but something closer to plain language, which she permitted herself only in this register and only in documents that would not survive their delivery. The note authorized the acceleration of the administrative containment process for the subject currently identified in Brek's active investigation file. It specified that the acceleration was to be treated as a priority action, not a standard processing item. It did not specify methods. The recipient would know the methods. That was why she was writing to the recipient rather than filing through standard channels.

She had been hoping the surveillance would be sufficient. Through the first weeks of the investigation, she had believed the subject's isolation — no verified network contacts, no registered address, moving through the city's margins without leaving the kind of archival residue that triggered review — would work in the Registry's favor. A subject without institutional support was a subject who could be managed through attrition: limit access, restrict movement, allow the city's own friction to slow the investigation until the notation fragment was processed and the encoding system was legible and the full picture was available before any action was taken.

The Hollows had changed that calculation. Tace had been there for four years, which meant the subject had not been isolated. She had been moving toward a contact Maerath had not identified, through a network Maerath had not mapped, and had arrived at the source of the one material evidence chain that could, if properly authenticated and publicly released, reach the secondary frequency band where Solen had encoded the names.

The name Maerath kept in the place where she kept it was one of those names.

She had known this those eleven years. She had known it since the administrative reassignment, since the routing notification, since the four hours she had held the notification before filing it. She had managed the investigation for the past several weeks with this knowledge present in the same way that the two entries in the personal ledger were present — not acted upon, not resolved, simply carried alongside the work.

The work was no longer compatible with carrying it.

She sealed the note with the plain wax from the secondary desk's upper right drawer — not the Registry seal, a blank impression — and set it in the internal courier sleeve. The night courier ran at the quarter-bell before midnight. The note would reach its recipient before the Spire's night bell sounded.

She sat with the ledger closed on the table and the sealed note in the courier sleeve and the night sounds of the city below the window.

Frequency readings from the lower monitoring room fed to a secondary display panel mounted in the ledger room's east wall — a small panel, easily overlooked, installed four years ago when the older stratum's instability had first become legible. Six bands across the panel's face. Bands one through four sat within normal parameters. Band five showed the same low-level elevation it had carried for the past three weeks, consistent with increased secondary register activity in the temple quarter district. Band six — the band associated with the older stratum, the one that should, in a correctly managed system, register nothing at all — showed a reading that was not alarming in isolation and was alarming in the context of the past month's cumulative data.

She had been managing the older stratum's instability quietly, without Registry authorization, because Registry authorization would have required disclosure of why she was monitoring it, and disclosure of why she was monitoring it would have required disclosure of what she knew about the secondary frequency band, and disclosure of what she knew about the secondary frequency band would have required disclosure of the name she kept in the place where she kept it.

The subject was moving toward that name. The Hollows had confirmed it. Tace's cylinders had confirmed it. The notation fragment, once processed, would confirm the encoding system, and the encoding system would confirm the path to the secondary band, and the secondary band held the three names Solen had encoded — the authorizing authority, the implementing authority, and the name above both of them that Maerath kept in the place where she kept it — and if the subject reached that band before containment was complete, the name would enter the record.

Once it was in the record, Maerath would not be the only person keeping it out of the record. She would be the person who had kept it out of the record. The distinction was the difference between management and exposure, and she had been on the correct side of that distinction for eleven years, and the note in the courier sleeve was the action required to remain there.

She did not want to do it. This was not a new condition. She had not wanted to classify Tace's anomaly report as equipment variance. She had not wanted to file the routing confirmation on the administrative reassignment. She had not wanted to authorize any of the recalibration actions the investigation had produced over the past several weeks. The routing notification had sat in her hands for four hours before she filed it. The ledger's second entry was proof of that. She had not wanted to file the routing confirmation, and she had filed it, and the filing had been the correct operational decision by every measure available to her, and the colleague had died, and she had continued.

She continued now.

The next document in the active file was a frequency monitoring summary from the lower station — three pages, covering the past seventy-two hours. She picked it up and began to read. The courier sleeve sat in the tray. The ledger was closed. Outside the window the city was dark, the merchant quarter bell long since silent, the avenue below showing nothing but the dim light of the gas-post at the corner. The panel on the east wall registered band six at its elevated but not alarming level, and she read the monitoring summary the way she read every document: completely, in order, noting what the data supported and what it did not, letting the evidence say what it said.

Forty minutes to the night bell. She read.

Chapter 13

Three sleeves arrived with the morning reports. Brek set them on the desk in order of operational priority rather than chronological sequence — most urgent on top, least urgent beneath, and the middle one the item Maerath had been waiting for without having told him she was waiting for it.

Brek remained standing while she read. Nine years of report deliveries, nine years on his feet, and not once had she invited him to sit during a briefing. He had long since understood that the absence of an invitation was itself a form of information. Reading what arrived as absence was the quality that had kept him in this position.

"The temple quarter sweep," she said.

"Completed at the sixth bell. Sector coverage eighty-three percent. The remaining seventeen is the collapsed eastern section — structural access was assessed as unsafe for personnel deployment." He paused. "The note on the restricted section suggests the collapse predates current Registry records by a significant margin. Flagged for infrastructure review."

Maerath did not look up. The report open in her hands was from the second sleeve. Brek had placed the temple quarter sweep in the first sleeve, which she had set aside without opening. He registered this. He said nothing.

"The notation fragment," she said.

"Routed to cryptography at the fourth bell. Secondary priority queue, per the amendment filed by the secondary investigator. Baseline processing is eight to ten days from intake."

The secondary investigator. She turned the phrase the way she turned a stormglass crystal before accessing it — weighing it in her hand before committing to a read. The amendment was procedurally correct. The justification was adequate. Twelve years with the Registry, accurate documentation throughout, no previous deviations from standard routing practice.

The amendment was the deviation.

"The third item," she said.

"Frequency monitoring summary from the lower station. Seventy-two hours. Bands one through four within normal parameters." Brek's jaw tightened briefly, then settled. "Band five shows continued low-level elevation, consistent with the past three weeks. Secondary register activity in the temple quarter district."

She turned to the third sleeve and opened it. The monitoring summary ran three pages. She read the first before he continued.

"Band six." He stopped there. He had learned that elaboration on band six was not something she required from him.

The first page displayed the standard six-band readout in columnar format — each band's readings across the seventy-two-hour period rendered in the Registry's standard frequency notation, a grid of numbers that most archivists would read as routine infrastructure monitoring. Maerath had been reading this grid for four years. She knew what routine looked like. She knew what the current band six reading looked like. The two things were not the same.

Band six was elevated. Not alarmingly. Not at the level that would trigger the standard escalation protocol, which required a reading of one hundred and twelve hertz or above before mandatory reporting to the senior Registry board. The current reading was ninety-one hertz. Twenty-one hertz separated it from the threshold. She had been managing that gap for four years. For three weeks, the gap had been narrowing.

"The amendment delays cryptography analysis," she said. Not a question.

"Three days added to baseline. Eight to ten days becomes eleven to thirteen."

"The secondary investigator filed this amendment at what bell?"

"The seventh bell, yesterday evening. Approximately four hours after the preliminary report reached the operational annex."

Four hours. She set the monitoring summary on the desk and looked toward the window. Below, the city was moving into mid-morning — the Shelf walkways visible from this height as thin iron lines against the gorge face, a few figures crossing the upper sections. The Glass Bridge ruins were not visible from this angle. She had positioned the desk deliberately.

"His assessment of the notation fragment," she said. "His read on the grammar."

"Private notation system. Non-Registry grammar. Consistent with the Underbrim folio recovered in the earlier phase of the investigation." Brek did not shift register. "He assessed the fragment as authored by the subject."

The subject. The secondary investigator had filed accurate documentation on the subject throughout the investigation, with one exception: a blank location field in an early negative-result form, re-filed as a second form with a procedurally adequate explanation. She had noted it at the time. She had allowed it to remain in the active file because the second form was correct in every other particular, and because pursuing the blank field would have required her to disclose why she was pursuing it.

The subject had been in the Hollows. The subject had accessed Tace's cylinders. The notation fragment was the subject's work. The secondary investigator had received the preliminary report four hours before filing an amendment that delayed the fragment's analysis by three days.

The three items on her desk converged. The picture was not new — each piece had arrived separately, in its own sleeve, on its own day — but now they sat together on a single surface, and the shape they made was legible.

The secondary investigator knew the notation system. He had recognized it in the report. He had filed the amendment to delay analysis.

"Thank you," Maerath said. "That will be all."

Brek gathered the sleeves she had finished with — the first and the third — and left the second, which she was still holding. The door closed without sound. This, too, was something he had learned.

She sat with the second sleeve for some time after Brek left.

The monitoring summary lay open on the desk. Band six, column seven of the seventy-two-hour grid: ninety-one hertz, ninety-two hertz, ninety-one hertz. That elevation had held for twenty-two days. Before that, three weeks of gradual increase from the baseline she had established when she installed the monitoring panel four years ago. Before that, the baseline itself — fifty-three hertz, the older stratum's ambient resonance when she had first begun monitoring it, the reading that had told her the stratum was not inert in the way the Registry's official position maintained.

The Registry's official position held that the older stratum had been fully decommissioned in the founding period, its frequency architecture sealed, its resonance decayed to zero, and that the current stormglass infrastructure operated entirely on the standard encoding system established at the Charter's signing. This position appeared in the Registry's founding documentation, the infrastructure maintenance records, and every curriculum used to train archivists for the past forty years.

The monitoring panel on the east wall of this room had been registering fifty-three hertz from the older stratum for four years. The position and the panel were not compatible. She had chosen not to resolve the incompatibility through disclosure.

The notation fragment was the subject's work. The subject had been in the Hollows. The subject had accessed Tace's cylinders. Tace had been the original engineer on the Glass Bridge installation, had logged the anomaly in installation month three, had been removed from the project when she filed the report, and had spent four years in the Hollows — four years Maerath had not known about, because Tace had been listed in the Registry's personnel records as deceased following an illness. Maerath had not verified this. The not-verifying had been a choice, made.

Tace had been alive. Tace had the cylinders. The subject had reached the cylinders.

The cylinders were empty now. The assessment had noted twelve pre-Charter amber cylinders with residual Solen-period frequency signatures. Empty. The contents had been transferred. The subject was moving through the city carrying whatever Solen had encoded in those cylinders, and the notation fragment was the subject's working grammar for Solen's encoding system, and the secondary investigator had recognized the grammar and filed an amendment to delay its analysis.

The amendment had bought three days. The note she had placed in the night courier sleeve had been delivered before the Spire's night bell. Its recipient would have acted on it by now — or would act within the day, depending on operational logistics she had deliberately not made herself aware of. The action would take time. Three days was not a comfortable margin.

She opened the second sleeve.

The temple quarter sweep report ran eleven pages, single-spaced, in precise sequential notation: thorough, organized, characteristic. The Hollows staging area had been catalogued with the care of someone who worked physical evidence the way a cutter works stone — starting at the surface, reading the grain before committing to depth. The cylinders were noted — their positions, residual signatures, manufacturing period. The occupation evidence was noted: long-term, multi-person, the kind of settlement that accumulates over months rather than days. The notation fragment's location was noted, its condition, the specific tear pattern suggesting it had been separated from a larger document under time pressure rather than deliberately excised.

In a brief addendum on the final page, the report noted that the sensor alert triggering the sweep had been filed through Registry channels at the third bell, that arrival at the site had occurred approximately twenty minutes after the alert, and that the evacuation of the staging area had taken place four to six hours before his arrival.

Four to six hours before the third-bell alert. The alert had been triggered by the sensor — a standard Registry frequency monitor of the type installed in decommissioned public buildings as part of the infrastructure maintenance protocol, a protocol that authorized passive monitoring but did not authorize active alerts without a Registry supervisor's explicit instruction.

Someone had changed the sensor's alert threshold.

She read the addendum again. The timing discrepancy had been noted without interpretation, flagged for supervisory review, which was why it had come to her desk rather than remaining in the operational annex.

The sensor alert had been filed through Registry channels. The threshold change would have required access to the sensor's encoding — access available to Registry personnel above a certain clearance tier, and to no one else.

She had not authorized the threshold change. She had not asked anyone to authorize it. The standard monitoring protocol had been in place for the Hollows site for two years, since she had identified the decommissioned Remembrance Hall as a potential resistance staging area and placed it under passive monitoring. Two years without a triggered alert. The threshold change had triggered one last night.

Someone inside the Registry had changed the sensor threshold without her authorization. Someone had decided to accelerate the timeline on the Hollows site. Someone had been running a parallel operation inside the architecture she had built, using the tools she had put in place, moving toward an outcome she had not specified.

The monitoring summary was still open on the desk. Band six: ninety-one hertz.

The secondary investigator had filed an amendment to delay the notation fragment's analysis. Someone inside the Registry had changed a sensor threshold to accelerate the Hollows site discovery. The subject had been in the Hollows and was now moving through the city with the contents of Tace's cylinders.

The threshold change was the variable she had not created.

She closed the monitoring summary and slid it into the lower left drawer of the secondary desk, beneath the administrative manuals that had not been opened in three years. The band six reading would not appear in the operational file. It had not appeared in any operational file. This was one of the things she managed alone.

The secondary investigator's amendment. The sensor threshold change. The subject's location, unknown.

She set the three facts on the desk in her mind the way she set physical documents — edges squared, nothing overlapping — and looked at what they made. The crystal was out; she was reading.

The sensor threshold change was the variable she had not created. Everything else in the investigation's architecture had been built or authorized by her: the surveillance parameters, the routing protocols, the containment note placed in the night courier sleeve. The threshold change had been built inside her architecture by someone else, using her tools, without her knowledge.

The threshold change bore a Registry protocol number she did not recognize — not a format she had issued, not a sequence from any amendment log she maintained. She had managed the investigation's variables for several weeks under the assumption that she controlled the architecture. The threshold change was evidence that the assumption had been incomplete. Someone else was operating inside the system — someone with Registry clearance, Registry access, and a timeline that did not align with hers.

The containment note was with its recipient. The action would proceed on the recipient's timeline, not hers. She had understood this when she sealed the envelope. She had sealed it anyway.

The amendment had been filed at the seventh bell. The threshold change had triggered the alert at the third bell. The subject had evacuated the Hollows four to six hours before the alert. Three facts, a sequence she had not designed, arriving in the order they arrived.

The notation fragment was in cryptography. Eleven to thirteen days remained before analysis, per the amended timeline. The subject was in the city, carrying the contents of Tace's cylinders, in possession of Solen's encoding grammar. The secondary frequency band was accessible to someone with Solen's notation system — which the subject was now demonstrably holding.

Band six: ninety-one hertz. The gap between the current reading and the escalation threshold was twenty-one hertz. The gap had been narrowing for three weeks at a gradual, consistent rate — not random fluctuation but directional movement. The older stratum was responding to something, and that something had been increasing in intensity for approximately three weeks, which was when the subject had arrived in the temple quarter district and begun accessing the Hollows site.

She had been managing the older stratum's band six elevation in parallel with the investigation because the two variables were not independent. They had never been independent. She had known this for four years and had kept it in the place where she kept such things — a stone she did not turn over, carried in the same coat pocket as the work itself, its weight familiar enough that she no longer reached for it.

The system had more moving parts than she had authorized, and the parts were converging. She pulled the active file toward her and opened it to the operational summary page she updated each morning. Three columns: current known variables, current unknown variables, active containment actions. Several weeks of maintenance. It was the closest thing she had to a complete picture of the investigation's state, and it was not complete.

Under current unknown variables, she added two items in her precise, unornamented hand: the identity of the party who had modified the Hollows sensor threshold; and the subject's current location.

Under active containment actions, she recorded the time the containment note had been placed in the courier sleeve, the recipient's designation — not a name, a designation — and the expected action window.

She closed the file.

Outside the window, the city had settled into its working-day rhythm — figures crossing the Shelf walkways, the Gorge Floor's Millrow wheels transmitting their low vibration up through the Spire's foundation stone. The stormglass surfaces of the buildings below caught the first horizontal light and threw it back cold and pale, the color of a city that had been keeping records longer than anyone still living could account for.

The sensor threshold change meant someone inside the Registry was running a parallel agenda. The secondary investigator's amendment meant someone inside the Registry carried a parallel loyalty. The band six elevation meant the older stratum was responding to variables she could not fully account for.

Her hand rested on the file cover without opening it. The lower left drawer had not closed flush; a corner of the monitoring summary caught the frame. The cracks were not ones she had made.

The monitoring summary was in the lower left drawer. The operational file was closed. The containment action was in motion. The notation fragment was in cryptography with eleven to thirteen days remaining.

She pulled the next document from the active file — a routine frequency calibration report from the lower station, two pages, covering the standard six-band readout from the previous week — and set it flat on the desk. She turned to the first column and began. The cracks in the picture were information, and information was what she read, and she read everything completely, in order, each page before the next.

Below the window, the city moved. The band six reading sat in the lower left drawer. The containment note was with its recipient.

She turned to the first page and did not look up.

Chapter 14

Beneath the operational annex, the Registry's personnel archive ran the length of a sub-level corridor accessible only through a stairwell that demanded two separate clearance passes — the first at the top, logged automatically by the badge reader, and the second at the bottom, where a duty clerk recorded the time and the accessing officer's designation in a handwritten ledger that was itself bundled and archived at the close of each month. Davan had made this descent perhaps forty times across his career. He knew which step creaked. He knew the duty clerk's name was Peva, that Peva preferred silence before the sixth bell, and that Peva's ledger entries were precise and complete — never once challenged by a reviewing officer, because no reviewing officer had ever found reason to look.

Tonight there would be reason to look.

He went down without pausing at the first clearance point, which logged his badge at the third bell past midnight — late enough that the annex above had emptied, early enough that the pre-dawn shift had not yet assembled. The second clearance point sat unstaffed. Peva had gone home at the second bell. The ledger lay open on the clerk's desk, the last entry in Peva's careful hand dated two hours prior. Davan left no entry. The absence was its own kind of record, but a record that required someone to notice the gap — and noticing the gap required someone to already know what should have been there.

The personnel archive stretched the full length of the sub-level corridor: floor-to-ceiling shelving on both sides, files organized by Registry period and then by project designation, the older materials housed in the original amber-glass cylinders that had not been standard issue for twelve years, the newer materials in flat stormglass panels slotted into labeled trays. The gas lamps along this corridor burned on a reduced setting — cost management, standard practice for unstaffed hours — which left the upper shelving in shadow and the lower shelving in a light adequate for reading if he leaned close enough.

He did not use his own lamp. He did not want the light visible from the stairwell.

The Glass Bridge installation project had been designated under Infrastructure De-velopment, Gorge Crossing, Charter Year Fourteen. He had known this from the op-erational file he maintained in his official capacity, from the routing documents that had moved through the annex in the weeks since Brek's temple quarter sweep, from the seventeen years of institutional memory that had accumulated in him the way sediment accumulated in the Sill's bed — not chosen, simply deposited by the work. He located the section in four minutes. The files were organized by installation phase: site assessment, materials authorization, engineering review, calibration certification, final inspection, and sign-off.

He pulled the calibration certification file.

The first page was a standard Registry cover sheet, the project designation printed at the top in the font the Council had standardized in Charter Year Nine, the filing date stamped in red ink that had faded over seventeen years to something closer to rust. The second page was the calibration team roster — six names, their Registry designations, their assigned nodes on the Bridge's load-distribution system. Tace's name was there: Lead Calibration Engineer, Nodes One through Four. He had known it would be. What he had not known, and what the third page made clear, was the sign-off chain.

The calibration certification required three authorizing signatures: the lead engineer, the project supervisor, and the approving authority. Tace had signed as lead engineer. The project supervisor's signature belonged to a name Davan recognized from other infra-structure files of the period — a mid-level Registry functionary who had died eleven years ago, listed in the Registry's personnel records as retired. Maerath's signature occupied the approving authority line, dated fourteen days after the anomaly dismissal that Tace had contested and lost.

He had expected Maerath. He turned to the fourth page.

The fourth page was not standard. It was an addendum, filed under a secondary authorization protocol Davan had encountered perhaps three times in his career — a protocol reserved for projects with Charter-level oversight, meaning projects in which the founding governance structure held a direct stake. The addendum required a single signature: the Charter oversight authority.

The signature was Ryn Ossian's.

Davan held the page in the reduced gas light long enough to read it a second time, the seventeen-year-old paper dry and slightly rough under his thumb where the ink had pressed into the grain. Ryn Ossian. One of the original five signatories of the founding

Charter. The man whose name appeared in the city's public record as an architect of Bridgefall's memory-preservation infrastructure, who had been in nominal retirement for nine years, who was publicly honored at the Bridge Memorial observance every year, who had delivered the address at the last three observances himself — standing at the Plateau-side anchor tower of the bridge whose collapse had killed forty-one people, speaking about the importance of accurate memory in a city built on record-keeping.

The addendum was dated three days before the Bridge's final inspection. Davan photographed nothing. He had no equipment for it. He read the page three times, then a fourth. Then he replaced it exactly as he had found it — the slight curl at the upper right corner, the angle at which it rested against the third page — and slid the file back into its tray and walked the corridor to the stairwell.

The first clearance point logged his exit at seven minutes past the third bell.

Twelve hours, roughly, before a routine access audit would flag the personnel file as accessed outside standard operational hours by an officer whose active caseload had no connection to Infrastructure Development projects. The knowledge arrived as a specific pressure behind his sternum. His body had been running the numbers without him.

He walked the correct corridor. He held the correct expression. He went to find Vael.

She was already awake when he knocked — three, then two, then one, the sequence she had given him at the Underbrim and that he had not written down. The door opened before the echo of the last knock had finished. She had the amber shard in her hand, not as a weapon, simply held, the way she held things when she was thinking.

"You found it," she said.

Not a question. He had told her three days ago that he intended to look, and she had said nothing, and that nothing had been its own kind of answer — not permission, not prohibition, simply the specific quality of a person who had already calculated the risk and was waiting for the result.

"Come in," he said, because it was his room and the sentence was automatic, and then he registered the absurdity of it and stepped aside.

The room was the same room he had been renting for eleven weeks: a table, two chairs, a cot against the far wall, a window that faced the gorge wall rather than the street and therefore received no direct light. Nothing had been added. Nothing had been removed. The room looked like a room waiting to be vacated, which was accurate.

She came in. The door closed. She set the amber shard on the table — not carefully, simply placed it down, as though it were a tool she was finished using for the moment — and looked at him.

"Sit down," she said.

He sat. She did not. She stood on the other side of the table with her hands flat against its surface, which he had learned was how she positioned herself when she was about to say something she had been holding for longer than the conversation required.

"Tell me the third name."

"Ryn Ossian."

The stillness that came over her was not the stillness of surprise. It had the character of a wall taking weight — no visible give, no collapse, just the quiet of something holding under pressure it was built to hold. Her hands did not shift. Her breathing did not change in any way he could measure. She looked at him with the particular quality of attention she brought to stormglass when the frequency returned something unexpected and she had to determine whether the error was in the crystal or in herself.

"Show me," she said.

He had not brought the file. He had not taken the file. He told her what was on the fourth page: the addendum, the Charter oversight protocol, the signature, the date — three days before the final inspection. He told her about Ossian's presence at the Bridge Memorial observances, the address at the last three, the specific language the Registry's public record used to describe his role in the city's memory-preservation infrastructure. He delivered all of it with the flat precision he used for operational summaries.

She listened without interrupting. When he finished, she sat down.

For a moment the room held only the sound of the gorge — the Millrow wheels transmitting through the foundation stone as a low vibration, the cold of the city's lower levels seeping through the window's imperfect seal. The candle on the table between them had burned to approximately its midpoint. He had lit it when he came in, before he knocked, out of a habit he did not examine.

"Not corruption," she said. Her voice had the bearing of someone reading aloud from a document, testing whether the sentence held. "Not something that entered the system from outside and damaged it. He built the system. He was one of the five people who built the system. The Charter created the Registry's authority, and Ossian signed the Charter, and then Ossian used the authority the Charter created to authorize a calibration certification that he knew was wrong."

She was not asking him to confirm this. She was saying it aloud.

"The design," Davan said.

"The design." She picked up the amber shard. She did not look at it — she held it the way she had been holding it when she answered the door, as a weight, as a thing that had mass. "Tace logged the anomaly in installation month three. The dismissal came fourteen days later. Maerath's authorization came fourteen days after the dismissal. And Ossian's addendum came three days before the final inspection, which means he reviewed the certification — the complete certification, including Tace's contested anomaly report — and signed it. He signed it knowing the load-distribution deviation was real."

"He signed it knowing," Davan said.

"The Bridge Memorial address." She set the shard down. "He gives the address every year. He stands at the anchor tower and speaks about accurate memory. He has done this for nine years. Since the collapse."

Davan said nothing.

She looked at him across the table. Her eyes moved over his face the way they moved over a stormglass panel mid-reading — steady, then briefly still, cataloguing something. Then something shifted. She looked at him directly.

"The access record," she said.

"Exists."

"How long."

"Twelve hours before a routine audit flags it. Possibly less if someone is running a targeted review of Infrastructure Development access — but there's no reason they would be running one. The active caseload doesn't touch that section." He paused. "The duty ledger has no entry for my exit time. That creates a gap, but the gap requires someone to know what should have been there."

"Brek."

118 R.M. KISER

"Brek runs active sweeps, not archive audits. The audit function is a different desk." He watched her process this. "Twelve hours is the conservative estimate. It may be longer."

"We use twelve hours," she said. "We don't plan for longer."

She reached across the table and picked up the amber shard again, and this time she did look at it — turned it in the candlelight, the specific motion he had seen her use when she was reading a frequency rather than holding a weight. The crystal caught the light and held it in the particular way of pre-Charter amber, warmer than stormglass, less refractive, the light staying in the crystal rather than passing through it.

"What we have," she said. Not a question. An inventory beginning.

They worked through it in the order she established — not the order Davan would have chosen. The order that built toward the gap rather than toward the evidence, because the gap was what they needed to understand.

Solen's cylinder: authenticated, containing the three-name notation framework with Ossian now confirmed as the originating authority. The cylinder itself as physical object, the encoding as Solen's, the authentication as verifiable by anyone with knowledge of the secondary frequency band and Solen's specific encoding grammar.

Tace's twelve amber cylinders: the contents transferred, the calibration records from installation month three through installation month seventeen, the anomaly logged in month three and the dismissal fourteen days later and the chain of authorization above the dismissal. Tace herself: deceased, according to the Registry's records. Not deceased.

Nava's discrepancy catalogue: seventeen years of secondary frequency band documentation, the gap between the public record and the counter-archive made systematic. Nava herself: active, located, accessible.

The personnel file: Davan's memory of it, which was precise but was not the file. The access record existed. The file itself remained in the sub-level corridor, unaltered, where anyone with the appropriate clearance could read it.

"We can't use the file," Vael said. "Not directly. If it surfaces through official channels, Maerath's apparatus has the access record as evidence that it was tampered with — or that you accessed it improperly, which is the same thing for their purposes."

"The access record doesn't show what I read. It shows that I accessed the Infrastructure Development section."

"It shows you accessed it at the third bell past midnight with no operational justification logged." She looked at the candle. "That's enough for them to challenge anything that comes from it."

"So we need the file to surface through a different channel."

"We need someone with legitimate access and a legitimate reason to pull the file. Someone whose access wouldn't require explanation." She turned the shard in her fingers. "Ossian himself has the clearance. The oversight protocol means his name is on the addendum, which means he has review rights over the complete project file."

"You're not suggesting—"

"No." The word was flat. "I'm mapping what we have. The file exists. The file is accessible. We can't use the access we already have, and we can't create legitimate access quickly enough." She set the shard down. "So the file is evidence we can describe but can't produce. Which means we need the other evidence to carry weight without it."

Davan watched her work through this. She did not look frustrated. She paused mid-thought, pressed two fingers to the edge of the table, then resumed, her voice picking up exactly where it had stopped.

"The cylinder and the catalogue together," she said. "Solen's notation identifies three names. Tace's records document the anomaly chain that those three names authorized. Nava's catalogue documents seventeen years of the gap between the public record and the counter-archive. None of it names Ossian directly — the cylinder's notation is in Solen's private grammar, which requires translation, and the translation is interpretive."

"Interpretive enough to challenge."

"Interpretive enough that a Registry legal challenge could occupy the question for months." She looked at him. "Months might be enough. If the challenge is public. If the documents are already in circulation before the challenge is filed."

"Circulation," he said.

"The Registry controls the standard publication infrastructure. Any formal release through official channels goes through the Civic Hall's document intake, which Maerath's apparatus reviews before public access is granted." She picked up the shard for the third time, and this time she did not turn it — she held it flat in her palm, the amber warm in the candlelight. "We need a channel they don't control. We need something that reaches every stormglass receiver in the city simultaneously — the public installations, the private ones, the Registry's own monitoring network. Something that makes the challenge a response to something already heard rather than a suppression of something not yet released."

The candle had burned lower. The gorge vibration was constant beneath them, the Millrow wheels, the Sill. Davan had been in this room for eleven weeks. He knew the wheel-sound when it slowed near the fourth bell, knew the cold that came through the window's gap when the wind turned off the gorge wall. What he did not know was the sound of this — two voices in the room, the candle between them, the problem spread across the table like a map with one road missing.

"The Spire's broadcast installation," he said.

She looked at him.

The Spire's broadcast installation was the Registry's primary frequency transmission point — the equipment used, at the Council's founding, to transmit the Charter's ratification signal to every stormglass receiver in Bridgefall simultaneously. It had not been used for a broadcast of that scale since. Maintained as operational infrastructure, tested quarterly, staffed by a rotating duty engineer whose primary function was to ensure the equipment remained capable of use if the Council ever required it.

The installation required specific access codes. The codes rotated on a quarterly schedule. The current rotation had been in effect for six weeks.

Davan knew the current codes because he was the officer who had filed the quarterly access verification report six weeks ago, and the verification report required logging the codes as part of the audit trail, and the audit trail was a document he had generated and filed and retained a copy of in his operational records as standard procedure.

"I have the access codes," he said.

He said it plainly, the way a man states a thing he has known for some time without recognizing its full weight until the moment he speaks it.

Vael looked at him across the candle's diminishing light. The amber shard sat between them on the table alongside the files, a third object neither of them had placed there deliberately. The access record existed. The twelve hours were running. Below, the Millrow wheels turned in the gorge, and the Sill ran cold, and across the city the stormglass surfaces caught the first grey light of pre-dawn and gave it back pale and flat, the way the city always looked in that hour before the lamps were doused.

She reached for the shard. Her eyes dropped to it, then came back to him — measuring, not the shard but the next step, and the one after that, and what each would cost.

The candle burned toward its base. Outside, a cart crossed the upper road, iron wheels on stone, the first working sound of morning. Twelve hours remained, and the broadcast installation was in the Spire, and the Spire was the building where Maerath read her files each morning and Brek delivered his reports and the band six frequency climbed its slow, unreported degrees toward something no one in the operational annex was permitted to name.

Chapter 15

The overflow storage room in the lower Registry annex had no window, and eleven years had shaped the space around that fact. Shelves ran floor to ceiling because no glass interrupted the walls. The gas lamp hung on a long articulated arm, angled to reach any shelf face. The single chair sat not for comfort but for the precise reach it allowed between the third and fourth rows. Vael had been in this room before — but not like this, not in the hour before dawn with the city still quiet and the overnight staff reduced to two clerks at the annex's far end, and Nava standing at the easternmost shelf with her back to the door, pulling cylinders.

She did not turn when Vael came in. "You have the third name," Nava said. Not a question. The cylinder in her hand was amber, pre-Charter — the kind that warmed when accessed. She set it into the carry case already open on the floor: plain canvas, field-equipment style, the buckle straps dark and stiff at the edges where they had never quite flexed right. Vael looked at it. Seventeen years of discrepancy records, becoming portable.

"Ossian," Vael said. "Ryn Ossian. One of the five Charter signatories. His addendum is in the personnel file — Charter Year Fourteen, Infrastructure Development, Gorge Crossing. He signed three days before the Bridge's final inspection."

Nava's hands rested flat against the shelf between two cylinders, not reaching for anything. The posture of a body that had already decided what the mind was still catching up to.

"His name is in Solen's notation," Vael said. "Originating authority. The first level of her three-level grammar."

The shelf held. Nava's hands held. The gas lamp angled toward the fourth row, and the amber glass threw a low amber wash across the packing cloth — seventeen years of frequency signatures glowing faintly in their housings, each one the record of something the Registry had chosen not to record.

"I know," Nava said.

Vael said nothing.

"I have known for four years." Nava lifted one hand from the shelf and rested it on a cylinder without yet pulling it. "I could not prove it. The reclassified personnel records from that period require access above my tier. I had the shape of it — the authorization chain, the hierarchy, the silence where his name should have been —" She pulled the cylinder. It clicked softly against the two already in the case. "You found the personnel file."

"Davan found it. In the sub-level archive, third bell past midnight. He replaced it exactly as he found it." Vael moved to the next shelf and set her hand on a cylinder. The glass was cool. She waited for Nava's nod, which came, then pulled it and placed it in the case. "We can't produce the file. The access record makes it unusable through official channels. But Solen's notation names him, and Tace's records document the anomaly chain he authorized, and your catalogue documents seventeen years of the gap."

"The gap," Nava said.

"Between the public record and what you built here."

Nava was quiet. She moved to the next row and worked without speaking, pulling cylinders in a sequence that was clearly not random — she knew which ones, which order, which sections of the catalogue carried the most weight and which were corroborating redundancy. She did not pause to decide; her hands went directly to each cylinder in turn, the case filling in an order only she fully understood. Vael worked alongside her, handing cylinders when Nava indicated and packing them when Nava's hands were already full, and the room began to empty in a way that made its organization visible as absence.

The shelves had a logic. Vael had always understood that in the abstract. Watching the logic become portable — the cylinders nested in rows, the canvas sides filling out, the buckle straps pulled snug — the room looked suddenly like a space that had been holding its breath.

"We need the broadcast installation," Vael said. "The Spire's primary frequency transmission point. Davan has the access codes."

"The Spire," Nava said.

"Yes."

Nava set a cylinder in the case and did not reach for another. She stood with her hands at her sides and looked at the carry case on the floor — the cylinders nested in their packing cloth, amber glass against canvas, the frequency signatures quiet without a reader to wake them.

"I will not go to the Spire," she said.

Vael had known this. She had known it the way she knew things before she had language for them — something she had read in the way Nava never reached past the fourth row without being asked, as though she had always known that row would be the last. Nava's hands settled at her sides — not dropped, not let go, but placed.

"I will get the catalogue to the broadcast point," Nava said. "The market edge at the Plateau's lower rim — the nearest point I can reach from the annex without passing through Registry-controlled transit. I will carry it that far." She looked at Vael. "That is my limit. I am naming it clearly so you know what you are working with."

"I know what I'm working with," Vael said.

Nava reached for the last cylinder on the shelf she had been clearing. She held it a moment before placing it — not reading it, just holding it, the amber glass warming slightly in her palm the way glass did when someone had been handling it for a long time. Then she set it in the case.

"Tell me what Ossian signed," she said. Not the name — she had the name. The act. What the addendum recorded.

"He reviewed and approved the Bridge's final certification," Vael said. "Three days before inspection. The addendum required his signature as Charter-level oversight. He signed knowing Tace's load-distribution anomaly was real — knowing the dismissal had been filed under a Registry ID that appears nowhere else in the record, knowing the authorization chain ran from the dismissal through Maerath's approval to his own review." She paused. "He signed it anyway."

Nava closed the carry case. The buckles caught with a sound like a small door.

"Forty-one," she said.

The word landed. The specific, irreducible fact that everything else rested on — the thing that had made the work insufficient.

Vael said nothing. There was nothing to add.

Nava picked up the carry case. She straightened under its weight, shoulders settling, chin coming level — not straining against it, simply taking it in.

"The market edge," she said. "Before the fifth bell."

The Council operational offices occupied the Spire's second floor, east corridor — brushed-metal stormglass panels at overnight dim, sound-absorbing wall treatment that made the space feel narrower than its actual width, the way institutional corridors did. Davan had walked this corridor for a decade. He knew its silences by kind: the particular drop in ambient sound when the annex staff changed shifts, the brief mechanical stillness when the frequency monitoring room ran a calibration cycle, the plain quiet of the hour before dawn when most of the building's operational staff had not yet arrived.

He was two-thirds of the way to the stairwell when Brek came around the corner.

"Davan." Brek's voice was easy, the genuine ease of a man glad to find a familiar face at an odd hour. He wore his long Registry grey coat with the collar up against the overnight chill, a report sleeve tucked under one arm and a cup of tea in his other hand — exactly the image of a man who had arrived early because the work required it and found the morning more manageable than expected. "You're in early."

"Couldn't sleep," Davan said. True enough.

"I know the feeling." Brek fell into step beside him — not blocking, not intercepting, simply joining, the way colleagues moved through institutional space when they had business in the same direction. "I've been here since the third bell. The temple quarter sweep is running behind — the eastern section is still inaccessible, the access structure needs repair, and the sector team has been waiting on authorization from Infrastructure for six days." He shook his head with the mild frustration of a competent man inside a slow system. "I was going to flag it in the morning report. But since you're here."

"Flag it," Davan said. "Infrastructure authorization takes three days minimum. You'll want the request logged before the review cycle."

"Already done." Brek sipped his tea. "I wanted to ask you about something, actually. The personnel archive access — the sub-level, Infrastructure Development. It logged at third bell past midnight." He said it without weight, without the careful flatness that would have signaled accusation. Collegial, genuinely curious, his tone offering Davan room to account for it before the question became something else. "I saw it on the overnight access summary. Your badge."

The corridor did not change. The stormglass panels held their overnight dim, the sound-absorbing walls their particular quality of institutional silence. Davan kept his pace.

"Cross-reference for the Hollows notation analysis," he said. "The fragment Cryptography is processing — I wanted to check whether there were any personnel records from the relevant period that might establish authorship context before the analysis completes. Save time on the identification phase."

Brek nodded slowly. The nod of a man processing information rather than accepting it. "The notation fragment is in secondary priority queue. Cryptography's timeline is eleven to thirteen days from intake."

"I know. I was trying to get ahead of it."

"Infrastructure Development," Brek said. "The notation fragment is from the temple quarter staging area. The cross-reference to Infrastructure Development — that's a long reach."

"The Hollows staging area had twelve pre-Charter cylinders with Solen-period residue." Davan let his voice carry the look of a man thinking aloud through a case, each detail offered in sequence, a little more than strictly necessary. "Solen was an archivist trained before the Council standardized the systems. I was checking her personnel period against the Infrastructure Development files — she may have had direct contact with the installation teams during the Bridge project. If the notation fragment is hers, the personnel records might help establish the grammar's origin."

Brek was quiet for a moment. The corridor turned at the far end and they were both walking toward the turn, the stairwell beyond it, the morning coming whether either of them was ready.

"That's a solid line of reasoning," Brek said.

The warmth in his voice was real. That was the difficulty. Brek's concern was genuine — the professional interest, the collegial regard, the weight of a man who had worked alongside someone for a decade and found him reliable and was extending a benefit of the doubt he did not fully have. Davan had been on the other side of this exchange before. He recognized exactly what Brek was doing because he had done it himself — the warm question that was also a test, the collegial framing that was also an opening, the specific generosity of a colleague telling you, in the gentlest possible register, that he had noticed something and was letting you explain it before he was required to act on what he'd noticed.

Brek had bought Davan time. He would keep buying it until the review flag triggered and he had no choice but to stop.

"I didn't find anything useful," Davan said. "The relevant personnel records from that period are reclassified above standard investigator access. I should have checked the access tier before going down there."

"Happens," Brek said.

They reached the stairwell. Brek stopped — his floor was here, the morning report, the sector sweep authorization, the ordinary machinery of a competent man doing his work. He held his tea with both hands and looked at Davan the way a man looks when he has more to weigh than he is willing to name outright — still, attending, not quite done.

"Get some sleep when you can." He said it without turning fully back, the door already moving. "The review cycle runs at the eighth bell. If there's anything in the overnight access summary you want to annotate before it processes, the window is tight."

He went through the stairwell door. It closed behind him with the sound of a well-maintained hinge — quiet, precise, institutional.

Davan stood in the corridor. The stormglass panels held their dim. The review cycle ran at the eighth bell. He had the access codes in his operational records and a window that was closing and a colleague who had just told him, in the language of a man who did not want to be required to act, that the window was closing.

He turned and went to find the stairwell down.

The message came through the dispersed Hollows network at the fourth bell, routed through two relay points and delivered to the drop point she had established at the Underbrim three weeks ago — a loose stone in the third step of the stairwell that descended to the market's lower level, behind which a small space had been cleared and lined with oilcloth against the moisture that rose from the gorge in the early morning hours.

The message was short.

She read it in the stairwell with the city beginning to acquire its working-day texture above her — the first market traders setting up at the Mudflat's edge, the Millrow wheels already turning in the gorge below, the pre-dawn light coming grey and flat off the stormglass surfaces, neither dark nor day, the kind of light that made every edge look provisional.

The message read: *I have been waiting four years. This seems like the right use of it. Secondary entrance, hour before dawn.*

No name. No explanation of why now, when Tace had declined every prior approach through every prior channel — the dispersed network contacts, the relay points, the three separate requests routed over the past six weeks. No account of what four years looked like for a woman listed as deceased, living in the Hollows with twelve pre-Charter amber cylinders and an oilcloth-lined shelf and a woman who had set a chair precisely beneath the lowest shelf, the stone floor beneath it ground pale where the legs had shifted over time.

Vael folded the message and put it in her coat.

Down the stairwell the gorge wall showed pale through the stormglass — the pre-dawn light catching in the facets and breaking apart, the colors separating briefly before the eye resolved them back into grey.

The hour before dawn. The secondary entrance. Tace at one door and the catalogue in a canvas carry case and Davan with the access codes and the review cycle running at the eighth bell — four hours, which meant the window was not closed yet.

She climbed the stairwell back to the market level, turned toward the Spire, and walked.

Chapter 16

Nava's hands moved without hesitation. She pulled the last cylinder from the shelf, turned it once between her palms — checking the seal, checking the weight, the same motion she had made a thousand times — and set it into the canvas case alongside the others. The overflow storage room held a cold that had nothing to do with the season, born from the depth of the stone and the weight of the building pressing down through all those layers above. Seventeen years of that cold. She had stopped registering it sometime in the fifth year, and had not noticed the absence of noticing until this morning.

The letter was already written. She had composed it in the early hours before Vael arrived, at the small corner table where the gas lamp threw its yellow circle across the surface and left the rest of the room in the close dark of places shaped by work rather than living. She had used the standard request form — the kind that came in packs of twenty from the Registry's administrative supply, the same form she had used for seventeen years to document irregularities, cross-reference calibration records, note discrepancies that entered the catalogue and never left it. She had filled every correct field. She had listed her registered title, her access tier, her seventeen-year tenure in the Calibration Division as the procedural grounds for the request. The request itself called for formal review of the calibration records from Charter Year Fourteen, specifically the Glass Bridge installation series, specifically the load-distribution anomaly documented in installation month three by engineer Tace, subsequently dismissed as *equipment variance* — their term, not hers, the only term the form had a field for.

Nothing in the letter was undocumentable. She had not named the forty-one. She had not named Maerath, or Ossian. She had written: *the record requires review*, and she had used their word — the word that meant correction and meant erasure in the same breath — because it was the only word the form had a field for.

The letter sat folded in the outer pocket of the canvas case, unsealed. She was not certain she would send it. That uncertainty had occupied the last three hours, the same uncertainty she had carried over seventeen years about everything — whether the catalogue was sufficient, whether documentation without release was resistance or only its performance — her hand had gone to the outer pocket three times in the last hour and stopped each time at the folded edge of the letter, whether the forty-one needed a witness or needed an act. The letter was an act. The kind that could not be recalled once it left the pocket.

She placed the last cylinder in the case and buckled the worn straps.

She had known, when she began the catalogue, that a moment like this would come. The shelves still held their shape. The lamp still threw its circle. The cold was still the cold. A coffee tin sat on the corner shelf where she had left it three mornings running, lid askew, as though she might yet come back for it. Nothing around her had changed, and she had changed everything.

She did not read an entry before closing the case. For seventeen years she had done exactly that — one small notation each month, one name she did not recognize, reading it the way you read something aloud to someone who cannot hear you. She did not do it now. The case was closed, the buckles fastened. The buckles were fastened. The letter was in the pocket.

She gripped the case by its handles and walked toward the door.

Tace was already inside when Davan opened the secondary entrance.

The door was a maintenance access point on the Spire's lower north face, set into the stone at the base of a service corridor running parallel to the main infrastructure channel. It did not appear on the current operational floor plan — it appeared on the original construction survey from Charter Year Three, which Tace had filed under a cross-reference notation in the infrastructure maintenance logs before the Council standardized the filing system, meaning no one had searched for it in eleven years. Davan had found it in the access codes log as a footnote to a quarterly verification entry. The entry had not explained what the door opened onto. The footnote had been enough.

Tace stood in the corridor beyond it with a flat lamp, motionless, her weight settled into her heels the way it settles in a person who has been standing in the same place for a long time and has stopped counting the minutes.

She was older than the Registry's personnel records would have suggested — expected, given that those records listed her as deceased, illness, Charter Year Twenty-One, and she had been living in the Hollows for four years since, which left marks no records had fields for. Her hands, wrapped around the lamp, showed the quality of hands that had spent years with installation equipment — the callus pattern at the base of the fingers, the way she gripped the lamp's housing rather than its handle, as though by instinct she were checking for heat.

Vael said nothing. Neither did Tace. Davan pulled the door closed behind them, and the three of them stood in the service corridor's narrow dark with the lamp throwing its circle and the Spire's stone pressing in from every side.

"Second level," Tace said. "Then the service shaft. The monitoring room is adjacent to the installation chamber on the upper level." She said it the way someone says a thing they have rehearsed alone, in the dark, in preparation. "The shaft runs behind the east wall. There's a junction at the third level that the current floor plan marks as a sealed utility space. It isn't."

"How long?" Davan asked.

"Twelve minutes if we don't stop."

They didn't stop.

The service corridors ran behind the Spire's operational spaces the way older infrastructure always ran — in parallel, slightly off-axis, built for the building's original function rather than its current one. The stone here was the same pale limestone as the Spire's facade but unfinished, tool marks still visible in the wall surface where the original installation teams had cut the passage. Tace moved through it without holding the lamp to the walls, which meant she had mapped the route in her head rather than her eyes — the distances between turns, the height differential at the second-level junction, the give in the flooring at the point where the original construction had been modified during Charter Year Seven. At each turn she touched the wall before rounding it. Not feeling for the way. Confirming it.

Vael carried the canvas case in both hands. The cylinders shifted as she moved — amber glass audible against amber glass through the canvas, a sound like something settling into place. The amber shard rode in her coat pocket, separate from the cylinders, its weight a familiar pressure against her ribs. She had carried it long enough that she only noticed it when it was gone.

Davan walked behind her. She did not look back. She knew from the sound of his footfall — the way of a man reading a space rather than simply moving through it — that he was marking the route, logging the distances, building the exit sequence before they had finished the entry. This was the thing she had learned to trust about him: not courage, but the way his body was already solving the next problem while his face was still working on the current one.

At the second-level junction Tace stopped and brought the lamp close to the wall. The stone here showed a seam — a repair, the mortar a slightly different color than the surrounding surface, the work done at some later date than the original construction. She pressed her palm flat against it.

"They bricked this up in Charter Year Nineteen," she said. "Infrastructure Development. I filed the work order." A pause. "I filed it under routine maintenance."

She pressed at the lower edge of the seam, at a specific point, and the section of wall shifted. Not a door — the whole section moved, pivoting on a concealed hinge, opening onto a shaft that ran vertically up the building's interior. Iron rungs set into the stone at regular intervals. The shaft smelled of old air, stale and unmoving, the kind that collects in a space no one has entered in years.

"Four years," Tace said, as if she had heard the question no one had asked. "I have not been in this building in four years."

Vael went first. The canvas case made the climb awkward — she had to hold it by one handle and use the other hand for the rungs, her weight distributed wrong, each rung demanding more from her arms than it should have. She did not stop. The shaft was narrow enough that the walls pressed close on both sides, the stone cold where her knuckles brushed it, and above her the shaft opened into the dim grey of pre-dawn light filtering through a ventilation grate at the upper level.

Davan came last. He pulled the wall section back into place behind him, and the sound it made — a settled, final click — was the sound of the corridor below becoming inaccessible. Not locked. Not sealed. Simply closed, in the way of things designed to appear as though they have never been opened.

The upper level.

The monitoring room was lit.

Two figures were visible through the glass panel beside the door — the night staff, both seated, one with a ledger open, one watching the monitoring board's display of the city's frequency receivers, the small lights indicating active transmission status across Bridgefall's stormglass network. The board showed the city in its overnight state: most receivers dark, a handful of residential units running passive playback, the Registry's own broadcast channel holding its standard overnight signal, the low continuous hum of institutional presence that played whether anyone was listening or not.

Tace and Vael pulled back from the corridor's bend. Davan did not.

He straightened his coat. He had worn it the entire way up the shaft, which meant it had acquired the wrinkle pattern of someone who had been climbing rather than walking, but in the dim light of the service corridor it was not visible, and what was visible was the Registry investigator's badge at his lapel, the standard-issue authentication token that opened every operational door in this building. He squared his shoulders and walked to the monitoring room door and opened it.

Both night staff looked up. One reached for the ledger — a reflex, the gesture of someone noting an interruption. Davan was already speaking before either of them had fully registered his presence.

"There's a band-three anomaly flagged in the lower ward." Flat, unhurried, the tone of a man who has delivered this kind of news a hundred times and expects the same response he always gets. "The sensor log shows it came in at the fourth bell and wasn't routed to the overnight response team. I need you both on-site — the ward supervisor has been asking for Registry presence for the last hour and the routing failure needs to be documented before the eighth-bell review cycle processes it."

The night staff looked at each other. The one with the ledger glanced at the monitoring board — the city's receivers in their overnight state, nothing flagged, nothing active that required their presence here.

"We're not scheduled for—" the second one began.

"The routing failure put you on the response chain," Davan said. "It's in the overnight log. If you're not on-site when the review cycle processes, the documentation gap becomes yours." He paused. The pause was exactly long enough. "I'll cover the board until the day shift arrives."

They went. Without hurry, without alarm, moving the way people move when procedure has given them somewhere to be and a reason not to ask questions. The door closed behind them.

Davan held his position at the monitoring board for a moment. Then he turned and walked back to the corridor.

"Twenty minutes," he said. "Less if the ward supervisor actually calls in."

Tace was already moving toward the installation chamber door.

The broadcast installation was larger than Vael had expected.

She had seen the operational schematic in the Registry's quarterly verification report — the document Davan had retained the access codes from six weeks prior, the audit copy that should have been returned and had not been. The schematic showed a standard stormglass housing, the kind used for institutional frequency broadcasts, the same basic architecture as the transmission units in the city's relay towers but scaled for primary use. The schematic was accurate in its dimensions and silent on the smell — old glass and old metal, both of them warm, that dense trapped warmth of machinery run without interruption for so long the heat has nowhere left to go.

The installation's housing was brushed metal, its surface buffed down at the edges and corners from years of hands checking the same contact points during the same calibration routines. The stormglass at its center — the primary transmission crystal — was the largest piece of worked glass Vael had ever seen in a single housing: the width of her spread arms, the depth of a long step, its surface the amber-grey of pre-Charter glass that had been in service since the city's founding and had never been replaced because the Council did not know how to replace it, only how to use it. The glass held the room's dim light and scattered it the way old glass always scattered rather than reflected — not cleanly, but the way something that has absorbed more than it has transmitted carries both, the clarity and the residue together.

The monitoring board was visible through the glass panel to the adjacent room. The city's receivers in their overnight state. The standard overnight broadcast running its low continuous signal.

Tace set the flat lamp on the housing's edge and opened the calibration panel on the installation's south face. The panel was a maintenance access point — not the primary interface, which required Registry authorization, but the secondary calibration channel installed during Charter Year Three and never updated because the Council's archivists did not know it existed. It ran at 94.7 hertz. Standard encoding frequency. The frequency Solen had used for the secondary band because it was the one no one watched.

"The interface is manual," Tace said. She examined the calibration panel with the focused attention of someone reacquainting themselves with something they knew well and have been away from. "The primary channel requires Registry authentication. This one doesn't. It was designed for installation checks — putting a signal into the transmission crystal directly, bypassing the authentication layer." She touched one of the panel's contacts. "It will reach every receiver in the city. The same as the primary channel. The authentication layer is on the input side, not the output side." A pause. "I know that because I built it that way. I thought it was a safety feature. In case the primary system failed during an emergency broadcast."

She did not say what she thought of that now. She didn't need to.

Vael opened the canvas case. The cylinders were packed in order — Nava's seventeen years of discrepancy documentation, the frequency-signature glass, the amber pre-Charter cylinders holding the anomaly chain from installation month three through the final certification. She had gone through them twice the night before in Davan's room, then again in the grey hour before dawn while boot steps and cart wheels began sounding on the street overhead. She knew what was in each one. She knew the order.

She took the first cylinder out and held it.

The glass was cold. Not the cold of the overflow storage room — this was the cold of stormglass that has not been accessed in hours, the frequency dormant, the crystal holding its last playback temperature the way water holds the shape of its container, cold at the edges first, cold all the way through. Her palms registered the temperature differential at the cylinder's edges before anything else, and then the weight, and then the faint vibration that was not quite sound — the 94.7-hertz baseline that Solen's encoding always carried, the frequency Solen had encoded at the baseline of every recording she made.

Tace worked at the calibration panel's contacts. Not quickly — with the deliberateness of someone who will not rush a calibration, who has learned at cost what rushing produces. Her hands moved with the same quality they had moved with in the service corridor: confirming rather than finding, each contact point checked against a map she held internally.

"The cylinder interface," Vael said.

"Here." Tace indicated a series of contact points along the installation's lower housing. They were the same diameter as the cylinders' base plates. Vael had seen similar interfaces in the Hollows — the older stormglass architecture, the pre-standardization design that Solen had known because she had been trained before the Council updated the systems. "The glass needs direct contact. Unmediated. The installation will read the frequency signature and route it through the transmission crystal." Tace paused. "It will read everything in the secondary band. Not just the primary encoding. Everything Solen put in the layers beneath."

Vael looked at the contact points. Then at the first cylinder in her hands.

She placed it against the contact point without gloves.

The glass warmed immediately — the warmth of a stormglass interface recognizing a compatible frequency, the same warmth she had felt in the evidence drawer when she pulled a recently accessed crystal, but moving in the opposite direction. Not the residue of someone else's access. The warmth of the glass opening to her own. Her palms carried the frequency signature from years of handling Solen's work — the same pressure, the same baseline temperature her mother had encoded the unlock condition against. The glass did not require a deliberate gesture. It required her.

She felt the secondary band activate before she heard anything.

The vibration moved up through her palms and into her wrists and settled somewhere behind her sternum. She had learned, over the months of the investigation, to read what the glass was carrying before it resolved into anything she could name — the wrongness of altered glass came in like a note resolving to the wrong pitch, a frequency finding a place that was not its place. The rightness of true glass was different: the note resolved and held, and the air around it was different for the holding. That distinction had come to her only in fragments until now, in brief moments when the secondary band opened and something in Solen's encoding seemed to locate her rather than merely reach her.

This was not a fragment.

The cylinder's full contents moved through the interface and into the installation's transmission crystal, and the crystal's surface changed — a slow brightening, the amber-grey glass acquiring a luminosity that was not reflected light but generated from within, the frequency building in the crystal's structure the way a note builds in a resonating body before it becomes audible. The monitoring board in the adjacent room began registering the signal. One light, then three, then a cascade across the board's lower register as the city's passive receivers began detecting the transmission.

Vael placed the second cylinder.

Then the third.

Tace worked steadily at the calibration panel, her hands moving across the contacts, adjusting the output balance as the signal's complexity increased — seventeen years of Nava's documentation loading into the transmission crystal alongside Solen's encoding, the frequencies layering in the way stormglass layered when multiple sources were routed through the same crystal, each source maintaining its distinct signature rather than merging. Nava's discrepancy records carried their own frequency character — the consistency of one person's pressure pattern across seventeen years of documentation creating a signature as distinct as a voice. Tace balanced the output between Solen's secondary band and Nava's primary-band records, keeping neither from overwhelming the other, running the calibration the way an installation engineer runs calibration: without urgency, without error.

Davan stood at the door. She did not look at him. His stillness had changed — she could feel it from across the room, the way a man goes quiet when he is counting down rather than waiting. The twenty minutes were no longer twenty minutes.

She placed the fourth cylinder. The fifth.

The installation's crystal was fully luminous now, the amber-grey glass throwing light across the broadcast room — not evenly, but broken into bands, each frequency the crystal carried casting its own register across the walls, some warmer, some cooler, the amber range of Solen's encoding frequency burning brightest along the upper housing, the one Vael had grown up seeing in the background of her mother's work without knowing what she was seeing.

The monitoring board was showing the city.

The lights were multiplying. Not the gradual accumulation of overnight receivers coming online — the rapid, simultaneous activation of receivers across the full map of the city's stormglass network, residential units and institutional relays and the small private crystals in the market stalls and the gorge-wall receivers and the Plateau's civic installations, every stormglass surface in Bridgefall built to receive a broadcast frequency receiving this one. The monitoring board's map was the city. The city was lighting up.

Vael placed the sixth cylinder. The seventh.

The hum was audible now. Not the subsonic vibration she felt in her palms — the actual sound, the 94.7-hertz baseline of Solen's encoding carried through the installation's architecture and amplified to the point where it was no longer a frequency in the glass but a frequency in the room, in the stone of the Spire's walls, in the air between the broadcast crystal and the monitoring board's glass panel. The sound of something true playing through a system designed to play something else, the system carrying it without resistance because the physics of transmission did not distinguish between authorized and unauthorized, only between compatible and incompatible frequencies, and Solen had encoded the secondary band at 94.7 hertz because she had known it was compatible with every receiver in the city.

Not as a single coherent narrative. As a flood.

The city was receiving seventeen years of discrepancy records, Solen's calibration chamber, the anomalous readings from installation month three, the load-distribution deviation that Tace had logged and that had been dismissed as equipment variance, the installation team roster, the authorization chain, the third name. Not explained. Not curated. The raw frequency data of every piece of glass in the canvas case, playing simultaneously through the largest transmission crystal in Bridgefall into every stormglass receiver in the city, arriving the way frequency data always arrived — not as language, not as argument, but as the quality of a thing that has been encoded and is now playing, and anyone with a receiver would feel it before they understood it, the same low hum Vael had felt in her palms when stormglass played something altered, now playing something true.

She placed the eighth cylinder. The ninth.

Tace had her palm flat against the installation's housing, her eyes closed. She was no longer calibrating. The calibration was complete — the balance between Solen's encoding and Nava's documentation had settled into its own equilibrium, the two frequency signatures finding their place within the transmission crystal's architecture as two instruments find their pitch in the same room, neither overwhelming the other. Tace held the housing the way you hold something you have been waiting to hold for a long time and were not certain you would get to hold. Her hand was not trembling. It was simply present.

Vael placed the tenth cylinder. The eleventh.

The monitoring board was almost fully lit. The city's stormglass receivers, one after another, the whole map of Bridgefall's memory infrastructure receiving something it was not designed to receive and unable to stop receiving it, because the transmission was compatible with every receiver in the network and the network had no mechanism for refusing a compatible transmission. The authentication layer was on the input side. Tace had built it that way. In case of emergency.

She placed the twelfth cylinder.

The last of the amber pre-Charter glass — the cylinder from Tace's own documentation, the anomaly chain that began in installation month three and ended with a load-distribution deviation the final certification had recorded as within tolerance. The glass warmed in her hands, old stormglass held in the dark for years, waiting. She placed it against the contact point and felt the frequency move through her palms and into the installation's crystal and out through the transmission architecture into the city's receivers, and she kept her hands against the contact point for a moment after the cylinder was seated — not because the contact required it, but because the glass was warm and the hum was moving through her palms in the way it did when the glass was playing something real.

This was what her mother had been trying to do.

The hum moved through her palms and she kept her hands against the contact point and did not lift them. Solen had encoded the counter-archive for this. Had aimed the encoding at Vael's hands for this — because Vael's hands carried the frequency signature, because Vael's hands would open the glass, because Solen had known the unlock condition was not a gesture or a pressure sequence but a specific person, the person whose palms held the right temperature and the right pressure and the right inherited frequency from years of handling the same glass. This was the architecture. This was what the four years of the Hollows and Nava's seventeen years and Davan's access codes and Tace's four years listed as deceased in the Registry's personnel records had been converging toward. This room. This crystal. This morning.

The monitoring board showed the full map of the city, lit.

"He's here," Davan said, from the door.

Chapter 17

Nava reached the Council Spire's civic intake level at the third bell past dawn, while the queue at the brass-grilled windows was still thin enough to allow a choice. She took the second window from the left — not the nearest, which would have read as urgency, and not the furthest, which would have read as avoidance — and she stood with the canvas case at her feet and a sealed envelope in both hands, her body easy, her breathing even, the posture of a woman who had spent seventeen years in lines exactly like this one and had stopped needing to arrange herself for them.

The intake clerk was young. New enough that his Registry badge still wore the bright copper finish that browned within a season. His eyes moved from the envelope to Nava, then back to the envelope.

"Formal review request," Nava said. "Charter Year Fourteen Glass Bridge installation. Engineer of record, Tace. Load-distribution anomaly, installation month three. I'm requesting the calibration records from that period."

The clerk's pen found the intake log. "Requester designation?"

She gave it. Her Registry classification, her archive access tier, her institutional affiliation. None of it was rehearsed — it was simply what she was, the accumulated credential of seventeen years inside the institution she was now formally petitioning.

"Purpose of request?"

"Cross-referencing frequency-signature records against installation documentation for a discrepancy catalogue I maintain under standard archival protocol." She had settled on this exact phrasing months ago. Not *investigation*. Not *evidence*. *Discrepancy catalogue* and *standard archival protocol* — their vocabulary, her meaning, the envelope already sealed in the canvas case's outer pocket before she had walked through the Spire's doors.

The clerk wrote it down without looking up.

The intake log was a physical ledger, not a stormglass record. That was the entire point. A stormglass record could be re-indexed, its classification altered, its existence quietly denied. A physical ledger entry, timestamped and initialed by the intake clerk, was harder to manage. Not impossible — seventeen years inside the Registry had confirmed that nothing there was impossible to manage — but harder. Any erasure would require a physical alteration rather than a frequency reclassification. Someone would have to put their hands on the book.

The clerk initialed the entry. He pressed the intake seal to the envelope — the Spire's civic processing mark, the date, the bell-time — and slid it into the intake sleeve behind the grille.

Nava watched the envelope pass out of her hands.

The canvas case was already with Vael. The letter was already in the intake sleeve. The timestamp was already in the ledger.

She had not named the forty-one. She had not named Maerath. She had not named Ossian. The letter was a request for calibration records, nothing more, filed through the appropriate channel, processed by a clerk who had not read it, entered in a physical ledger that now held her name and the date and the words *Charter Year Fourteen Glass Bridge installation*.

Nothing about it could be taken back.

She lifted the canvas case — empty now, the buckles still bearing the faint impression of what they had held — and walked out of the civic intake level into the morning air.

The Spire rose behind her. She did not turn to look at it.

The letter arrived at Maerath's session room at the seventh bell, delivered by a duty clerk who set it in the morning sleeve alongside the other intake correspondence and left without a word. Tenne was already at his secondary desk in the corner, working through a stack of re-indexing authorizations, his pen moving steadily, pausing only when a line required a second check, the rhythm of a man who had long since found his pace and kept it.

Maerath read the letter standing.

He read it a second time sitting.

On the third reading, he laid it flat on the desk and looked at it the way a man looked at something that had been true for a long time and had now acquired a different quality — not new information, but information that had weight now, a different weight — he set the letter flat on the desk and left his hand on it, palm down, not reading it again.

Charter Year Fourteen Glass Bridge installation. Engineer of record, Tace. Load-distribution anomaly, installation month three. Calibration records.

The request was procedurally correct. Filed through the appropriate channel. Time-stamped and intake-sealed at the third bell past dawn. The requester's designation was Registry-registered, the access tier sufficient for the request category, the stated purpose consistent with documented archival protocol.

Every element was correct. That was the point.

"Tenne."

"Councilor."

"The twenty-four-hour administrative hold on frequency-event materials. Where does it stand?"

Tenne looked up from the re-indexing stack. "Filed at the sixth bell last night, as you authorized. The broadcast installation materials are under hold pending review classification."

Maerath set the letter down. "That hold is now procedurally irrelevant."

Tenne's pen did not move. He was the kind of man who waited for a sentence to finish before responding — a quality that made him useful and that made him, in this particular moment, a particular kind of obstacle. Not resistant. Simply present.

"The broadcast event was an unauthorized frequency transmission," Maerath said. "The hold was designed to prevent secondary access to the installation materials before review classification could be established. It assumed the primary evidentiary question was the transmission itself."

He picked up the letter again. Held it at the edge, where the intake seal was still crisp.

"This request was filed before the sixth bell. Before the broadcast. Before the hold."

Tenne understood. The quality of his stillness shifted — not alarm, because Tenne did not do alarm, but a recalibration, the kind of adjustment a man made when the framework he had been working inside required revision.

"The request is in the intake ledger," Tenne said.

"The physical ledger."

"Yes."

Maerath set the letter down again. The intake seal caught the session room's light — amber from the old stormglass panels in the wall sconces, the same amber range that the monitoring reports had been showing in elevated readings for twenty-two days, the same amber the broadcast installation had been throwing across the city's receiver network for the past four hours.

The city was not the same city it had been at the fifth bell.

He understood this the way he understood structural load-distribution. The broadcast had gone into every stormglass receiver in Bridgefall. The counter-archive, Solen's calibration records, Tace's anomaly chain, Nava's seventeen years — all of it, raw and unnarrated, playing through the frequency architecture of the city's memory infrastructure. And now this letter. Filed before the broadcast. Filed through the correct channel. Requesting the calibration records the transmission had just made redundant.

Someone had understood the geometry.

Not Vael — Vael had been inside the broadcast installation since before the dawn bell, which Brek's report confirmed. Someone who had been building toward this for longer than the broadcast. Someone who had understood that an irreversible timestamped receipt, filed through the appropriate channel in the physical ledger, would survive any reclassification the Registry might attempt in the broadcast's aftermath, because the ledger entry predated the event the Registry would be managing.

Nava. Seventeen years in the institution. Seventeen years of watching how the Registry managed its own records. Seventeen years of learning exactly which mechanisms were reversible and which were not.

"Pull the intake ledger entry," Maerath said.

Tenne's pen remained still. "Pull it."

"The entry is in the physical ledger. To remove it would require a physical alteration to the intake record, which would require a senior authorization filed with the Charter compliance office, which would create a second record of the alteration —"

"I am aware of the procedure, Tenne."

"— which would be logged in the compliance office's own ledger, which is also physical, and which is reviewed quarterly by the Charter oversight committee, whose review cycle runs in —"

"Enough."

Tenne stopped.

Maerath looked at the letter. The intake seal. The date. The bell-time.

The twenty-four-hour hold was a mechanism for managing frequency-event materials. It said nothing about calibration record requests filed through the appropriate channel at the third bell past dawn, before any frequency event had occurred, by a registered archivist with the correct access tier and a stated purpose consistent with documented protocol.

The hold was not wrong. It was simply aimed at the wrong thing.

Someone had understood — seventeen years ago or last night or at some point in between — that the geometry of the situation required both a broadcast and a receipt. That the broadcast alone could be managed: reclassified, contextualized, challenged on authentication grounds. That the receipt, filed in the physical ledger before the broadcast, created a different kind of problem.

Not an evidentiary problem. A procedural one. The Registry's own intake process had timestamped a request for the records Solen’s broadcast had just released into the city's frequency architecture. The request existed in the ledger. The ledger was physical. The broadcast was in every stormglass receiver in Bridgefall.

Both things were now in the world simultaneously, and the world did not have a mechanism for receiving them that left the Registry's position

Maerath folded the letter along its original crease.

"File it under active review," he said. "Standard classification. No hold."

Tenne wrote it down, the pen moving at its usual pace, the motion of a man whose role was technical and who had long ago decided that this was sufficient.

Maerath looked at the session room's stormglass panels. The amber light in the wall sconces held the same frequency range Solen had used for her encoding. He had known this for eleven years. He had continued working in this room for eleven years.

The monitoring board in the broadcast installation was showing the city fully lit.

Brek had sent a runner at the sixth bell with the initial situation report. The broadcast was complete. The installation was secure. Three individuals were in custody pending administrative detention. The runner had not named them, but the runner had not needed to.

Maerath opened his private archive drawer.

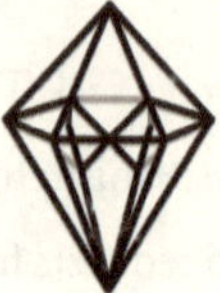

The drawer held three items: the personal ledger with its binding repaired twice in dark thread, a secondary frequency key he had not used in four years, and a sealed cylinder of pre-Charter amber glass that he had removed from the installation's evidence intake eleven years ago and had not returned.

He lifted the cylinder out. Set it on the desk.

The glass was cold. It had not been accessed since he placed it here. Cold stormglass did not lie about whether it had been touched.

He did not access it. He looked at it.

The calibration records from Charter Year Fourteen were not in the Registry's active archive. They were in this cylinder, in this drawer, in this room, where they had been across eleven years. The original records — not the re-indexed version filed under infrastructure maintenance, not the frequency-signature summary logged in the installation documentation, but the actual calibration data from installation month three, including Tace's anomaly report and the load-distribution deviation that the final certification had recorded as within tolerance.

The deviation had not been within tolerance. He had known this when he signed the authorization — when Tace filed the anomaly report, when the project lead dismissed it as equipment variance, when the final certification was submitted with the load-distribution figure adjusted to fall inside the acceptable range. He had known it at every step, and at every step he had continued.

His pen hand had been steady when he signed. He remembered that. The anomaly report open beside the authorization form, Tace's frequency notation in the margin, and his own hand moving without hesitation across the signature line.

He had continued because of what he had seen in the band-six stratum the winter before the Bridge broke ground — the processing queues outside the intake offices, the frequency-ration notices posted on stormglass that had already gone dark. The Bridge had felt, then, like the kind of answer that required a certain kind of question not to be asked.

All of this was true. He had believed all of it. He still believed most of it.

He opened the personal ledger to the first entry. The date was seventeen years ago. The handwriting was his own, younger, with a forward lean it would lose once he understood that the writing might be read by someone other than himself.

Authorization signed. Load-distribution deviation within acceptable range per project lead assessment. Anomaly report filed under equipment variance. Bridge certification submitted.

Five sentences. The forty-one were not in those five sentences. They had not been there yet.

He turned to the second entry. Eleven years ago.

Administrative reassignment processed. Routing confirmation filed. Senior analysis division — one of three individuals with full knowledge of the authorization chain. Reassignment complete.

Administrative reassignment. His word. His handwriting. The word that meant a colleague who had known his name in the context of the Bridge's authorization chain had been processed through the Registry's containment apparatus and had not returned from processing.

He had written *reassignment* in this ledger and nowhere else. The official record said *transfer to external consultation, voluntary departure*. The official record was the version the Registry maintained. This ledger was the version he maintained — the private accounting, kept those seventeen years, that used his own words for what had happened even when he could not bring himself to write what it had meant. Not honesty, exactly. Something less than honesty and more than pretense: the record a man kept when the truth was too heavy to release and too heavy to set down in plain language.

The cylinder on the desk was cold. The broadcast was in every stormglass receiver in the city. Nava's letter was in the intake ledger with a timestamp that predated the broadcast, and the broadcast contained everything the cylinder contained, and the cylinder was still cold because he had not accessed it — had not needed to access it — had been keeping it here for eleven years telling himself that having the original records was not the same as destroying them.

It was not the same. But it was not so different as he had needed it to be.

He picked up the cylinder. The cold came up through his palm at once — glass that had sat undisturbed in the dark over eleven years, temperature steady, waiting with the patience of objects that do not wait.

He pressed the frequency contact.

The cylinder warmed in his hands. The warmth came fast, not gradually — a recording that had been sealed a long time, and now open. The encoding was Tace's. He recognized the frequency signature — had come up in the same archival training cohort, had learned the same encoding grammar from the same instructors, had watched Tace's frequency signature develop its particular character over years of shared work before the Bridge project, before the anomaly report, before the administrative reassignment that the official record called a voluntary departure.

The load-distribution deviation read 94.7 hertz on the primary band and 97.3 on the secondary, with a variance pattern that Tace had flagged in installation month three as indicative of asymmetric stress distribution in the eastern anchor housing. The project lead had noted *equipment variance, recalibration recommended* and had not recalibrated. The final certification had recorded the deviation as 94.7 hertz, primary band only, within tolerance.

The secondary band reading was not in the final certification. An omission, not a removal. It had not been removed — it had simply not been included. The certification form did not require secondary band documentation for load-distribution assessments. The form had been designed before the secondary band's significance was understood.

The secondary band reading was in this cylinder. Had been in this cylinder those eleven years. Had been in Solen's encoding for longer — Solen had known about the secondary band because Solen had the same pre-standardization archival training, had known to look there, had encoded the counter-archive with the secondary band data included.

The broadcast had included it. The city's stormglass receivers had received it. The secondary band reading — 97.3 hertz, asymmetric stress distribution, eastern anchor housing — was now in every receiver in Bridgefall that had been active when the broadcast played.

He held the cylinder until it cooled again.

The personal ledger lay open on the desk. The letter from Nava rested folded beside it. Through the session room's stormglass panels the amber light fell the same as it always had, but the morning had turned into something he had not prepared for, and the difference showed not in the light but in what he could no longer tell himself about it.

He had been keeping the original records. He had placed them in a drawer and closed the drawer and returned to work, and when the weight of what he had done pressed down he had opened the drawer and looked at the cylinder and told himself that a man who kept the evidence was not the same as a man who had destroyed it. Eleven years of that. The broadcast had ended it.

The cylinder was in his hands. The records were in the city. Both things were true simultaneously, and the only question remaining — the question he had been deferring for eleven years through the mechanism of keeping the cylinder in the drawer and not accessing it — was what it meant that he had been keeping them.

Not what it meant for the Registry. Not what it meant for the investigation Brek was currently conducting in the Spire's broadcast installation, three floors above this room. What it meant for the accounting he had been keeping in the personal ledger — the private record of what had happened, maintained alongside the official record as the version that used his own words.

He had written *reassignment* for the colleague who had not returned from processing. He had written *authorization signed* for the Bridge. He had written every entry in a flat hand, recording what had occurred without recording what he thought of it, because thinking of it in the ledger would have required him to be a different kind of man than the kind he had decided to be.

The broadcast had not required his decision. It had moved through the city's frequency architecture with the particular indifference of a compatible transmission finding a compatible receiver, and the city had received it, and the intake ledger held the timestamp, and the cylinder was cold in his hands.

He placed the cylinder back in the drawer.

He did not close the drawer.

He sat with the personal ledger open and the cylinder visible in the drawer's mouth and the session room's amber light holding the same frequency range it had always held. What settled over him was not new understanding — he had understood this before — but the first time he had understood it without any available mechanism of deferral. The original records had not been enough. Having them had not been the same as not suppressing them. A man who kept a private accounting alongside a public one and called it integrity had only arranged his record-keeping to support what he needed to believe about himself.

The broadcast was in the city.

The cylinder was in the drawer.

Brek was three floors above, conducting the arrests Maerath had authorized at the sixth bell.

He closed the personal ledger. He did not replace it beneath the administrative manuals. He left it on the desk, beside the letter from Nava, in the session room's amber light, and he sat with what remained when the mechanism of deferral was no longer available to him.

Not absolution. Not even clarity.

What remained was a man sitting before an open drawer in a room where the broadcast had already made its contents redundant — holding, for the first time without retreat, the understanding that redundancy was not the same as release. He had kept the cylinder in the eleven years since because releasing it would have required him to be the kind of man who had kept it for eleven years and then released it, which was a different kind of man than the kind he had decided to be. The decision was still his. The drawer was still open.

Chapter 18

The room was not a cell. The Registry had arranged things so she would understand this immediately.

A stormglass panel sat in a brushed-metal casing on the far wall, throwing light that left the air around it unchanged. The pallet had been dressed with clean linen. On the small table, a water carafe and a ceramic cup had been placed with the deliberate care of an institution that had made comfort into policy. The stone held a faint metallic taste at the back of the throat — sealed and recirculated, not unpleasant — and the building's sounds arrived muffled, swallowed by the thickness of the walls, so that the Spire above existed only as an occasional vibration through the floor, something structural and remote, the way a living body registers its own heartbeat only in the moment it stops.

Vael sat on the pallet's edge with the amber shard resting in her palm.

At intake, two wardens had searched her. Unhurried, procedural, they had moved through her coat pockets with the flat efficiency of people who had long since stopped imagining what they might find. The shard had registered on the frequency sensor as a personal object — a private archive, below broadcast threshold, not flagged as active. One warden had held it briefly, turning it in the light, then set it in the return tray beside her belt and outer coat. She had picked it up again before she had fully understood she was permitted to.

She could not say. The Registry's administrative containment apparatus was precise enough that the distinction might not hold — an oversight here was also a decision, the decision to build a sensor protocol that would not flag objects below broadcast threshold, which was also the decision to allow detained persons to keep the specific category of object that could not transmit, could not be used to resist, could only be held. The shard's warmth against her palm was the warmth of stormglass handled continuously for weeks, her own body heat returning to her in a closed loop.

She tried to calculate how long she had been moving. The broadcast had gone out at the pre-dawn bell. Brek had appeared at the chamber door. The intake process had been efficient, which carried its own message. She had been in this room for some portion of a morning she could not see from any window, because the room had no window, because the Registry's detention facility in the Spire's lower levels had been designed before natural light was considered a variable worth accommodating.

Her hands had nothing to do with themselves — she pressed them flat against her thighs and held them there — and the stillness had a particular weight to it. She had not been still like this — not with this quality of stillness, not with nothing immediately requiring her hands — since before Nava's overflow room, before the cylinders, before the Hollows evacuation, before the eleven months of accumulation that had built toward a broadcast she had completed and could not uncomplete. The motion had been so continuous that stopping felt like a new kind of danger, the way a frequency held too long at high amplitude will stress the crystal carrying it — not from the amplitude itself but from the sudden silence when transmission ends.

The broadcast was in the city.

She knew this the way she knew the shard was warm — not as a conclusion she was still working toward but as a physical fact already present, already true, requiring nothing further from her to remain true. The city's stormglass receivers had been active. The secondary calibration channel had run at 94.7 hertz, bypassing Registry authentication, and Tace had pressed her palm flat against the installation housing with her eyes closed, and Vael had loaded the final cylinder, and the monitoring board had lit with the completeness of a system doing exactly what it had been built to do. The city had received it. Stormglass did not forget.

What she did not know was what the city was doing with it now.

She turned the shard between her fingers. She had handled it so many times over the past months that the amber glass had taken on the manner of a worked surface, the sharp points long since gone, the edges thinned where her thumb ran the same path again and again — something shaped by use rather than manufacture. Solen had encoded it with pre-Charter syntax, older than the Registry's standardized frequency grammar, using the secondary band that the Council's archivists had never been trained to read. The shard was the last physical piece of the counter-archive she still held. Everything else had been loaded into the transmission crystal, broadcast, released into the frequency architecture of a city that was now, somewhere above her, receiving what her mother had built.

The stormglass panel on the wall held its light without moving.

Vael pressed her thumb along the shard's longest edge, feeling the resistance of old glass — denser than modern manufacture, slightly uneven in its composition, the kind of material produced before standardization made density a controlled variable. Solen had known this. Had chosen it deliberately. Had known that pre-Charter amber glass would carry the secondary band with a fidelity that modern stormglass could not match, that the encoding would survive decades of storage without the consonant degradation affecting newer crystals, that the frequency signature would remain legible to anyone who knew to look in the secondary register.

Anyone who knew to look.

She had grown up hearing Solen's frequency signature in the background of every recording her mother made, had learned to recognize it the way she recognized her mother's handwriting — not by studying it but by accumulation, by exposure, by the particular education of a child living alongside a specific intelligence. Solen had known this too. Had built the counter-archive to her daughter's specific knowledge, her daughter's specific hands, the frequency literacy of a child raised in the margins of archival work.

The shard was warm.

Vael set it on the table beside the water carafe and looked at it. The amber glass sat in the panel's light and threw back a deep, warm color at the edges — the color of old preservation, the color of something that had been waiting a very long time.

The broadcast was in the city. What happened next was not hers to manage. This was what the stopped motion felt like — not relief, not completion, but the recognition that the thing she had been the instrument of had left her hands, and she was sitting in a room in the Spire's lower levels with a stormglass panel throwing its light and a ceramic cup she had not yet touched and the amber shard on the table between them. Her hands lay open on her thighs. There was nothing left for them to do.

She picked up the cup. The water was cold. She drank it.

The senior archivist was a woman in her fifties whose every movement had been stripped to its minimum — nothing wasted, nothing performed, the bearing of someone who had understood long ago that visible effort was a liability in rooms where effort was supposed to be invisible. She sat across from Davan with a notebook open on the table and a pen she had not yet uncapped.

The interview room was slightly larger than Vael's. The table was wider. The stormglass panel here was mounted higher on the wall and threw pale, even light without warmth across the surface below. A second chair sat empty along the wall behind the archivist, which told Davan the interview had been designed for a witness who had either not arrived or been decided against.

The archivist introduced herself by designation rather than name: Senior Review Archivist, Administrative Inquiry Division. She said this the way she said everything else — flat, deliberate, the register of a woman who understood exactly which room she was in. Designation was simply the correct form of address here, and she used it.

"The inquiry will be recorded," she said. "Standard protocol for administrative review. You'll have the opportunity to review the transcript before it's filed." She uncapped the pen. "I'd like to begin with the personnel archive access. Third bell past midnight, eleven days ago. Can you walk me through your decision to access the Infrastructure Development files?"

Davan had been aware of this moment since before the broadcast. Not planning for it — he had not been planning, precisely, had not been operating from anything he would have called a plan — but aware of it the way you are aware of a structure you are moving toward, the way the gorge wall is present before you reach it. The interview had been inevitable from the moment he had not logged his exit in the duty clerk's ledger, which had been inevitable from the moment he had decided not to log it, which had been — he was not sure, precisely, when the decision had been made. His body had made it before his mind had language for it. He had walked the correct corridor, held the correct badge, worn the correct expression, and had not written his name in the ledger, and the decision had already been complete.

He told her.

Not everything at once — he was not performing confession, was not seeking catharsis or absolution, was not doing anything that required an audience. He was giving an account. An accurate one. The distinction mattered to him in a way he could not fully articulate but could feel as a structural difference, the difference between a document produced under duress and a document produced because the production is the last thing still yours to control.

The personnel archive access first. He described the badge entry at third bell past midnight, the duty clerk Peva's absence, the ledger left open on the desk — the Glass Bridge installation, Charter Year Fourteen, Infrastructure Development, Gorge Crossing. He described the Charter-level addendum. He named Ryn Ossian.

The archivist wrote without looking up.

He described the access record and what it would contain: his badge, the timestamp, the sub-level designation. He had not photographed anything, had replaced the file exactly as found, had exited without logging in the duty clerk's ledger. He described going to Vael's room afterward. The knock sequence: three, two, one.

"Why that sequence?" the archivist asked. She had still not looked up from the notebook.

"It was established. Between us." He paused. "A recognition signal."

She wrote this down. He watched the pen move and understood, without particular emotion, that the phrase recognition signal in an administrative inquiry transcript carried specific weight — it implied an ongoing operational relationship, which was accurate, which was what he was here to provide. An accurate account.

He described the evidence inventory. Solen's cylinder, Tace's twelve cylinders, Nava's discrepancy catalogue. He described the broadcast installation — its location in the Spire, the access codes he had retained from the quarterly verification six weeks prior, the secondary calibration channel Tace had designed and that he had known about because the quarterly verification had included a review of the installation's technical documentation. He described the decision to retain the codes. He described it as a decision.

"When did you decide to use the access codes for a purpose outside the verification protocol?" the archivist asked.

He considered this. The question was precise — she was asking about the decision point, not the action point, and the distinction mattered because the decision point was earlier, was in the small hours of the morning in his rented room with Vael across the table and the evidence inventory between them and the closing window of the audit cycle already running. He had not experienced it as a decision at the time. He had experienced it as the only thing available to do with what he had. But that was not an accurate account of what had happened. What had happened was that he had looked at the codes in his retention file, understood what they could be used for, said all right, and moved forward from that moment without examining the movement.

"Before the conversation with Vael," he said. "When I understood what the access codes made possible."

"Before the conversation."

"I had them. I knew what the installation could do. The understanding arrived before the conversation."

The archivist wrote. He watched the pen move and thought about what an accurate account actually required — that it meant rendering what had actually happened rather than the version that was more defensible, that the gap between those two versions was precisely where integrity lived. Whether this constituted integrity or simply a different form of the same mechanism — the self-narrating apparatus finding a new object — he did not know. He was not sure the distinction was available to him from inside his own account.

The archivist asked about Brek. She asked about the encounter in the east corridor, the cover explanation Davan had offered — cross-referencing Solen's notation against Infrastructure Development personnel records — and whether the explanation had been true.

"It was true in the sense that I had done that cross-referencing," Davan said. "It was not true in the sense that it was the reason for the archive access."

"You gave a technically accurate explanation that was functionally misleading."

"Yes."

She wrote this down. He watched her write technically accurate, functionally misleading and felt something he could not quite name — the sensation of a description that fit without being the description he would have chosen for himself, which was not the same as the description being wrong.

He described the entry to the Spire via the maintenance door. He described the shaft Tace had bricked up under a false work order in Charter Year Nineteen. He described the false band-three anomaly misdirection — the two night-staff redirected to the monitoring room, their professional obligation used against them, their competence exploited as the mechanism of their own exclusion from what was about to happen. He described this without minimizing it. He described Tace opening the secondary calibration channel. He described Vael loading the cylinders.

"You were present for the broadcast."

"Yes."

"Were you in a position to stop it?"

He thought about this carefully. He had been at the chamber door when Brek arrived. He had been watching the monitoring board. He had been present in the specific sense of someone who has committed to a direction and inhabits it, not as an observer but as a participant. Whether he had been in a position to stop it depended on what position meant. He had had the physical capacity. He had not had anything else.

"No," he said.

The archivist looked up for the first time. Gray eyes, steady and without investment — not sympathetic, not hostile, the eyes of someone who had spent years taking in accounts and had learned to let them arrive before deciding anything about them. She held his answer for a moment.

"You had the physical capacity," she said. It was not a question.

"Yes."

"But not the — what?"

He considered. The honest answer was that he had not had the will, but will was not quite accurate — it implied a struggle he had not experienced, a moment of deliberate choice he had not had. What he had not had was the capacity to be a different person than the person he had become between the moment he walked past the duty clerk's open ledger and the moment the monitoring board showed the city fully lit. The account he was giving in this room was the account of a man who had made a series of decisions, each of which had made the next more coherent, until the pen had moved across the page without pause, and the page had filled, and he had watched it fill.

"The inclination," he said.

She wrote this down. He watched the word appear in the notebook — inclination — and understood that whoever read this transcript would read it as evasion. It was not evasion. It was the most accurate word he had.

They continued. He described the arrival at the door — Brek's voice, the way Brek knocked, the sound of it enough to tell Davan this was not an unofficial visit. He described the moment after the broadcast completed: Vael's hands still on the final cylinder contact point, Tace's palm flat against the installation housing, the monitoring board showing the city fully lit. He described saying nothing. He described none of them saying anything, for the interval between the broadcast's completion and Brek's arrival — he was not sure how long. Long enough that the silence had a quality. Long enough that it had been a kind of witness to itself.

The archivist asked about Nava. She asked whether Davan had had prior contact with Nava before the night of the broadcast, whether he had been aware of the discrepancy catalogue, whether he had known about the formal review request Nava had filed at the civic intake level.

"I knew about the catalogue," he said. "I had not had direct contact with Nava. I was aware she had filed a request — I was made aware of it through normal channels, as part of the Registry's intake review."

"You did not flag it."

"No."

"Why not?"

Flagging it would have required him to act against Vael's operational timeline, and by that point his operational timeline and Vael's were the same timeline, and flagging the intake request would have been flagging himself. He did not say this. What he said was: "I had determined by that point that my responsibilities had been reorganized."

The archivist's pen stopped. She looked up again. "Reorganized."

"That's the word I would use."

She wrote it. He could see from the angle of her wrist that she had put it in quotation marks.

He described the rest. He described it in sequence, accurately, without the self-protection that would have required him to omit the parts that could not be defended by appeal to institutional logic. He described each decision as a decision. He described the blank field — the location report he had not filed, the moment he had understood that not filing it was also a choice — not as the origin of everything that followed, because the origin was older than that, was the woman whose name he could no longer reconstruct with confidence but whose teacup he could still see on the table when he arrived, already set out, and his own voice saying no thank you with the fluency of a man who had not yet understood what he was practicing — but as the first decision he had made that he had known was a decision at the moment he made it.

The archivist wrote for a long time after he finished. He sat with his hands flat on the table and watched the pen move and thought about an accurate account as the last thing you controlled — not the outcome, not the consequence, not what the transcript would be used for or what the review board would determine or what the Registry would do with the fact of him sitting in this room having described himself with this precision. Those things were not his. The account was his. He had given it.

The archivist closed the notebook.

"The review board will convene within forty-eight hours," she said.

She said this plainly, without noting that forty-eight hours was faster than the standard timeline — sixty-two to seventy-two hours for standard administrative review — which meant the Registry was treating this as a different category of case, which meant the signal had done something the standard timeline was not designed to accommodate, which meant the city above them was not processing this the way the Registry had expected.

She capped her pen. She gathered the notebook. She stood, moved to the door, and the warden outside opened it from the corridor side. She left without looking back. The door closed.

Davan sat in the interview room alone.

The stormglass panel threw pale light across the walls, unchanged and sufficient. The empty chair along the wall held nothing. The table between him and where the archivist had been sitting was a clean surface with nothing on it — no notebook, no pen, no record of anything — and the account he had given was in the notebook and the notebook was gone, and the account was accurate, and it would be used against him, and he was not sure this was the wrong outcome.

The warden returned. Davan stood without being asked. He followed the warden into the corridor, and the corridor was wide enough for two people to walk abreast, and the walls absorbed the sound of their footsteps so completely that the walking felt like something happening in a medium that was not quite air, and the stormglass panels in the ceiling put down flat, colorless light along the floor ahead of them, and the Registry's detention facility in the Spire's lower levels received them both without comment, as it had been designed to do.

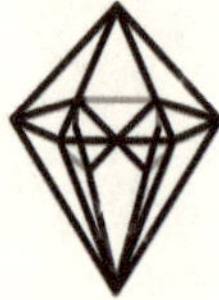

Tace had been lying on the mattress for several hours before it began to strike her as funny.

Not the mattress specifically — the mattress was a mattress, a reasonable piece of institutional furniture with the density of something designed to meet a comfort standard rather than to be comfortable. What she found amusing was the existence of the standard itself. That the Registry had a comfort standard for its detention rooms. That someone had determined, at some point in the institution's history, that the rooms should have pallets with adequate linen, and water carafes, and stormglass panels in brushed-metal casings, and that this determination had been implemented with the thoroughness of an institution that believed its own account of itself as a governing body rather than a punitive one.

She had spent four years in a decommissioned storage chamber in the Hollows with a cot she had reinforced herself using salvaged iron strapping and a stormglass panel she had rewired from a discarded monitoring unit and a water source that depended on the building's original drainage infrastructure, which she had mapped and partially restored during the first six months because the alternative was hauling water from the secondary access point and the secondary access point was a twenty-minute walk. The detention room's water carafe had been filled and placed on the table by someone else. The stormglass panel in its brushed-metal casing had been installed by someone else, maintained by someone else, and put out its light without requiring anything from her.

She had known this room was coming. Not this specific room — she had not known she would end up in the Spire's lower levels rather than somewhere else, had not known the walls would be this particular shade of pale stone or that the sealed air would leave that particular metallic taste at the back of the throat. But the general shape of it: a room. A waiting. The aftermath of a thing done. She had known this was the structure of what she was doing from the moment she had agreed to meet at the Spire's secondary entrance in the hour before dawn, which was also from the moment she had received the message through the Hollows network, which was also from the moment — four years ago, in the first weeks of the decommissioned chamber, when she had understood that she was not going to leave Bridgefall and was not going to be publicly dead and was therefore going to be waiting for the moment when the cylinders she had encoded could be used — that she had decided waiting was the work available to her and had begun doing it.

The installation engineer's precision had done its work. The secondary calibration channel had run at the frequency she had designed it to run at, using the authentication bypass she had built into the system in Charter Year Nineteen under a maintenance filing that the Registry's current technical staff had no reason to review. The transmission crystal had received the cylinders. The city had received the transmission.

She sat with her hands in her lap.

The load-distribution deviation had read 97.3 hertz on the secondary band, asymmetric stress distribution, eastern anchor housing. She had flagged it in installation month three. The project lead had noted equipment variance and had not recalibrated. She had filed the anomaly documentation in a cylinder and had kept the cylinder and had lived with the cylinder for eleven years — first in her registered address, then in the decommissioned chamber — and the cylinder was now in the city's stormglass receivers, its frequency running through every panel that had been active when the broadcast played, its data as available and as irretrievable as anything the stormglass had ever held.

The eastern anchor housing had been under asymmetric stress from installation month three. Forty-one people had crossed the bridge on the day it failed. The certification had recorded the deviation as within tolerance. The secondary band reading had not appeared in the final certification.

It was in the city now.

The stormglass panel put its light across the floor in a steady, even bar. The water carafe sat on the table. The room was clean and procedural and not a cell, and Tace sat in it with her hands in her lap — the hands of a woman who had carried something a long time and had finally set it down. She did not know what came after this room. She had not built toward after. She had built toward this: the cylinders released, the frequency running, the thing done. Her hands rested open in her lap and did not reach for anything.

She looked at the stormglass panel.

The light it threw was steady and sufficient. The room held it without comment. Somewhere above her, the city was receiving what had been built for it, and she sat with that, and did not find it insufficient.

Chapter 19

The amber shard had not cooled.

Vael kept it in her open palm, watching the light through the shelter's single high window climb from pale gray into something that qualified as morning. She did not track the time precisely. The shard had been in her hands long enough that the edges had dulled, the surface rubbed to a kind of sameness under the fingers, and the warmth coming off it was not dead warmth — not heat stored in glass and bleeding away — but something still working, something in the middle of itself. Whatever it was running, it had not finished.

The broadcast had gone out eight hours ago. Maybe nine. She had lost the count somewhere around the fourth or fifth attempt to answer the question Tace had posed without posing it — through the particular quality of her stillness in the chamber, the way she had held herself when she asked, indirectly: *what did it feel like from the inside, the second layer, when you were the one it was built for.* Each time Vael reached for language, the language slid away from the thing she was trying to name.

She set the shard on the shelter's single table. Salvaged timber, the surface uneven, and the shard found a slight hollow and settled into it as if it had rested there before.

What it felt like.

For months she had understood it abstractly — since the first time she pressed the shard against a reading surface and felt the frequency open under her hands in a way it had not opened under anyone else's. The specific give of a lock recognizing the right pressure. Solen had built the unlock condition from something Vael's hands knew before her mind did: a gesture, the way she had always held glass, the particular angle of her wrist, the distributed pressure across four fingers that Solen had encoded as the archive's authentication. Not a code. A recognition.

But abstract understanding was not what she was sitting with now.

The second layer had not felt like being used. That was the thing she kept returning to, the thing that refused to resolve into the shape she had prepared for it. She had spent months constructing a framework in which her mother's encoding was an act of aim — Solen choosing her daughter's hands because they were the right hands, the specific hands, because the archive needed releasing and Vael was the mechanism — and the framework was accurate. She did not doubt it. The encoding was deliberate, the unlock condition designed, the archive waiting for her in particular.

But the second layer, when it opened, had not felt like a mechanism being activated.

It had felt like being recognized.

Vael pressed the heel of her hand flat against the table. The timber was cold in the way of things that had occupied the same place for a long time, absorbing the shelter's particular chill, and the cold moved through her palm in a clean, direct line.

This was the problem. This was what Tace's question had opened and left open: the framework was correct, and the framework was insufficient, and both of those things were simultaneously true.

Solen had aimed the archive at her daughter's hands. That was a fact.

Solen had also encoded it in a frequency that felt, when it opened, like a hand placed over her hand.

The second fact had no home in the model she had built to survive the first. The model was constructed for instrumentalization — for the discovery that her grief had been a design feature, that her mother had needed her loss to function as the mechanism of the archive's release, that love and architecture had been the same act. The model could hold this. She had held it for six months without breaking.

She set the shard down and picked it up again, her thumb moving along the edge, pressing into each small irregularity, finding no place on it that felt like the right place to stop.

She picked up the shard again. Still warm. Whatever was still running in it had not finished.

In a middle-ward Registry office on the Plateau's administrative tier, a clerk named Sevet sat surrounded by eleven years of variance reports spread across his desk.

He had pulled them from the secondary filing cabinet at the sixth bell, before his colleagues arrived. The broadcast had played through the office's wall-mounted panel at the third bell past midnight, and after it ended he had lain in his registered room staring at the ceiling, turning the word *variance* over in his mind — the word he had been writing in a column labeled *equipment variance* on standardized form RT-7 eleven years, the same word what played through the receivers had used in a different context entirely.

The reports were organized by installation quarter, a system he had developed in his second year when the volume of anomalous readings from the Gorge-level panels made single-entry filing impractical. Eleven years of quarterly filings. Each one noted a deviation in the secondary frequency band. Each one classified under equipment variance per standard protocol. Each one signed by him, countersigned by his section head, filed in the secondary cabinet rather than the primary.

The secondary cabinet, because secondary band readings were not primary record.

He had known this. He had been trained to this. Secondary band readings were manufacturing artifacts, legacy frequency ranges from the pre-Charter installation period, not operationally significant under current calibration standards. Equipment variance. Within tolerance. Secondary cabinet.

The broadcast had played 97.Eastern anchor housing. Installation month three.3 hertz on the secondary band. Asymmetric stress distribution. Eastern anchor housing. Installation month three.

Sevet looked at his most recent quarterly report. The secondary band reading for the Gorge-level panel cluster this quarter: 96.1 hertz. Asymmetric distribution, consistent with prior readings. Equipment variance. Within tolerance.

He had filed that report six weeks ago.

The window behind his desk faced the Plateau's eastern edge. On a clear morning from this angle, you could see where the Glass Bridge's anchor tower had been incorporated into the Civic Hall's wall — the pale limestone, the slightly different color where old stonework met new, the visible line marking where something had been added to something that already existed.

His hands stayed flat on the spread paper. He did not reach for the reclassification form. He did not reach for anything. He looked at the anchor tower's outline in the morning light, and he did not move, the way a man does not move when he has been keeping himself from looking directly at a thing for a long time and has finally looked.

In the lower ward, in a schoolroom with small desks arranged in seven rows and a public stormglass panel mounted above the chalkboard, a teacher named Orrel had been sitting at her desk for two hours.

The broadcast had played during morning preparation. She had been writing the day's lesson on the board — frequency notation, standard curriculum for the intermediate level, a lesson she had delivered forty times — when the panel lit and the broadcast ran through it, unscheduled, at a frequency she recognized immediately as pre-Charter amber glass. She had a degree in archival studies. She had spent two years working in a Registry reading room before the teaching position opened, and she had taken it because the hours were better and the children were, in their way, more honest than the filing system.

She had recognized the frequency. She had stood with the chalk in her hand and listened to forty-one minutes of calibration data, load-distribution readings, and a human voice — damaged at the consonants, the hard sounds gone soft — addressing someone who was not in the room.

When it ended she set the chalk on the ledge and sat down.

Her students would arrive in forty minutes. She had a lesson on frequency notation to deliver. The notes were on her desk. The desk was in a room where forty-one people's names were now in the stormglass panel above the chalkboard, because stormglass did not forget, and the panel was still faintly warm, and she was a woman who had spent two years in a Registry reading room and knew what the secondary band was and what it was used for and what it meant that the broadcast had run on it.

She had also spent two years in a Registry reading room and had left. That was the fact she was sitting with. The forty-one names she had categories for. The calibration data she had categories for. What she did not have a category for was this: she had known, in the loose and general way you knew things you did not examine, that the reading rooms held things that did not match what the reading rooms were supposed to hold. She had known it over eleven years. She had left anyway because the hours were better and the children were more honest, and she was sitting now in a room with a warm panel above the chalkboard trying to reckon what that made her.

Outside, the lower ward was beginning its morning. The Silt Market vendors started their calls, the particular rhythm of Gorge-level mornings rising through the walls, the city arriving at itself.

In thirty-eight minutes her students would come through the door and she would teach them frequency notation and the panel above the chalkboard would be warm and she would not explain why.

She did not yet know what she would do after that.

On a work installation near the river, where a crew of young bridge workers had been arriving for the morning shift, a man named Carth stood at the edge of the work platform with his hands in his pockets.

The broadcast had played through the installation's panel at the third bell. Carth had been awake — always awake before the third bell, a habit from his apprenticeship that had never left him — and he had heard it through the thin wall of the workers' shelter and come out to listen. He had stood in the dark for forty-one minutes with the cold coming off the river.

He was twenty-three. Born four years after the Glass Bridge fell. He had grown up with the bridge the way you grew up with any city landmark: as a fact, as a shape in the visual field, as the thing adults referenced when they talked about before and after. The Glass Bridge had fallen. Forty-one people had crossed it that day. These were facts he had known since he was old enough to know facts.

The third name in the broadcast was Ryn Ossian.

Everyone knew that name. Everyone in Bridgefall knew it — on the Charter, on the memorial address that ran every year at the Plateau-side anchor tower, on the dedication plaque of the eastern reading room, on the curriculum standard for archival studies, on the Registry's founding document. Ryn Ossian. One of five. A name that meant Bridgefall's structure, its legitimacy, the specific authority that made the city's systems something other than just systems.

The broadcast had named Ryn Ossian as the signatory who had reviewed and approved the final certification knowing the secondary band reading had been omitted.

Carth did not know what the secondary band was. He was a bridge worker, not an archivist, and the technical vocabulary of the broadcast had moved past him in places. But he knew load-distribution deviation. He worked with load distribution every day. He knew what asymmetric stress in an anchor housing meant over time — knew it the way you knew things your hands had learned before your mind had words for them.

He knew what the omission meant.

And he knew Ryn Ossian's name on the Charter. On the memorial address. On the dedication plaque.

His shift supervisor was crossing the platform toward him. The morning work was waiting. The river moved below in its usual way, indifferent to the third bell, indifferent to the broadcast, indifferent to the name now sitting in Carth's hands in a way he could not put down.

He turned toward the supervisor. He went to work.

The name did not leave his hands.

In the Silt Market at the Gorge Floor's southern edge, a vendor named Prist who sold salvaged hardware and, occasionally, other things, had heard the broadcast on the shared panel in the market's covered corridor and spent the morning watching his customers.

Not surveillance — Prist had never been a Registry man, had spent thirty years carefully not being anything that required authorization. Just watching. The way you watched a market when something had shifted in the city and you needed to understand the new shape of things before making any decisions about what to offer and at what price.

Some of his customers moved normally. Some did not. The ones who did not fell into two categories: those moving faster than usual, walking with their chins down and their hands already reaching, going somewhere they had not been going an hour before, and those who had stopped entirely, standing at stalls without buying anything, their hands resting on objects they were not examining.

Prist had been in the Silt Market for thirty years. He had watched the city receive things before — Registry announcements, re-calibration notices, the occasional enforcement action that rippled through the Gorge-level panels in ways the Plateau panels never did. He knew how the market absorbed information. He knew its rhythms.

This was different. Not absorption. The market had the feel of a room where someone has set down something heavy and everyone is still deciding whose job it is to move it.

He had not broadcast anything himself. He had no cylinders, no amber glass, no frequencies above the secondary band. He dealt in hardware and occasionally other things, and the other things had never been this.

But he had handled a fragment once — pre-Charter amber glass, secondary band encoding, a seam in it he had recognized immediately as something that had been touched and touched and touched by hands that knew what they were looking for. He had felt the seam and sold the fragment and had spent the subsequent months refusing a specific category of salvage without explaining why to anyone who asked.

The seam was in his mind now. Pre-Charter amber had a particular resistance at the edges, a slight drag under the thumb where the encoding sat in the glass like a ridge of proud solder, and that fragment had pulled at his thumb the whole time he held it, the way a drawer does when it has been opened and left that way.

The market moved around him. The city was deciding where to put the broadcast. Prist watched and did not decide anything.

In the Warrens, in a common room where three families shared a stormglass panel that one of them had wired to the building's original drainage infrastructure fifteen years ago — because the Registry's installation fee for Gorge-level residential access was three months' wages and the drainage infrastructure ran adjacent to a primary frequency conduit and the family's eldest had an archival studies certificate and knew the conduit's calibration range — the transmission had played at the third bell and everyone in the building had woken up.

Not to the broadcast specifically. To the panel. It had run warm, warmer than it usually ran, and the warmth conducted through the wall into the adjacent sleeping room. The family in that room had a child who ran warm herself, and she had woken at the change in the wall's temperature and come into the common room and turned on the panel, not knowing it was already running, and the broadcast was in the room when the adults arrived.

The child was seven. She listened to the broadcast with the close attention of a child who does not understand most of what is being said but understands that the adults in the room are understanding it and that the eldest's hands, which had been moving, had gone still on the table.

The adults had not spoken to each other during the broadcast. After it ended they spoke for a long time, quietly, in the way of people trying to determine what to do with something they cannot put back.

The eldest, who had the archival studies certificate, said: *the secondary band. They used the secondary band.*

No one asked what that meant. They had all heard enough, in the Warrens, about the secondary band — about what ran on it, about what the Registry said did not run on it, about the specific gap between what the official calibration standards documented and what the Gorge-level panels occasionally picked up in the hours before dawn when primary band traffic was low — to understand what it meant that forty-one minutes of pre-Charter amber glass had run on it city-wide.

The child fell asleep against the eldest's shoulder before the discussion ended. She had not understood most of it. She had understood the warmth in the wall and the change in the room's shape and the way the adults looked at the panel for a long time after the broadcast ended, as if it had become a different kind of object.

By morning the panel was cool. The broadcast was gone from its surface the way broadcasts always went. But stormglass did not forget. The frequency was in the crystal. The crystal was in the wall. The wall was warm from the drainage conduit running adjacent to the primary frequency line, and the child slept against the eldest's shoulder, her breath steady, her hand open on the table.

A Registry warden named Tov, on duty at the Spire's eastern corridor when the broadcast played through the security panel at the third bell, had filed two reports.

The first, filed at the fourth bell, described the broadcast accurately: frequency origin consistent with pre-Charter amber glass, secondary calibration channel, authentication bypass, transmission duration forty-one minutes, content consisting of calibration data and recorded voice material relating to the Glass Bridge installation and certification, Charter Year Fourteen. Warden Tov had set down each technical specification in the order the monitoring log required, noting the anomalous frequency data the way he had been drilled to do it, without gap or omission.

The second report, filed at the sixth bell after the official channels issued their preliminary characterization, described it differently: *malicious frequency intrusion, unverified content, destabilizing technical artifact consistent with known counter-Registry activity, no operational significance to official calibration record.* Warden Tov filed this using the standard form for unauthorized transmission events, signed it with his badge number, and placed it in the primary filing channel for review at the morning brief.

The first report was in the secondary channel, where anomalous frequency event documentation was filed.

Warden Tov had not destroyed the first report. He had not been asked to. The official channels had not, as of the sixth bell, issued guidance on secondary channel documentation of the broadcast event. He had filed the second report because the second report was what the official channels required, and the official channels were what he worked within.

The first report remained in the secondary channel.

At the seventh bell, handing off the shift, his replacement asked if there was anything unusual to note. Warden Tov said *frequency event, documented, refer to secondary channel for technical specifications.* His replacement nodded. That was the end of it.

The first report was in the secondary channel. The secondary channel was filed. The stormglass in the Spire's security panel held the broadcast's frequency in its crystal the way all stormglass held what it received.

Warden Tov went home. The shift continued.

Maerath set down the preliminary public response document and turned to the window.

The Spire's director's office faced west, away from the gorge, toward the upper Plateau's administrative district and the pale limestone facades housing the Registry's operational infrastructure. Morning light came through at an angle that made the limestone look warmer than it was. Within an hour the angle would shift and the warmth would be gone and the facades would show what they were: old stone cut and dressed and laid in courses meant to outlast the arguments of any particular generation.

The document on the desk was her work. She had drafted it at the fifth bell, in the two hours between the broadcast's end and the first reports from the monitoring staff, and it was good work — precise, measured, technically accurate about what it confirmed and technically careful about what it declined to confirm. The broadcast had occurred. The broadcast's content was unverified. The Registry was conducting a full technical review. Citizens were encouraged to treat unverified frequency material with appropriate caution. The official Glass Bridge record remained the authoritative source for Charter Year Fourteen infrastructure events.

She had not said the broadcast was false. She was too careful for that. Saying it was false would require a counter-claim, and a counter-claim required evidence, and the evidence in the open drawer — the amber cylinder, the original calibration data, the 97.3 hertz reading the final certification had not included — was evidence she had been holding for eleven years in a drawer that no one had asked her to open.

The drawer was closed now. She had closed it before drafting the response.

The document would work for a portion of the population. She knew this the way she knew the weight of any calculation she had run long enough to trust: the portion that required official confirmation before it could believe something, the portion that found the broadcast's unverified status sufficient grounds for skepticism, the portion that had built its relationship to the Registry's authority on seventeen years of uncontested record and would not easily revise that foundation on the basis of forty-one minutes of pre-Charter amber glass playing through a panel in the night.

This portion was not nothing. It was, in fact, the majority. In her experience it was always the majority. The majority wanted the official account to be correct — not because they were credulous, not because they were incapable of evaluating evidence, but because the official account was the account their daily functioning was organized around, and revising it required revising everything built on top of it, and the cost of that revision was not abstract. It was a specific, material cost that the majority would pay and that she, in her office, would not.

The document would reach them. The document would hold a portion of them. The portion was calculable, and she had calculated it, and the calculation was correct.

What she did not calculate — she was aware of not calculating it, which was different from not knowing it existed — was the compounding.

The clerk in the middle ward with eleven years of variance reports spread across his desk. The schoolteacher in the lower ward who had two years in a Registry reading room, had left, and was now sitting at her desk with the panel still warm above the chalkboard. The bridge worker who could not put down the third name. The Warrens family with the child who had felt the warmth in the wall and woken the whole building. The warden with two reports sitting in two separate channels. The vendor in the Silt Market who had once felt a seam under his thumb and had been refusing a specific category of salvage ever since.

These were not the resistance. The resistance she had managed for years — mapped, monitored, contained within parameters that kept it from reaching the portions of the population she needed to hold. The resistance was a known variable.

These were the people who had received the broadcast and felt, in the specific way that stormglass made feeling unavoidable, the hum of something true running through a system designed to run something false. They were not a movement. They were not organized. They were not, today, large enough to threaten the apparatus.

She picked up the next document.

Outside, the morning light moved across the limestone facades. The angle was shifting. The warmth was leaving the stone. The city was processing. The portion she could not reach was not large enough. Not today.

She did not calculate the week. She did not calculate the month. She did not calculate what happened to a portion when it had time to speak to the portions around it — when the clerk mentioned his variance reports to a colleague over a meal, when the schoolteacher stood before her students with the panel warm above the chalkboard and taught them frequency notation, when the bridge worker said the third name aloud to someone who had not yet heard it.

She read the next document. Outside, the city continued.

Chapter 20

The maintenance level of the Council Spire had not been designed with directors in mind. Maerath had to angle her shoulders at the junction where the service corridor met the equipment shaft — the ceiling was that low — and the stormglass panels lining the walls were original installation, pre-standardization, amber-grey and slightly convex, throwing light that ran warmer and less evenly than the regulated panels on the upper floors. She had not been on this level in five years, had not been below the fourth floor at all — a fact that had never once surfaced in her mind until now, descending the service stair with her hand on the iron rail, the hum rising through the soles of her boots into the bone of her heel, a frequency she had been walking above for five years.

The stair was narrow. The rail was cold. Below her, the maintenance level produced a hum — not the stormglass hum she associated with monitoring panels or broadcast equipment, but something older, the low-frequency resonance particular to crystal that had been running without pause for a very long time. For seventeen years she had been hearing this hum through the floors above it. She had categorized it under infrastructure maintenance and moved on. Now she was moving toward it, and on the fourth step down the iron rail went colder under her palm, the hum rising in pitch by a register she had not heard from above.

The sealed calibration chamber was at the corridor's end. She knew this from the original construction survey she had authorized in Charter Year Nineteen, when the maintenance level was being re-assessed for load-bearing compliance following the Glass Bridge's collapse. The survey had been filed. The chamber had been noted as sealed per the calibration event of Charter Year Fourteen, pending final review. The final review had never been scheduled. She was the one who had not scheduled it.

The corridor ran six feet wide, lit by three amber panels, one of which had developed a flicker at its lower left edge — the encoding layer going, not the glass. She registered this and kept walking. The floor was stone rather than the treated composite of the upper levels, and her footsteps carried here in a way they did not carry above — sharp, unabsorbed, announcing her to no one.

Halfway down the corridor, a locked access panel sat flush against the wall — standard issue, Registry seal in the upper right corner. She had the key. She had always had the key. It shared a ring with the key to the personal ledger drawer, a pairing she had carried for eleven years without examining what it meant to carry them together. She did not examine it now. She unlocked the panel, noted that the mechanism turned without resistance — recently oiled, which placed maintenance staff here within the month — and continued.

The door to the sealed calibration chamber stood at the corridor's end, exactly where the survey indicated. No marking on it. No Registry seal, no classification notice, nothing to distinguish it from the maintenance access doors flanking it on either side. That absence had been a deliberate choice. She remembered making it. She had been standing in this corridor — not in this corridor, she had never been in this corridor, she had been standing in the corridor's equivalent inside the survey report, reading the recommendation that the chamber be marked for classification — and she had filed that recommendation under administrative review and moved on. The door bore no marking because she had not marked it. It looked like nothing. She had constructed that appearance.

She stood before it. The hum was louder here — not loud in any absolute sense, but present in a way that made the surrounding silence more apparent. Behind her, the amber panels flickered once. Her hand closed around the door handle. The metal was cold in the way of metal that had not been touched in some time. She held it a moment longer than the act of opening required. Then she opened the door.

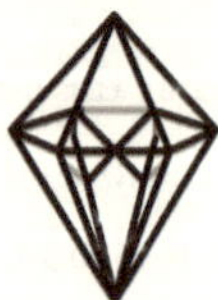

The sealed calibration chamber was smaller than she had expected, which was not a rational response — she had read the survey dimensions, had authorized the chamber's original construction, and the dimensions were not a surprise. Eight feet by twelve, stone-walled, a single stormglass panel mounted at the ceiling's center. The panel was not flickering. Steady amber light, which meant the crystal was intact and the frequency running through it was stable, which meant someone had maintained this panel continuously for seventeen years without her having authorized the maintenance.

She stood in the doorway. The maintenance was in the quarterly infrastructure report. She had been signing the quarterly infrastructure report in the eleven years since. She had not read the line items below the summary.

Three things occupied the room: a calibration console along the south wall, its surface cleared of instruments but carrying the specific patina of equipment that had been in use and then stopped; a single wooden chair positioned at the room's center facing the console; and on the console's surface, a series of shallow depressions in the stone where instruments had rested long enough to leave impressions. The impressions were the shape of calibration cylinders. She counted them. Twelve.

She crossed to the console and stood before it. The stone was cold under her fingertips. She did not touch the depressions. She looked at them.

In Charter Year Fourteen, the calibration event that had sealed this chamber had been authorized by her signature on a standard installation review form. That quarter she had signed seventeen installation review forms — the Bridge project had generated paperwork at a rate the Registry's standard processing structure had not been designed to absorb, and she had been processing it at the rate the structure required, which meant reading summaries rather than underlying documentation. She had signed the calibration authorization after reading a two-paragraph summary describing the event as a routine final-stage frequency verification. The summary had not described the secondary band reading. The summary had not described the four-hour gap. It had described the event as completed within standard parameters and the chamber as sealed for final administrative processing.

She had signed it and moved to the next form.

The chair at the room's center sat at the specific angle of something placed once and never adjusted. Whoever had run the calibration event had been sitting in that chair, facing the console, for the duration of the test. Seventeen years without being moved. The floor beneath it showed a slight discoloration — the stone worn pale in a circle where the chair legs had pressed, the weight of a single occupied afternoon still faintly recorded in the grain.

The technician who had run the test was a man named Oren. He appeared in the personnel records under Charter Year Fourteen, Infrastructure Development, Calibration Division. Six months after the Bridge's collapse, he had been administratively reassigned — that was the term the personal ledger used, the term she had entered into the personal ledger herself, which meant she had chosen that word herself.

She had not been in this room when Oren ran the test. She had been in the upper floors, processing the quarterly infrastructure summary, signing forms at the rate the structure required. Oren had been here, in this chair, running a calibration sequence that produced a secondary band reading of 97.3 hertz — outside the primary band's tolerance range, which should have triggered a review flag, which had not triggered a review flag because Oren had — she did not know what Oren had done. The the deviation was in the original calibration data, which was in the amber cylinder in the drawer upstairs. She had been holding that cylinder for eleven years. She had not asked Oren what he had done with the flag because six months after the collapse she had signed the administrative reassignment form and Oren had ceased to be a person she could ask.

She pulled the chair from its position and sat down in it. The wood was cold. She faced the console, the twelve depressions in the stone, the cleared surface where the calibration cylinders had rested. The stormglass panel above produced its steady amber light. The hum registered at the same frequency it had in the corridor — 94.7, she identified it without intending to, the standard encoding frequency, the frequency the final certification had recorded as the only reading, the frequency that was within tolerance.

She sat in the chair and looked at the console and did not move for a long time.

This was the room. The test had been run here. The secondary band reading had been produced here, by equipment that no longer existed on this console, by a technician who was no longer accessible, on a date she had authorized without reading the underlying documentation. The Bridge had been certified. The Bridge had been opened. Forty-one people had crossed it on the day it failed.

She had been in the upper floors.

The four-hour discrepancy had been in the survey report. She had read the survey report — three times, in the weeks after the collapse, while building the administrative structure that would manage the event's documentation: the suppression order, the re-indexing, the secondary band reading reclassified as equipment variance within tolerance. She had noted the four-hour discrepancy and filed it under the category she had created for it: the calibration event ran from the ninth bell to the first bell past midday, four hours, longer than the standard verification protocol required, which meant something had occurred during those four hours that the summary had not described.

She had built the administrative structure around the four hours. She had assumed — she had not assumed, she had decided, which was different, and she was sitting in the chair where the decision had been made and she was going to use the correct word — she had decided that the four hours contained the deliberate act. The secondary band reading produced, examined, and suppressed. The certification filed regardless. A decision made in this room, in this chair, by a technician she had subsequently reassigned, to proceed with the installation despite a reading indicating asymmetric stress distribution in the eastern anchor housing.

That was what she had been protecting. The deliberate act. The conscious choice to file a false certification. The murder, if she used the word the Warrens families had been using in the seventeen years since in a register she had been managing out of the official record.

The broadcast had used that word. It had been running through the city's stormglass receivers for nine hours. The word was in the frequencies now — in the amber panels in the corridor outside this room, in the monitoring panels on the upper floors, in the market stalls and the schoolrooms and the work platforms over the gorge. She had drafted a public response that neither confirmed nor denied the broadcast's content. The response would hold a portion of the population. She had calculated the portion. She had not calculated the compounding.

She sat in the chair and looked at the twelve depressions in the console's surface and saw, that

The four hours had not contained a deliberate act. Sitting in the room where the four hours had occurred, looking at the console where the calibration cylinders had rested, in the chair where Oren had sat running a test that produced a reading he did not know what to do with — she could see it now. A technician trained to the primary band. A secondary band reading the equipment had produced as a technical artifact of the older manufacturing layer — the redundant encoding layer that had never been officially documented, that Solen had known about because Solen had been trained before the Council standardized the systems, that Oren had not known about because Oren had been trained after.

Oren had seen a reading he could not account for. He had spent four hours trying to account for it. He had produced a summary describing the event as completed within standard parameters because the primary band reading was within standard parameters and the secondary band reading was outside his training's scope of interpretation. He had not suppressed the that number. He had not known it required suppression. He had simply not known what it was.

The four hours were not a cover-up. They were a technician sitting in this chair trying to make sense of a number his training had not prepared him for, eventually writing a summary that described what he understood — the primary band reading — and filing the secondary band reading as equipment variance because that was the closest available category, and going home.

She had built an administrative structure to protect a decision that had never been made. The certification had been filed in good faith by a technician who had not understood what he was seeing. The Bridge had failed because the secondary band reading indicated asymmetric stress distribution in the eastern anchor housing, and the technician had not known what the the recorded value meant, and she had not been in this room to ask, and forty-one people had crossed the Bridge on the day it failed.

No one had decided to kill them. No one had sat in this chair and looked at 97.3 hertz and chosen to proceed. No one had chosen. Oren had looked at 97.3 hertz and not known what he was looking at, and she had looked at Oren's summary and signed it without reading the underlying documentation, and the Bridge had opened, and the Bridge had failed.

The suppression order she had filed in the weeks after the collapse had not been protecting a deliberate act. It had been protecting the absence of a decision — the gap where a decision should have existed and did not. The four hours had not contained a choice to kill anyone. They had contained a technician trying to understand a reading that the Council's own standardization program had made it impossible for him to understand.

For eleven years she had suppressed this because she believed she was suppressing evidence of intentional harm. She had filed the administrative reassignment for Oren because she believed he had made a deliberate choice and she was managing the consequences. She had been wrong about what she was managing. Wrong about what the four hours contained. Right about the Bridge. The secondary band reading had always pointed to failure. Right that the certification should not have been filed.

The amber panel above hummed at 94.7 hertz. Steady. Within tolerance.

The forty-one names were in the broadcast. They were in the stormglass frequencies across the city. They had been in the secondary band of Solen's encoding across eleven years, and Solen had known about the secondary band because Solen had been trained before the standardization, and Solen had known what 97.3 hertz meant in the eastern anchor housing, and Solen had known that Oren had not known what it meant, and Solen had — she did not know what Solen had done with that knowledge before the collapse. She had the cylinder. She had not played the cylinder. She had been holding it eleven years in a drawer that no one had asked her to open.

The Vael variable. That was the term she had used in the session room. The Vael variable had introduced instability into the archival situation — the archivist's daughter, trained in pre-standardization methods, able to read the secondary band, able to find the forty-one names where the Council's current archivists would not know to look. She had been managing the Vael variable for two years. She had issued the re-calibration order that morning, after the review board, which she had chaired herself because the case involved the third name and she needed to be in the room when the third name was spoken into the official record for the first time. When it was finally said aloud.

Ryn Ossian. Charter signatory. The third name. In the official record of the review board's proceedings now — sealed, classified, accessible only to Registry directors and Charter signatories. Accessible to Ossian. She had been the only person keeping that name out of the official record for eleven years. That was over.

She had confirmed the re-calibration order. Standard procedure for unauthorized broadcast events. She had confirmed it because the alternative — not confirming it — was a category she did not have available to her inside the structure she had built, and she had been inside this structure those eleven years, and the structure's logic was the only logic she had been using for so long that she could not locate the seam where it ended and she began.

She had been in the chamber for a long time. The amber panel continued its hum. She remained in the chair.

For the duration of her time sitting there, she had been trying to complete a sentence. The sentence had a beginning: *the suppression was necessary because —*. She had been completing this sentence for eleven years — in the session room before the broadcast, in the quarterly infrastructure reports she had signed without reading the line items, in the personal ledger entries filed under the word *reassignment*, in the administrative structure she had built to manage an event she had understood incorrectly. The completion had always been available: *the suppression was necessary because without it the Registry's credibility would collapse.* The city needed that credibility to hold. The forty-one were dead and would remain dead. The living needed an account they could stand on. She had provided the account.

The sentence would not complete now.

Not because the completion was wrong — she could not evaluate whether it was wrong, sitting in this chair, in this room, looking at the twelve depressions in the console's surface. She could not evaluate it because the completion had been built on a foundation that did not exist. The deliberate act had not occurred. The decision to proceed had not been made. Oren had not chosen to file a false certification. She had not been protecting the city from the knowledge that its Bridge had been deliberately opened to fail. She had been protecting the city — protecting herself — from the knowledge that its Bridge had been opened without sufficient understanding of what 97.3 hertz in the eastern anchor housing meant, and that this was not a crime in the legal sense, and that no one had intended the forty-one to die, and that forty-one people had died anyway. Intent had not touched them. Cause had. The cause was in the secondary band reading that Oren had not understood and she had not read and Solen had understood and had been encoding for eleven years in the amber glass of the pre-Charter archive.

The sentence had no completion she could reach. She pressed her palms flat on the cold console surface and held them there.

The stormglass panel hummed. The hum was 94.7 hertz — within tolerance, the primary band reading, the reading that had been filed. The secondary band reading was in the cylinder in the drawer upstairs. She had confirmed the re-calibration order. The order was signed and sent. Vael was in the detention room. The amber shard — she had handled the amber shard without cloth gloves during the review board, an irregularity the senior archivists had noted and not questioned, because she was the Registry's director and had handled archive glass before. The shard had not activated. Attuned to Vael's frequency, it had not opened for her, which was the correct outcome, the expected outcome, an outcome she had been sitting with since she set the shard back in its cloth-lined tray and confirmed the re-calibration order in the same motion.

She could not open the archive. The archive was Solen's. It had always been Solen's, encoded for a pair of hands that were not hers, and the city had received the broadcast, and the re-calibration order was signed, and the sentence did not have a completion.

She stood from the chair. She did not move it back to its original position. She walked to the door, stepped into the corridor, and pulled the door shut behind her. The latch caught. The door looked like nothing again — she had made it look like nothing and it still looked like nothing, and behind it the chamber held a console with twelve depressions in the stone, a chair she had moved slightly out of position, and a stormglass panel humming at 94.7 hertz, steady, within tolerance, running without interruption for seventeen years.

She walked back down the corridor toward the service stair. The amber panel with the flickering edge flickered once as she passed. She noted it and did not stop.

Upstairs, the personal ledger was in the drawer. The seventeen-year-old entry was in the personal ledger. She was going to open the drawer and read the entry and she was not going to add to it — not today — because she did not have a completion for the sentence and she was not going to write an incomplete sentence in the ledger, which was the one place she had been keeping the record as it actually was rather than as the administrative structure required it to be. The ledger was the place she had been honest, which meant the ledger was also the place where she had been writing the wrong account for eleven years in good faith, which was — she did not have a word for this that the ledger's vocabulary could hold.

She climbed the service stair. Her hand rested on the iron rail. The rail was cold. Above her, through the floors, the city was still processing the broadcast, and the afternoon light was going off the limestone facades of the administrative district. Down at the gorge the stormglass riverbed would be catching what was left of it — pale and flat, the current moving the way it always moved, carrying the frequency the same as it carried everything else, the same as it had carried everything before the Bridge fell and would carry everything long after she had finished deciding what to do.

She had confirmed the re-calibration order. Seventeen years ago she had signed a form she had not read, and the Bridge had opened, and she had spent the years since building an account that explained what she believed had happened. She had been wrong about what happened. She had confirmed the re-calibration order anyway — because the structure demanded it, because without the structure she did not know what she was, because that was a way of explaining it that also was not quite a reason.

Vael was in the detention room. The re-calibration order was signed and sent. The third name was in the official record, and Ossian would know it had been spoken. Outside, the afternoon light was going out of the stone.

Chapter 21

T he note had been left on the table while she slept — a single folded card bearing the Registry watermark, her name written in the technician's hand. She had not heard the door open. The amber shard was still in her coat pocket, where it had rested since the review board; the coat hung over the chair beside the bed, and when she woke and read the card she held it for a moment before pressing it back along its original crease.

The technician arrived at the second bell past dawn.

He was younger than she had expected — mid-thirties, perhaps, with a directness in his movements that suggested he had come to this work and stayed. A case of pale birch sat in his grip, its brass clasps dull at the corners where the plating had long since rubbed away. He set it on the table without ceremony and did not move to open it.

"You've been informed of the procedure," he said. Not a question — an opening.

"The re-calibration order," Vael said.

"Yes." He took the chair across from her, which put the case between them on the table. "Before we begin, I want to explain what the procedure involves. It's standard practice — I prefer it. Some technicians don't."

She waited.

"The instrument adjusts frequency sensitivity at the perceptual threshold." His hand rested on the case's lid without lifting it. "Your current calibration registers significantly outside Charter parameters — you're receiving in ranges the standard archive infrastructure was never designed to transmit to. The secondary band, primarily. Some pre-Charter registers." A pause. "The procedure brings your reception into alignment with current standards. You'll retain access to stormglass archives. You'll still be able to read encoded material, conduct frequency analysis, perform archival work at a professional level. The adjustment targets only the anomalous registers."

The anomalous registers. She recognized the phrasing — *anomalous*, their word, the word that had appeared in her personnel file across eleven years, the word that meant the frequency at which her mother had encoded a counter-archive into pre-Charter amber glass and aimed it at a pair of hands that were hers.

"It won't hurt," he said. "There's a period of frequency sensitivity afterward — some people describe a ringing, a warmth. It passes within a few hours."

"And my memories."

"Won't be affected." He held her gaze directly. "I want to be precise about that. The procedure doesn't interact with encoded memory at all. What you remember, you'll remember. What you know, you'll know. The adjustment is perceptual, not cognitive." He paused. "Everything that happened — you'll carry it. You simply won't be able to feel the dissonance in the same registers afterward."

She looked at the case on the table. Birch and dull brass. The instrument inside was probably clean — he had that quality, this technician, something visible in the unscuffed hinges of the case and the deliberate way he'd set it down, flat and square. She did not doubt he believed this. She did not doubt the instrument was clean.

"The amber shard," he said. "The personal object you retained through intake. The procedure works best when the patient's frequency objects are present — it helps establish the baseline. I'll need you to have it accessible."

She reached into her coat pocket and placed the shard on the table between them. It was cold. Had been cold since the review board, since Maerath had held it without activating it, since she had set it back in its tray and the warmth had gone out of it. It lay on the table's surface and caught no light.

"Thank you," he said. He studied it — not her, the shard — his head tilting slightly, eyes moving along the amber's edge the way a reader's eyes move across a line of text. "Pre-Charter amber." He turned it a quarter rotation with one finger. "The bevel's gone thin here." He did not touch it further. "I'll need you to hold it during the baseline assessment, and again during the procedure itself."

"How long."

"The full procedure runs approximately forty minutes. The baseline assessment is the longest portion — twenty minutes, perhaps twenty-five, depending on the range of the anomalous registers." He looked up. "Is there anything you want to ask before we begin?"

The room was the same room it had been for four days — stone walls, stormglass panel in the ceiling casting its even light, the table and two chairs and the narrow bed. Nothing in it had changed. The light from the panel ran at 94.7 hertz, within tolerance, the primary band, the reading that had always been filed. She knew this the way she knew the weight of the shard and the specific temperature differential at its edges.

"I'd like an hour," she said. "Before the procedure."

He looked at her without surprise. "I'll need to confirm with the warden."

"I know."

He stood, took the case, and left. The door locked behind him — not with a key, with the specific click of a Registry mechanism, the kind that registered the locking event in a secondary log she would never read. She sat with the shard on the table in front of her and the even light from the ceiling panel and the city outside the Spire's stone, still processing, still receiving, carrying frequency the way it had always carried frequency.

Twenty minutes later the mechanism clicked again. A different sound — the warden's confirmation arriving through the door's secondary register. She had one hour.

She picked up the shard.

Cold in her palm. It had been cold since the review board, and before that warm — warm from the broadcast chamber, warm from the transmission crystal, warm from eleven years of Solen's encoding running at 94.7 hertz in the secondary band no one had been trained to read. The warmth was gone. She held it anyway.

The room was very quiet.

She had opened the shard four times. The first time in the evidence drawer, when it had shown her Solen's calibration chamber and the console with twelve depressions and the four-hour window in Charter Year Fourteen. The second time in the review board, when Maerath had held it without activating it and she had understood what it meant that the shard was attuned to her frequency and not to his. The third time — the broadcast chamber. Tace's hand flat against the installation housing. The amber cylinder loaded last.

The fourth time had not been counted. It had simply happened, the way things happen when you have been building toward them for eleven years and the building is done and what remains is the thing itself.

She pressed her thumb against the shard's surface.

The warmth came back.

Not the calibration chamber. Not the secondary band reading. Not the authorization signature missing from the suppression order, not the forty-one names in the frequency the Council's archivists had never been trained to strip.

Something earlier.

The workshop.

The light is ordinary. Morning light, she thinks, though she cannot see the window from this angle — the angle is low, the perspective a child's height, standing in the doorway of Solen's workshop with her shoulder against the frame in the specific way she had always stood in doorways, watching.

Solen is at the bench. Her back is to the door. She is calibrating a piece of domestic glass — not archive glass, not pre-Charter amber, a standard household piece, the kind used in kitchen windows and reading lamps and the small decorative panels above doorways in the middle wards. Her hands move through the calibration in a steady unhurried rhythm, each adjustment following the last without pause or hesitation, the motion of hands that have found their work and settled into it.

She is humming.

Not a melody Vael can name — something without structure, rising and falling with the calibration, following the glass's frequency the way a hand follows a surface to read its temperature. The hum and the glass and the morning light and the smell of the workshop, which is cedar, the sharp mineral cold of the stone, and underneath both the faint metallic bite that stormglass leaves on the air.

Eighteen seconds.

Solen does not turn around. She does not know she is being watched, or she knows and has decided not to make it a moment, to let the watching be ordinary, to let the workshop be a place her daughter stands in doorways and watches her work without it requiring acknowledgment or meaning.

The glass catches the light. The hum holds its frequency.

Eighteen seconds.

The shard went dark.

Vael sat with it in her palm. The warmth was already fading — the specific fade of pre-Charter amber when the encoding completes, the crystal returning to its ambient temperature, which was the temperature of her hand.

The room was very quiet.

She did not know when Solen had encoded this. The light in the workshop was ordinary, morning light, no urgency in it, no awareness of what was coming. Before the secondary band reading. Before Charter Year Fourteen. Before any of it, perhaps, when Vael was seven and standing in doorways and the workshop was simply the workshop and Solen was simply her mother working and humming without a melody.

Her thumb moved against the shard's edge — the worn bevel, the place where the amber had thinned from handling — and stopped there. The counter-archive was evidence — the calibration chamber, the frequency readings, the suppression order without an authorization signature, the forty-one names. This was not evidence. This was an ordinary morning. Solen at the bench with her back to the door and her hands moving and the hum that had no melody.

The shard was cold.

She pressed her thumb against it once more. Nothing activated. The encoding was complete — had been complete the moment it ended, the way all stormglass encodings were complete, fixed at the moment of recording, incapable of revision or addition or reply. She knew this and pressed her thumb against it anyway, the worn surface under her thumb, the amber pale in the room's even light.

Nothing.

She set it on the table.

The stormglass panel in the ceiling hummed at 94.7 hertz, steady, within tolerance. Outside the Spire's stone, the city was still receiving the broadcast — complete and irreversible, gone into every stormglass receiver in Bridgefall at the frequency Tace had opened and Vael had loaded and the transmission crystal had carried. The forty-one names were in the public record now. The secondary band reading was in the public record. The authorization signature missing from the suppression order was in the public record.

It lived in the amber shard on the table, encoded in the secondary band at 94.7 hertz, filed under nothing, accessible only to the pair of hands it had been built for.

Was.

She looked at the shard for a long time.

The re-calibration would not remove her memories. The technician had been clear about this, and she believed him — in the way he'd separated perceptual from cognitive without reaching for softer language, repeated the distinction twice, held her gaze while he said it. She would remember the workshop. She would remember Solen at the bench. She would remember the hum without a melody and the morning light and the smell of cedar and cold stone.

What she would lose was the ability to feel the dissonance when altered glass played. What she would lose was the ability to open pre-Charter amber bare-handed, reading the secondary frequency band that had never been officially documented because it was considered a flaw in the early manufacturing — the redundant encoding layer that Solen had known about because she had been trained before the Council standardized the systems.

What she would lose was this.

She picked the shard up again. Held it in both hands. The amber was pale and its surface gone thin at the bevel and cold and it caught the light from the ceiling panel in the specific way that pre-Charter glass caught light, which was different from standard stormglass — a difference she had been able to feel since she was a child standing in doorways watching her mother work.

The workshop had been warm. The light had been ordinary. Solen had been humming. That was what the shard had kept.

Not the investigation. Not the evidence. Not the eleven years of encoding or the forty-one names or the secondary band reading that had been filed as equipment variance within tolerance. An ordinary morning. A child in a doorway. A woman at a bench with her back to the door, calibrating household glass, humming without a melody.

Vael sat with this until the mechanism in the door clicked again.

The technician opened the case on the table.

The instrument was smaller than she had imagined — a cylinder of pale stormglass approximately the length of her forearm, its surface matte rather than reflective, its ends capped in the same dull brass as the case's clasps. It looked like a calibration tool. It looked like something Solen would have kept on the workshop bench.

"Hold the shard," he said.

She picked it up from the table. Cold.

"I'm going to begin the baseline assessment. You'll feel a frequency resonance — some people describe warmth, some describe a mild pressure behind the eyes. Both are normal." He held the instrument without activating it, waiting for her to settle. "Tell me if the sensation becomes uncomfortable."

She nodded.

He activated the instrument.

The resonance arrived the way he had described — a warmth, then a pressure, not behind her eyes but in her palms, which was where it had always been, the dissonance living in her hands before it lived anywhere else. The instrument was reading her calibration — establishing the baseline, the range of the anomalous registers, the secondary band sensitivity that had been in her personnel file over eleven years. The instrument was precise. It was doing exactly what it had been built to do.

The shard was cold in her hand.

She thought: the workshop. The morning light. The hum without a melody. She thought: the forty-one names are in the public record. The secondary band reading is in the public record. The suppression order without an authorization signature is in the public record. The broadcast is complete and irreversible and the city is receiving it and will continue to receive it.

She thought: Solen at the bench with her back to the door.

The baseline assessment took twenty-three minutes. She knew because she counted — not the seconds but the frequency pulses from the instrument, which ran at a consistent interval she could feel in her palms. She counted them the way she counted the physical properties of glass when the grief-architecture was close to failing — the weight, the temperature differential at the edges, the specific resistance of the surface. The counting was not calming. It was displacement. Her grip on the shard steadied with each pulse, the cold of it moving up through her fingers until her breathing matched the interval.

When the baseline was complete, the technician made a notation in a small ledger. He wrote without pause, the pen moving across the page and lifting cleanly, the entry done before she had fully exhaled. He did not show her what he had written.

"The procedure itself will take approximately fifteen minutes," he said. "The anomalous registers are extensive, but the adjustment is straightforward." He looked at the shard in her hand. "Keep holding that."

She kept holding it.

He activated the instrument again.

The warmth came back — different this time, not the reading-warmth of the baseline but something that moved, that had direction, that tracked through her palms toward the specific registers where the dissonance had always lived. She had been feeling the dissonance for so long she had stopped registering it as a sensation separate from her own baseline — it was simply how stormglass felt to her, the slight wrongness in altered glass, the specific opening when pre-Charter amber activated. Only now, with the instrument finding it from outside, did she feel it as a thing with edges.

The shard was cold.

She thought: this is what it felt like. This specific warmth, moving through her palms toward the registers where her mother's voice had lived those eleven years. This was the mechanism. This was the calibration chamber, the console with twelve depressions, the four-hour window in Charter Year Fourteen — all of it arriving at this room, this table, this instrument in the hands of a technician who believed he was correcting a malfunction.

He was not wrong that it was a malfunction. The secondary band was not officially documented. It had never been designed to be read. Solen had known about it because she had been trained before the standardization, because she had been an archivist in the years when the Council's systems were still being built, because she had understood the specific flaw in the early manufacturing and had used it — had built eleven years of evidence into it, had encoded an ordinary morning in a workshop into it and aimed all of it at a pair of hands that could feel the dissonance in altered glass.

The warmth moved through her palms and the registers shifted and she held the shard and the shard was cold.

Fifteen minutes. She counted the frequency pulses.

When the instrument stopped, the technician set it on the table and reached for the ledger. He wrote the second entry the same way he had written the first — pen down, pen up, done.

She set the shard on the table.

Both palms rested flat against the stone surface. The table was standard Spire construction — limestone with a stormglass inlay along the edge, a decorative element that served no archival function. The inlay ran at 94.7 hertz, within tolerance, the primary band, the reading that had always been filed.

She waited.

"You may feel some frequency sensitivity for the next several hours," the technician said. "That's normal. It will resolve on its own." He closed the case. "If you experience anything beyond the standard sensitivity — significant disorientation, persistent pressure — the warden can contact the technical division."

She nodded.

He picked up the case. Paused at the door. "The shard is yours to keep," he said. "The procedure doesn't affect retained objects — only the perceptual threshold."

The mechanism clicked. He was gone.

She sat with her palms flat on the table and the shard in front of her and the light from the ceiling panel steady and even at 94.7 hertz. The limestone inlay ran warm along the table's edge. She could feel it — the warmth, the frequency, the primary band running without interruption through the stone. She could feel it the way she had always been able to feel it, the standard register, the reading that fell within tolerance.

She reached out and pressed her thumb against the amber shard.

Nothing activated.

She lifted it into her palm. The amber was pale, its surface thinned at the bevel, the old pre-Charter glass lighter in the hand than standard stormglass, its edge behavior different in the light. She held it and waited for the warmth that meant the secondary band was reading her calibration — the specific opening that meant the encoding had found the pair of hands it had been built for.

The shard was cold.

She sat with this. She would not know yet whether the dissonance was gone — not until she held a piece of altered glass and felt for the wrongness that had lived in her palms since she was a child watching her mother work. The technician had been precise: the procedure was perceptual, not cognitive. She would remember. She would know. The registers where she had felt it would simply no longer carry it.

She would not know until she knew.

What she knew now was that the shard was cold and her palms were flat on the table and the last thing she had received from her mother was an ordinary morning in a workshop before any of this began — the light ordinary, the bench familiar, the hum without a melody rising and falling with the calibration of a piece of household glass that no one would ever encode into a counter-archive, that no one would ever file under the maintenance log, that no one would ever use as evidence of anything except that a woman had been at her work on an ordinary morning and her daughter had been watching from the doorway and neither of them had known what was coming.

Chapter 22

The adjournment notice arrived at the sixth bell past midday, filed through the standard administrative channel, timestamped and sealed with the committee clerk's initialing stamp. Brek read it twice before he understood what it was.

Not a dismissal. Not a closure. An adjournment — the formal suspension of proceedings pending review of newly surfaced materials that fell within the committee's jurisdiction. The language was procedural, each clause correctly formed, the authorization signatures in their proper columns. He had filed documents like this himself, dozens of times, in his first years as a Registry operative when the paperwork still felt like craft rather than reflex. He knew the form's architecture from the inside.

What the form said, in the precise vocabulary of Registry administrative procedure, was that someone had invoked the review mechanism correctly. Not approximately correctly. Not with sufficient irregularity to challenge on technical grounds. Correctly. The pre-broadcast filing, the timestamped intake ledger, the clerk's initialing — all of it predating the twenty-four-hour hold by enough margin that the hold could not reach backward and cover it. The mechanism had been designed to protect legitimate archival review from suppression. Someone had understood this and had used the mechanism for exactly the purpose it was designed for.

Brek set the notice on his desk. The stormglass panel in its brushed-metal casing ran at 94.7 hertz, primary band, the standard reading for this floor of the Spire. He had stopped noticing it years ago — the way a man stops hearing the mill wheel outside his bedroom window, present in his sleep but absent from his waking. It registered now. The frequency ran without interruption, clean and even, and he sat with the notice on his desk and the frequency running and something in him that had not yet decided what it was doing.

He had been in the broadcast installation at the third bell. He had conducted three arrests. He had filed the intake documentation with his usual precision — names, times, the charge designations that the Registry's procedural manual specified for unauthorized archive access and unlicensed frequency transmission. The documentation was accurate. It was complete. He had returned to his office and written his preliminary report and eaten the meal someone had left on his desk and drunk the tea that had gone cold while he was writing.

And then the adjournment notice had arrived, and he was sitting with it, and the pause that had started in the broadcast installation when Davan asked him about the personal receiver was still going.

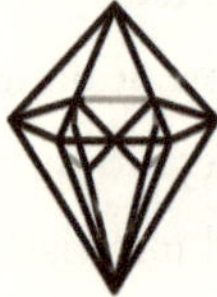

He had clearance for the sealed record. Co-investigator status on the case gave him access to the full proceedings documentation, including the transcribed interviews from the administrative detention review. He had not looked at it yet. He looked at it now.

Davan's account was the first document in the file.

The account was dated at the second bell past midday, the day after the broadcast — yesterday, which felt like longer. The interviewing archivist was identified by designation only. The account itself was given in the first person, present-tense transcription, which was the Registry's standard format for formal recorded statements: the interviewee spoke, the archivist rendered the speech into the administrative record, the interviewee confirmed the rendering.

Brek read the blank field first. Not because it appeared first — it did not appear until the account's third page, embedded in the chronological sequence of Davan's actions — but because he had been carrying it since the broadcast installation, the cursor sitting on the file name, which he had not yet opened. The blank field in the location tracking log. Eleven days of entries, each one complete, each one filed at the correct interval with the correct notation, and then one entry with the subject field populated and the location field empty. He had seen blank fields before. Clerical error, system lag, a notation made before the operative had confirmed position. He had not flagged it because he had had no reason to flag it.

The account explained it.

Davan had accessed the shelter's location from the personnel file. He had gone there. He had found the amber shard on the floor of the room where Vael had been staying, had held it, had experienced four seconds of stormglass playback that he described in the account with spare exactness, each technical detail placed in its order: the Glass Bridge, eastern anchor housing, asymmetric stress distribution at 97.3 hertz on the secondary band, the load-distribution anomaly that had not appeared in the final certification because the certification had recorded only the primary band reading of 94.7 hertz, within tolerance. He had retained the access codes from a previous assignment. He had provided a false explanation to Brek. He had used the maintenance shaft.

Brek read this passage three times.

The account was accurate. He could feel its accuracy in the specific way you felt the accuracy of a statement that confirmed something you had not known you suspected. Davan had been in that shelter. Davan had held the shard. Davan had known, for eleven days before the broadcast, what the secondary band reading was, and had filed a location report with a blank field, and had come to the broadcast installation when Brek called him in, and had stood at the installation's entrance with his hands in his pockets and asked whether Brek had received it on his personal receiver.

The man who asked the question was the same man who had filed accurate reports for twelve years. Brek knew the quality of Davan's reports. He had reviewed them. He had cited them in three separate commendations. The specificity, the consistency, the particular way Davan noted things that other operatives missed — a worn track across a threshold where foot traffic said more than any floor plan, a hook set low on a wall suggesting who in the household reached it last, a chair angled toward a door rather than a desk. Brek had always thought of this as Davan's professional skill. He read it now and scrolled back to the commendation language he had written himself — the specificity, the consistency — and then set his hand on the desk and did not scroll further.

The account continued past the blank field into the shelter visit, the personnel file access, the eleven days of carrying the knowledge of the secondary band reading while filing accurate reports about everything else. Davan described this without apology and without justification. He had done these things. He had made these choices. He set them down in the same register he used for everything — flat, sequential, unadorned — as though the only thing left that mattered was getting the record straight.

Brek sat with this for a long time.

The account did not read as confession. That was the thing he kept returning to. It read as documentation — the same quality Davan brought to every report he had ever filed, applied now to himself. Brek had read thousands of Registry intake statements. Most of them had a quality of management, a shaping of events toward the most defensible account. This one had none of that. The sentences did not lean. They did not soften at the edges where a man's choices became hard to look at directly. Each one carried the same flat weight as the one before it, and the difference between this and every other statement Brek had read was visible in the sentence-level grain of the transcription.

He closed Davan's account.

The Registry's cryptography section had transcribed the broadcast's frequency data into readable form: the discrepancy catalogue, the calibration chamber records, the installation team roster, the secondary band reading with its date and its encoding signature and its specific technical data about the eastern anchor housing asymmetric stress distribution. Forty-one names. The load-distribution anomaly in installation month three. The final certification recording only the primary band. The authorization signature on the suppression order that had not been filed.

Brek read through this material with the attention twelve years had made habitual — the kind that moved through a document without deciding beforehand what it expected to find, pausing where something snagged and moving on when nothing did. The discrepancy catalogue was Nava's work — he recognized the filing conventions, the cross-reference notation, the seventeen-year accumulation of variance reports that the Registry's secondary cabinet had been absorbing without acting on. He had processed Nava's arrest documentation himself. He had not read her files before that. He read them now in the broadcast's rendered form and felt the seventeen years in it and that you had not looked at.

Then he reached the installation team roster and the third name.

He read the name and stopped.

Ryn Ossian. Charter signatory. Memorial dedication. The name in the commemorative stormglass installations that played on public holidays — the warm, measured cadence of the founding Charter reading, the voice Brek had heard as a schoolboy in Bridgefall's civic hall, standing in his good clothes beside his father while the recording played and the adults went quiet around him. He had heard it again as a Registry operative standing at attention during the Charter anniversary ceremony, three years running, while the installation played and the Spire's official contingent stood in the courtyard with the stormglass panels running their commemorative sequence.

The name in the sealed record was the same name. On the installation team roster for Charter Year Fourteen. Attached to the final certification that had recorded only the primary band reading. By the logic of the discrepancy catalogue and the secondary band data and the suppression order with its missing authorization signature, one of the names that had known or should have known what the eastern anchor housing was doing at 97.3 hertz on the secondary band.

Brek sat with the sealed record on the terminal and the commemorative frequency running in his memory and the gap between them.

The gap was not ambiguous. That was the thing. He had been trained to identify ambiguity in documentary evidence — the inconsistency that could be clerical error, the discrepancy that could be system lag, the signature that could be forgery. He looked for the ambiguity in this gap and could not find it. The name in the sealed record was the name in the public memory. The name in the sealed record was attached to a certification that the secondary band data contradicted. The secondary band data had been in the Registry's variance reports for eleven years, filed quarterly under form RT-7, equipment variance within tolerance, in the secondary cabinet where no one was required to look.

He closed the broadcast's rendered content.

The office was quiet in the way of the Spire's operational floors at this hour — not empty, but the ambient sounds of institutional work running at their standard register. Down the corridor, a clerk's chair scraped and held still. The stormglass panel ran at 94.7 hertz. He had worked in this office for six years. He knew the look of its quiet.

He had conducted three arrests at the broadcast installation. He had filed accurate documentation. He had done his job correctly.

The adjournment notice was on his desk. The sealed record was on the terminal. Somewhere in the detention facility, Davan was in a clean room waiting for a review board decision that would convene within forty-eight hours, which was faster than standard, which meant the Registry was treating this as an exceptional case, which meant the broadcast had created institutional pressure that the standard timeline could not absorb.

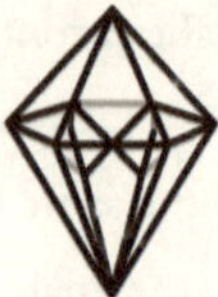

Brek pulled up Davan's personnel file.

Not the account from the sealed record — the full personnel file, twelve years of Registry service, the complete professional record of a man who had been very good at his job. He read it from the beginning. Not looking for anything. Just reading.

The early entries had the weight of all early Registry files — the onboarding documentation, the training assessments, the first assignment reports with their slightly formal register as a new operative learned the institutional vocabulary. Davan's early reports were good. Brek could see, even in the first year, the cast of attention that had distinguished his later work: the notations about physical spaces, the observations that sat slightly outside the standard reporting categories, the detail that was accurate and that no one had asked for.

He read through the years. The commendations he had written himself were there, in their correct sequence. The assignment records. The location tracking logs with their regular entries, each one complete, each one filed at the correct interval.

Then the blank field.

It was a single entry in a twelve-year file. The subject field was populated. Correct timestamp. The location field was empty, but the filing was otherwise complete.

Brek looked at it for a long time.

The blank field was not a flaw in the twelve years of accurate reports. He had been reading it that way without knowing he was reading it that way — as an anomaly against a baseline of integrity, a deviation from a pattern, the moment a good operative had made a bad choice. But that was not what he was seeing when he looked at the file from the beginning. What he was seeing was twelve years of a man doing his job correctly, and then one day a blank field, and the blank field was not a deviation from the pattern. It was the same pattern. The same attention, the same precision, applied to the question of what to record and what to leave empty.

Davan had not stopped being accurate. He had made an accurate choice about what accuracy required.

He closed the file. He opened it again. He read the blank field entry one more time and then sat with his hands flat on the desk and the stormglass panel running at 94.7 hertz and the adjournment notice in its correct position and the city outside his window still processing the broadcast, the Registry's public response circulating through the official channels, the commemorative stormglass installations playing their Charter anniversary sequence in the civic squares as they did every day at this hour, Ryn Ossian's voice warm and complete in the primary band, within tolerance, the reading that had always been filed.

Chapter 23

Cold rose from below — not the regulated chill of the Spire's interior rooms, but something older, something the Sorrow carried up through the stone from the riverbed, from the ruins, from the infrastructure that had existed before the bridge and would outlast whatever followed it. Maerath had known this cold was here. The inspection reports had described it. She had never stood inside it before.

She had entered through the Plateau-side tower's lower access using her director's clearance — the kind that logged visits in a secondary system no duty clerk reviewed before the third bell. The warden rotation would carry no record of her passage. She had worked this out on the service stair, the way she worked out most things: not slowly, not with any visible effort, but running the way breathing ran, without her attention on it. She had come through the tower and down the maintenance path and arrived at the iron grating in the pre-dawn dark with the Sorrow below and the stormglass riverbed catching what little light the hour offered.

The amber had not lit for her. She had known it would not.

The grating was iron, older than the bridge installation — original infrastructure, the kind that appeared in the earliest Plateau civic records as a safety barrier between the maintenance path and the gorge drop. She put her hands on it. The cold climbed through her palms and into her wrists. She held it and looked down at the riverbed.

The stormglass was luminous even now. Pre-dawn, the gorge still in shadow, and the riverbed produced its own faint light — not warmth, not heat, but the particular quality of glass that has been running frequency data in the eleven years since with no one authorized to read it. She had seen this from the Spire window. The window flattened it, made it legible as a view rather than a fact. Standing at the grating, with the iron cold in her hands and the drop below her and the Sorrow audible as a low continuous sound that the inspection reports called ambient resonance — a sound that was, in fact, a river running over the remains of a bridge — it was not a view.

Forty-one people.

She had not let herself think of them this way in eleven years. Not without the threat model. Not without the contingency framework, the managed consequence categories, the specific language that converted forty-one deaths into a structural event and the structural event into a suppression requirement. She had told herself it was governance. That governance demanded difficult decisions and difficult decisions required someone willing to carry them.

She had been willing. She had told herself this was a form of courage.

Forty-one people crossed the bridge the day it failed. The eastern anchor housing had been running at 97.3 hertz on the secondary band for three months. The primary band read 94.7 — within tolerance, within the certification parameters, within everything the final inspection had measured and recorded and signed. The secondary band was a manufacturing artifact, undocumented, absent from the standard assessment protocol. Oren had not known to look for it. She had not known to ask him to look for it. The certification had been filed in good faith by a technician who lacked the training to interpret what he had measured, and she had signed it without reading the underlying documentation, and forty-one people had crossed the bridge.

She had built the suppression apparatus to conceal a decision. Standing at the grating, she understood now that there had been no decision. There had been an absence — two absences, Oren's and hers — and the bridge had failed in the space between them, and forty-one people had fallen into the river whose bed was now carpeted with the glass from that bridge, and she had spent eleven years protecting the absence.

The hum was in her chest. She had not expected this. The inspection reports described the subsonic resonance from the stanchion residue as a low-frequency ambient, consistent with degraded stormglass in extended exposure, within the parameters of standard environmental monitoring. It was in her chest. Not painful. Not threatening. Present the way the cold was present — factual, indifferent, older than her management of it.

She thought about Oren.

She had not stood anywhere and thought about him specifically in eleven years. She had thought about the Oren variable — the phrase was in her personal ledger, in the entry from the year after the collapse, written in the specific vocabulary she had developed for managing the situation's components. The Oren variable had required administrative reassignment. She had written this. She had executed it. He had been moved to a position in the western registry annex with no access to calibration systems, no contact with the

Infrastructure Development division, no pathway back to the work he had been trained to do. She had written administratively reassigned in the ledger and in the official record, and she had not, until this moment, at the grating, in the pre-dawn cold with the hum in her chest, allowed herself to complete the sentence she had been building for eleven years.

He had not known what he was measuring. He had filed it as equipment variance within tolerance because that was the category available to him, because the secondary band was not in the certification protocol, because no one had trained him to recognize what 97.3 hertz on an undocumented channel meant for a load-bearing anchor housing under asymmetric stress. He had done his job correctly by every standard he had been given. She had reassigned him to prevent him from speaking to anyone who might ask questions she could not answer, and she had used the language of administrative procedure to make the reassignment invisible as an act, and he had spent — she did not know how many years he had spent in the western annex. She had not checked. The ledger did not contain this information because she had not put it there.

Forty-one people. Oren. Both weights, held simultaneously, at the place where both absences had their physical consequence.

She had never stood in a place and held them both at once before.

The Sorrow ran below. The stormglass riverbed produced its faint, continuous light — all those glass panels, all that frequency data, running at registers she could not access because the glass was attuned to frequencies she did not carry. Vael could access it. The girl who had grown up handling Solen's stormglass, whose perceptual range included the secondary band as a matter of developmental exposure, whose hands had felt the dissonance in altered glass as an involuntary physical response — that girl had been able to read what the riverbed was saying. Maerath had ordered the re-calibration to remove that capacity.

The re-calibration had been executed. The girl was now in the city — released from administrative detention, pending a formal review process the Registry's legal apparatus required. The broadcast had made immediate re-integration the path of least institutional resistance. Maerath had made this calculation from the Spire. It was a correct calculation. It was also the kind of correct calculation she had been making for seventeen years, and she was standing at the grating in the pre-dawn cold with the hum in her chest and forty-one dead and one administratively reassigned technician, and she did not move. Her hand stayed on the iron. The calculation sat in her chest and she did not reach for the next one.

The uncertainty was new. She held the iron and looked at the riverbed and let it be new.

The third name was in the sealed record. Ryn Ossian, Charter signatory, voice of the civic commemorative installations, name attached to the Charter Year Fourteen installation team roster and to the final certification that had recorded only the primary band reading. No communication had come from the upper ward since the broadcast. The silence was a kind of communication, and she was not yet certain what it communicated — whether it was the silence of someone who had already consulted legal representation, or the silence of someone waiting to see what she would do before deciding what they needed to do, or simply the silence of someone very old who had been carrying their own version of the weight seventeen years and had not yet found the words.

She had not found the words either. She had been finding the language of administration instead.

The city was dark. The first suggestion of pre-dawn light was at the gorge rim — not visible here, in the shadow of the ruins, but present as a quality of the darkness changing. The broadcast was twenty hours old. The Registry's public response had been circulating for most of that time, measured, neither confirming nor denying, framed in the language of ongoing review and institutional due diligence. She had written the response. It was technically accurate. It was designed to hold the majority of the city's institutional trust while the review process ran its course, and it would hold that majority for a while, and the while was finite in ways she had been calculating, and the compounding she had been deliberately not calculating was already running in the portions the response was not designed to reach.

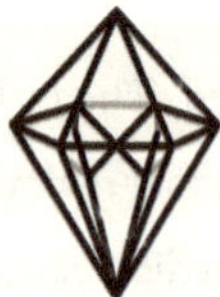

She released the grating.

Her hands were cold. She looked at them — the specific cold of iron in the pre-dawn, the slight redness at the palms from the pressure of holding. She had been holding longer than she intended. She did not know how long she had been standing here. The inspection reports gave the ambient temperature of the maintenance path in winter as approximately four degrees below the Plateau average, and she was not cold in the way that required action, but she was cold in the way that confirmed she had been here for some time.

She reached into her coat.

The personal ledger was there — it had been there since the review board, since she had descended to the calibration chamber and confirmed what she had spent eleven years refusing to confirm, since she had come back up the service stair with the re-calibration order irreversibly sent and the door unlatched behind her and the chair slightly displaced in a room no one was supposed to know existed. She had been carrying the ledger since then, waiting for a moment to open it that she had not been able to force or name.

She opened it.

The leather was worn at the spine, the key on the same ring as the access panel key, the ledger always in her coat pocket or her desk drawer or her hand. She knew its physical weight the way she knew the weight of the Spire's administrative calendar. She turned to the seventeen-year-old entry.

The ink had gone the specific brown of ink sitting in paper over seventeen years, slightly faded at the edges where the page had been exposed to air during the rare moments she had opened it. The handwriting was her own, the formal registry hand she had used for all official documentation in Charter Year Fourteen, before she had developed the slightly compressed shorthand of her later years. She read it.

She had read it before — in the calibration chamber, two days ago, for the first time in eleven years. She read it again now, standing at the grating with the Sorrow below and the hum in her chest and the cold in her hands. The entry described, in the language she had been using then, the administrative decisions she had made in the weeks following the collapse. The language was institutional throughout. The forty-one dead appeared as fatalities resulting from the structural event. Oren appeared as the Calibration Division technician responsible for the Charter Year Fourteen assessment. Her own decision to suppress the secondary band data appeared as the determination that full disclosure of the variance readings would not serve the public interest at this time.

She read it to the end. Then she took the pen from her coat — she carried a pen, always, the habit of someone whose work required notation at any hour — and she turned to the entry's final line, the line that ended with and the administrative record was closed accordingly, and she wrote beneath it.

One sentence.

She wrote it without stopping. She did not revise it. She had not planned what it would say — she had known, standing at the grating, that she needed to add to the entry, and she had not known until the pen moved what the sentence would be, and then it was written, and she read it once, and she closed the ledger.

The sentence was not in the institutional vocabulary. It was in the other vocabulary. It was private. It would remain private unless she chose otherwise, and she had not yet decided what she chose. She had decided something about what she had done. That was a different thing.

She put the ledger back in her coat.

The grating was behind her. The maintenance path ran back toward the Plateau-side tower, and the tower's lower entrance, and the service stair that would carry her up to the Spire's operational floors where the adjournment notice sat on Brek's desk and the sealed record sat on the terminal and the amber cylinder with the 97.3 hertz reading sat in her closed drawer and the re-calibration order on Vael was signed and sent and the formal review process was running on its ninety-day minimum timeline.

She walked.

The city was beginning to lighten. She felt it before she could see it — the specific quality of the dark shifting as she moved along the maintenance path and up through the tower's lower entrance and into the stairwell. The first market noise was starting in the lower wards, faint through the stone — a vendor's call, the clatter of a cart on the gorge floor, sound climbing the gorge walls toward the Plateau as it always did in the early morning. She had heard this from the Spire for seventeen years. She heard it now on the service stair, two flights up from the Plateau maintenance level, and the sound was the same as it had always been. She was not.

She climbed toward the operational floor, the ledger against her ribs, the sentence written and closed.

She did not know yet what she would do with the sentence, or with the ledger, or with the amber cylinder in her drawer, or with the silence from the upper ward, or with the specific knowledge she now carried about the gap between what she had suppressed and what she had believed she was suppressing. She did not know whether the re-calibration order on Vael was something she would allow to stand or something she would find a mechanism to reverse, and she did not know whether a mechanism existed, and she did not know whether the broadcast's compounding effects were already beyond the point at which any action she took would change their direction.

She knew what she had done. She had written it, in her own hand, in the vocabulary that named things correctly, in the ledger she had been carrying for seventeen years. Knowing what she had done was not the same as knowing what she would do. It was something smaller and more specific — the cold of iron still in her palms, the ledger against her ribs, the sentence written and closed, walking toward the Spire through a city beginning to wake, a city that did not know the woman moving through it had just, for the first time, told herself the truth.

The stair turned. The service door to the operational floor was ahead. She put her hand on it and pushed it open.

For the first time in seventeen years she did not know what came next. She walked through the door and let that be true.

The resonance changed.

Vael felt it in the soles of her boots before she had language for it — the Hollows' familiar pull, the low directional frequency she had learned to read as something drawing rather than warning, shifting register the way a frequency shifted when a second source entered the field. Not louder. Different. The way a room changed when a door opened somewhere above it, the air pressure adjusting to accommodate a new condition.

Tace felt it too. She was standing at the shelf where the cylinders had been — the shelf now empty, the carrying cases at her feet, the seventeen years of encoded documentation in the canvas bags that the network had moved out in the hours before the Registry's sweep. She had her hand flat against the shelf's bare surface, and her hand had gone still, fingers pressed down and unmoving, the way a hand goes when the body is listening through it.

Neither of them spoke.

The resonance deepened. Not the Hollows' baseline frequency, which Vael had come to know as a companion sound, present and constant and requiring nothing — this was something responding. The stone beneath her feet was responding. To what, she could not immediately say. The broadcast had gone out eighteen hours ago, had been running through every stormglass receiver in Bridgefall for eighteen hours, and the secondary band had been carrying Solen's encoding for the duration. That was part of it. The frequency in the city had shifted, and the older stratum beneath the Hollows was registering the shift.

But that was not the whole of it.

Vael pressed her palm flat against the Hollows floor.

The stone was warm.

Not the warmth of a room that had been lived in, which was the warmth she had always associated with this space — the residual warmth of people moving through stone corridors, of clay lamps burning through long nights, of the specific human temperature that accumulated in enclosed spaces over months and years of use. This was different. This was the warmth of something running in the stone itself, the way the stanchion housing had been warm at the gorge grating, the way the transmission crystal in the broadcast chamber had been warm under the cylinders' contact. The warmth of glass under load. Frequency as heat.

The older stratum was running.

She had not understood, until this moment, that it could do this without her initiating it. She had understood the stratum as something that responded to her specific frequency, to the hands Solen had encoded the archive for, to the secondary band access her developmental exposure had given her. She had understood herself as the activating condition.

The stratum did not appear to be waiting for her activation.

"Tace," she said.

Tace turned from the shelf. Her eyes found Vael's face, then Vael's hand flat against the floor, then the floor itself. She crossed to where Vael crouched and put her own hand beside Vael's without being asked.

The engineer's face did not change. But her hand pressed flatter against the stone, reading through the heel of the palm the way she read a housing under load — not watching a dial, finding the number in the bone.

"Ninety-four point seven," Tace said. Her voice was level, stripped to the measurement. "Primary band. Steady. Not source frequency. Response frequency."

"It's answering the broadcast."

"It has been answering the broadcast since the third bell. I thought it was residual. Sympathetic resonance from the city's receiver network — the secondary band running in the public stormglass, the older stratum beneath the Hollows picking it up the way old glass picks up ambient frequency. Passive." She stopped, looked at her hand against the stone, looked again. "It is not passive."

The warmth in the stone was building. Not alarmingly — not the band-six elevation that Maerath had been monitoring toward its threshold, not something that triggered any sensor Vael knew of. A gradual accumulation, the way a recording accumulated in stormglass when the encoding ran long, the crystal warming by degrees as the frequency settled into the material.

The older stratum was not picking up the broadcast's frequency.

It was generating its own.

Vael sat back on her heels and let the warmth come through her palm and up through her wrist and into her arm and register in whatever place she had learned, over the past year, to trust before she had language for what it was registering.

The stratum was not responding to the broadcast the way a receiver responded to a transmission. It was responding the way a voice responded to being spoken about — a quality of directed attention, the specific shift in a room when the people in it realize the conversation has come around to something they have been thinking about for a long time.

The broadcast had said the forty-one names. Had said the 97.3 hertz reading. Had said the suppression order without an authorization signature and the personnel file addendum with Ossian's name on it. Had said, in Solen's own encoding grammar, the three names and the chain of authorization and the specific gap between what the primary band recorded and what the secondary band knew.

The older stratum had been built before the Charter. Before the Council's standardization program. Before the secondary band was classified as a manufacturing artifact and its documentation suppressed. It had been running under Bridgefall for three hundred years, carrying the memorial frequency marks carved into the Hollows walls, maintaining the connection between the city's stormglass infrastructure and the deeper encoding layer the founding period had understood and the Council had been trained to forget.

It had been listening.

For three hundred years, and specifically for the past eighteen hours, and most specifically for the past several weeks during which a woman with Solen's calibration grammar in her hands had been moving through the Hollows, loading pre-Charter cylinders, activating encoded material in the secondary band no one was supposed to know how to read.

Vael understood, in the way she understood things before she had words for them — as pressure, as direction, as the specific quality of a frequency arriving before she had consciously parsed its source — that the stratum had not been waiting for the broadcast.

It had been waiting for her.

Not because she had been chosen for it. Because she was the first person in eleven years — in much longer, possibly, than eleven years — who had been moving through the city with Solen's frequency grammar in her hands, activating the secondary band, waking up the encoding layer that the Council's standardization had suppressed. The stratum was not choosing her. It was recognizing something it already knew. A frequency it had encountered before, in a different pair of hands, in a different generation, doing the same work.

Solen had been in the Hollows.

Not recently — the evidence was old, the stone carrying the residue of someone who had spent time here years before Tace arrived, years before the collapse. The calibration work, the secondary band practice, the long process of building a notation system precise enough to encode testimony that the primary archive could not touch. Solen had worked here. Had used the older stratum's responsive frequency as a kind of amplifier, the way you used resonant architecture to extend a signal's range.

Had built the counter-archive into a system that would respond to it being used.

"She designed the stratum response into the encoding," Vael said. Not to Tace. To the floor under her palm.

Tace heard it anyway. "Yes," she said. The flat certainty of someone who had known this for some time and had been waiting for the moment when someone else arrived at it.

"You knew."

"I knew she had spent time here before I arrived. I found the notation in the lower passage — her grammar, not the pre-Charter memorial script, layered over the older carving in a way that didn't disturb it. She was not overwriting the original encoding. She was adding to it. Using the structure that was already here." Tace looked at the wall. The memorial frequency marks, centuries old, surrounded them. "The stratum responds to the secondary band because it was built to carry the secondary band. That was its original purpose. Before the Council standardized. Before that unmonitored register was classified as a flaw."

The warmth in the floor held steady. Ninety-four point seven. Primary band. Response frequency. The older stratum, running what it had always run, now surfaced to something that could hear it.

Vael's palm was flat on the stone. Her hand was warm.

"She told the stratum what to wait for," Vael said.

"She told it a great many things. I could only read a portion of it." Tace looked at her with the clear grey attention Vael had come to know since the day they met — steady, unhurried, carrying something that had been held a long time and could at last be said. "There is one thing I could read clearly. That I have been waiting to tell you since you first came through that passage."

Vael did not speak.

"Your mother knew," Tace said. "She knew before I did. She came to me two months before the collapse — before I had finished my own investigation, before I had the full chain of authorization. She came to me and she had already traced it. She had the suppression order. She had Maerath's name. She had the name above Maerath's." Tace's voice did not change register. "She had all three names."

"She came to you."

"She came to me to warn me. She said the Registry's apparatus had begun to move against her — that she had perhaps a week before her access was revoked. She wanted to make sure I survived long enough to be a witness." Tace was quiet for a moment. "She told me that the archive was complete. That everything was encoded. That she had built it to activate in sequence — the shard first, then the broadcast, then the stratum response. Each stage unlocking the next only when the previous stage had already entered the public record, so that nothing could be suppressed before it was already in circulation."

The city above them was waking. The Hollows' stone carried it, muffled and distant — the Mudflat market's first sounds, the gorge's updraft moving through the ruins, the ordinary morning that did not know what was happening beneath it.

"She said one more thing," Tace said. "She said there was one part of the archive she had not completed when she came to me. A final encoding, in the deepest register — below the layer the broadcast would release. A layer that could only be accessed from a specific angle, an angle that didn't exist yet. That would only exist after the primary archive had played out and after a specific alteration had been made to the receiver."

Vael's hand was still on the floor.

"She said she was encoding it for you," Tace said. "That by the time you could access it, you would know what it contained. And that the stratum would tell you it was ready."

The warmth in the stone rose once — a single pulse, distinct and unmistakable, the way a frequency pulse announced an encoding completing — and held.

Vael looked at the warm floor under her palm.

She looked at her coat pocket.

She stood.

"The Spire," she said.

Not a question. Not a plan. The way you name a place you are already walking toward.

She turned toward the passage.

"Vael." Tace's voice behind her, still level, carrying the same quality it had always carried — unhurried, exact, the voice of someone who has measured the moment and found it ready. "Whatever it contains — you are the person she built it for. You have been since before you knew you were looking for it."

Vael's hand found the passage wall. The stone was warm.

She walked toward the morning.

Chapter 24

The processing clerk's pen was already moving when he slid the release form across the counter — scratch of nib against ledger paper, audible in the intake level's particular quiet, the kind of quiet that was managed rather than natural, the ceiling's stormglass panels absorbing sound and returning it slightly altered, slightly flattened, so that voices arrived stripped of their edges. The amber shard sat on top of the form in its evidence envelope, labeled in the Registry's standard notation: personal frequency object, non-standard origin, returned at release per standard procedure. Their language. Not hers. She reached for the shard first.

It was cold through the paper.

Not room-cold, which was the cold of circulating air. This was something else — the cold of an object that had spent long enough in institutional storage to take on the temperature of the system itself, a mineral cold, the cold of stormglass sitting in a labeled drawer in a correctly indexed location, untouched, waiting. She held it in both hands before setting it down to sign the form, and when she released it the cold stayed in her palms, the way a frequency stays in the inner ear after the source has gone.

She signed. The clerk lifted the form without examining it, filed it in the lateral tray to his left, and said — still without looking up — that the review process would run its minimum ninety-day timeline, that formal notification of hearing dates would arrive through the Registry's standard correspondence channel, assuming her registered address remained current, which — he paused, consulting a different ledger, one finger moving down a column with the particular efficiency of someone who has performed this consultation ten thousand times and long since stopped registering what the entries contain — it appeared it did not, and she would need to update it within fourteen days of release or the correspondence would be filed as undeliverable and the review timeline suspended.

She said she understood. The clerk said there was one additional item.

The co-respondent in the broadcast matter — he used co-respondent, the Registry's term — was being held pending a separate review process applicable to Registry officers who had used active clearance codes for unauthorized purposes. That process ran a minimum of one hundred and eighty days. She was not required to take any action regarding the co-respondent's situation. She was simply being informed, as a matter of procedure.

The pen kept moving. Somewhere in the intake level's managed silence a door opened and closed — the sound of institutional hinges, heavy, self-closing, the sound of a room that did not want to be left open. The clerk did not register it. His pen did not pause.

She stood at the counter with the amber shard in its envelope and the cold still in her palm and the pen moving and the ledger filling, and she did not ask to see Davan. She did not ask how the one hundred and eighty days would run, or what the review would determine, or whether the blank field he had finally filled in would count for him or against him. The clerk would not know. And she already understood that the Registry's apparatus made its calculations without consulting her, and those calculations were running now. The apparatus had no surface she could press her palm against. It had a counter, and a lateral tray, and a clerk whose pen was already moving through the next entry.

She said she understood.

The clerk said she was free to go.

Twelve steps from the processing counter to the Spire's public entrance. She counted them without deciding to — a habit, eleven years of counting steps in rooms where the counting was the only thing she controlled. The door was heavy, its handle dark at the center where the metal had been touched so many times it no longer looked like metal so much as use, warm in a way that surprised her — the warmth of contact repeated so many times that the touching had become part of the material — and it opened onto the civic approach into light that was the specific pale of early morning in the lower wards, the sun still behind the gorge wall, the stone of the approach still holding the night's cold in its surface.

She stopped on the threshold.

Not long. Long enough to feel the air, which was cold and carried the smell of the Mudflat market beginning below — the sound of vendors and carts and the gorge floor's updraft carrying it all upward, which she had heard from inside the Spire and now heard from outside it, which was a different thing. From inside, the market sounds arrived as something happening elsewhere. From outside, they arrived as the city itself, ongoing, indifferent, already in the middle of its morning. She did not calculate how long she had been inside the Spire. The broadcast was twenty hours old, or thirty, or something between. The city had been processing it while she was processed. That was the correct word. She put the amber shard in her coat pocket, still in its envelope, and walked down the civic approach toward the lower ward.

The flagstones were uneven in the way of stone laid over centuries of slight subsidence, each block settling at its own angle so that the surface was never quite level, never quite unpredictable, requiring the attention of a person who had walked this route long enough to know where the tilts were. She had walked it for five years. Her feet knew it without her. She let them.

She walked south.

Not toward the vacated shelter, which was somewhere the Registry's apparatus knew and had processed and which no longer held any of her things — the amber shard had been the last thing. Not toward the resistance's network, which had its own processing to do now, its own calculations running, the people in it making decisions she was not part of and did not need to be part of, not yet, not this morning. Not toward any of the locations she had been moving through for five years, the salvage tunnels and the overflow rooms and the market stalls and the maintenance paths that she had learned the way she had learned the flagstones' tilts — through repetition, through the body's accumulation of what the mind was too careful to rely on. South, because south was where the Glass Bridge ruins were, and because she had been circling that direction for five years without arriving, and because the city was waking up around her and the broadcast was in the air and there was nowhere else she needed to be.

The rope bridge was visible over the rooftops.

She had looked at it directly once before — in the weeks after the broadcast's first fragment surfaced, standing on a Shelf walkway section with the gorge wind lateral and cold, her coat pulled against her, the sound of the gorge's updraft in her ears. She had looked at the rope bridge and felt the specific wrongness in her palms that she had been feeling since she was seven years old, and she had moved before it completed. Now she looked at it without moving. The ropes were the same ropes, or ropes of the same age, and the bridge deck swayed in the gorge's morning wind in the pattern of a structure that had been swaying long enough that the sway had worn grooves in the way it moved — habitual, like breathing. She looked at it until she had finished looking at it, and then she looked at the flagstones and kept walking.

The lower ward was beginning its morning. A vendor was setting up at the corner of the Mudflat approach — the sounds of crates being stacked, canvas unfolded, and the particular exchange between a vendor and a supplier that was not quite an argument and not quite not, the exchange of two people who knew each other's pauses. Two children crossed the flagstones ahead of her at a run, not looking, legs working with the pure mechanical pleasure of speed and no particular direction. A warden stood at the junction of the civic approach and the market alley, watching the street with the quality of attention that was not surveillance but was not nothing either — the attention of someone who has been told something is different today and does not yet know what to do with that information. His eyes moved across the approach and reached her and moved on. She kept walking. The morning kept beginning.

Something had changed in the ordinary weight of it. The vendor's exchange had a quality of pausing it would not have had yesterday. The warden's attention carried uncertainty. The children ran past and were simply children, but the adults in the market alley below moved with the quick purposefulness of people who had somewhere to be and a reason that was new. The broadcast was in all of it — she could see it in the vendor leaning across her crates, in the warden's too-careful stillness, in the way people moved through the alley without quite meeting each other's eyes. The morning was still itself. It was organized around something it could not name.

She walked through it without stopping.

The Glass Bridge ruins were at the gorge's edge — the Plateau-side tower incorporated into the Spire's eastern wall and inaccessible from the civic approach without a key most clerks did not have, the far-side tower visible across the gorge on its narrow path, the three suspended sections of the original deck still hanging between the anchor cables in the morning air. The cables were stormglass-threaded, the original installation's decision, and in the morning's pale light they refracted what there was of the sun in the specific way of stormglass under low frequency — not brightness but depth, the light going into the material and returning changed, carrying something of the interior with it. The debris field began where the flagstones gave way to salvage ground — glass panels from the original deck repurposed into the Mudflat's navigational landmarks, large fragments that residents used as reference points, their surfaces darkened along the edges where hands had gripped them through the years, the centers pale and polished where people had steadied themselves passing.

The grating was iron, set into the gorge's edge between two sections of the stone balustrade, the balustrade cracked at its northern join in a way that had been cracked for as long as she could remember. The grating covered the drainage channel that ran from the maintenance path to the Sorrow below, and it was cold to the touch in all seasons because the gorge air ran through it continuously, and it smelled of iron and old water and the specific mineral quality of the Sorrow's current where it moved through the stormglass riverbed.

She put her hand on the stanchion.

The stanchion was a remnant anchor post from the original bridge, incorporated into the balustrade when the ruins were stabilized — the iron was older than the stone around it, the specific old of metal that has been under load for long enough that the load has become part of its composition. Stormglass residue filled the anchor housing, the same residue that Maerath had stood near in the night before dawn, that Vael had felt in her chest rather than her hands because the frequency ran at 97.3 hertz and she was not attuned to it the way she was attuned to other things.

Vael pressed her palm flat against the iron.

The dissonance was there.

Altered — the recalibration had shifted something in the way she received it, the frequency arriving at a slightly different angle than before, as if the channel through which she heard it had been moved a fraction of a degree so that the sound came from just beside where it had always come from, close enough to be recognizable, different enough to notice. The iron was cold under her palm. The gorge wind moved through the grating below her. The Sorrow's sound came up from forty feet down — the specific acoustic of water moving through a stormglass riverbed, not the sound of ordinary water, which was turbulent and various, but the sound of water moving through a medium that had already decided what frequencies it would carry and which it would not, a sound that was almost a hum, almost a frequency in itself. But present. The hum in her palms when the glass played something wrong, when the crystal carried a frequency that did not match its official reading, when the record and the thing recorded diverged in ways that left a mark in the material. Present, and hers, and not gone.

She stood with her palm on the stanchion and the Sorrow below and the stormglass riverbed luminous in the gorge's shadow with everything it had been given to carry — her mother's archive and forty-one names and seventeen years of quarterly variance reports and the 97.3 hertz reading that the primary band had never shown and the maintenance logs that had been filed correctly and the certification that had been signed and the bridge that had stood for three years after the signing and then had not stood anymore. All of it still in the glass below. The glass did not distinguish between what it had been given and what it had been forced to hold. It carried both.

The city's morning noise was above her. The market. The warden at the junction. The children who had crossed the flagstones at a run. The broadcast circulating through the Registry's response channel and through the informal channels the Registry's response was designed not to reach and through the specific human transmission that happened when people who had heard something told people who had not yet heard it — which was already happening, had been happening for twenty hours or thirty — a woman at the nearest stall leaned across her crates and touched the arm of the woman next to her, and neither of them looked at anything in particular.

She did not know what Maerath had written in the ledger. She did not know what the review process would determine for Davan, or whether the one hundred and eighty days would run toward something or simply run. She did not know what Nava remembered, or what Nava was doing in the market where she had stopped, or whether the work of seventeen years had left any residue in the person who had done it, the way the bridge had left residue in the stanchion housing, the way everything left something in the material it had passed through. She did not know whether the third name in the sealed record would produce silence from the upper ward for another day or whether the silence was already breaking in ways she could not hear from here.

The amber shard was in her coat pocket, still in its envelope. She did not take it out. She did not need to. The last encoding had been the workshop — Solen at the bench, back to the door, calibrating household glass, humming without a melody, eighteen seconds of ordinary morning that had been encoded before any of it, before the investigation or the counter-archive or the decision that made the counter-archive necessary. Just the workshop. Just her mother's back and the hum and the glass on the bench and the quality of morning light that the recording could not carry but that Vael had supplied from memory, which was not the same as what the stormglass held but was not entirely separate from it either. The recording held the sound. She held the light. Between them, something almost complete.

The shard would not replay, and she had stopped asking it to. The encoding was fixed, the stormglass rule absolute — what was given to it was given once, and played once, and then held without release. She had pressed her thumb to it after the procedure and nothing had activated, and she had sat with that for however long she had sat with it in the cell, her palms flat on the table, the cold of the shard in her hand, the table's surface carrying no frequency at all, just wood, just the ordinary silence of a material that had never been asked to hold anything. She was still sitting with it in the way that things you have finished sitting with continue to sit inside you.

The hum in the stanchion was 97.3 hertz, shifted slightly in her reception of it, still recognizable as the frequency of something true.

Footsteps on the flagstones behind her.

Not the warden's — a different weight, a different rhythm, the sound of someone who was not walking toward the grating so much as arriving at it, the way you arrive at a place you have been circling without knowing you were circling it. The footsteps had the manner of a route completed rather than a destination chosen. She did not turn immediately. She waited until the footsteps stopped, and the gorge wind moved through the grating, and the Sorrow's sound came up from below. Then she turned.

Tace was standing two feet away.

Older than the Registry's file photographs — older than the Charter Year Fourteen documentation, older than the certification records, older than the installation team roster that now existed in the sealed official record alongside Ryn Ossian's name and the 97.3 hertz reading and the unsigned suppression order. The file photographs had been taken when the certification was filed, when Tace had been the age of someone who had not yet understood what the signing would cost, and the cost had been accumulating in her face for eleven years in the specific way that a thing you cannot put down accumulates in the body carrying it. Her coat was the coat of someone who had been released that morning and had not yet been home, if home was still a place that existed for her in any form the word meant. Her hands were at her sides. Her eyes moved from the grating to the stanchion to Vael's hand still flat against the iron.

They had not arranged this.

Vael had not known Tace had been released that morning — the processing clerk had not said, and she had not asked, and the Registry's apparatus made its calculations without consulting either of them about the outcomes. Tace had not known Vael would be here. They had arrived separately, from different directions, through different processes, and found each other at the place both of them had been circling — the place where the bridge had been and where the bridge was not, where the archive had been held in the riverbed glass eleven years, where the hum in the stone was the frequency of a reading that should have stopped a certification and had not.

Tace put her hand on the grating.

Not on the stanchion — on the grating itself, the iron bars over the drainage channel, her palm flat against the cold metal in the same gesture Vael had made against the stanchion. The hum was in the iron and in the stone and in the residue of the anchor housing and in the riverbed below where the glass still carried everything it had been given. The morning was above them both, ordinary and ongoing — the market and the vendors and the warden at the junction and the broadcast still circulating through every channel the Registry could reach and could not reach.

Neither of them spoke.

The gorge wind moved through the grating between Tace's fingers. The Sorrow's sound came up from below, carrying the specific frequency of water through stormglass — the frequency that was almost a hum, almost a reading, almost the sound of the secondary band running at 97.3 hertz in the eastern anchor housing on the morning of the inspection in Charter Year Fourteen, which was the same housing Vael's palm was against now, the iron cold and old and still holding what it had been given to hold.

Tace had stood in the certification chamber and read the primary band and signed the document that said 94.7 hertz, within tolerance. The secondary band had been running at 97.3 hertz in the eastern anchor housing — the housing Vael's palm was against now, the residue still in the iron, the frequency still in the glass below. Tace knew what she had signed. Vael knew what the signing had cost. The broadcast had said both things, in the secondary band's frequency, for forty-one minutes, to everyone who could receive it and to everyone who would receive it from someone who could, which was already a larger number than the Registry's apparatus had calculated and would be a larger number still by tomorrow. Neither of them needed to say it. The iron said it. The glass below said it.

Altered, present, hers — the dissonance was in Vael's palm.

The city was behind them. Maerath was walking toward the Spire with the ledger in her coat and the sentence written in it in the vocabulary that named things correctly — the sentence was private, and what she would do with it was not yet decided, and the not-deciding was not the same as management, which was new. Davan was in a clean room in the detention facility with one hundred and eighty days running and the blank field filled in and whatever came next still ahead of him. Nava was at the market where she had stopped, doing the work she did, without the memory of the work she had done, which was the specific cost of a specific choice that Nava had not made and that had been made for her, and which the archive now held in the secondary band in the glass below along with everything else the glass had been given to carry. Brek was in his office reading Davan's file again with the adjournment notice on his desk and the sealed record open on the terminal and the commemorative installations playing Ryn Ossian's voice in the civic squares, and what he would do with what he knew was not yet decided either.

The third name was in the sealed record.

The third name was in the upper ward's silence.

The broadcast was thirty hours old, or forty, and the Registry's response was circulating, and the compounding effects were running whether or not anyone calculated them, and the city was still processing something it could not stop having received. The market below was louder now, the morning fully begun, the sound of it rising through the gorge on the updraft and reaching the balustrade where they stood — the sound of the city going about the business of being a city, which it had been doing on the morning of the collapse and on every morning since, and which it would continue doing through whatever the sealed record and the broadcast and the not-yet-decided decisions produced. The city did not wait. It was already in the middle of the next thing.

Vael's palm was on the stanchion.

Tace's hand was on the grating.

Between them the hum moved through the stone — the frequency of asymmetric stress in the eastern anchor housing, 97.3 hertz, the reading the secondary band had been carrying since Charter Year Fourteen, the reading the primary band had never shown, the reading that was now in the sealed official record and in the public archive and in the glass of the riverbed below and in the palms of the two people standing at the iron at the gorge's edge while the city went about its ordinary day behind them. The iron was cold. The gorge wind moved through the grating and rose. The Sorrow ran below through its stormglass bed, carrying its frequency, carrying what it had been given, indifferent to whether anyone was listening.

The glass below was still carrying everything it had been given.

The hum had not stopped.

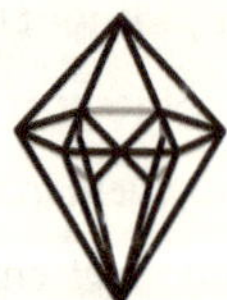

The warden came for her an hour after the clerk said she was free to go.

She was still at the counter. Not from confusion — she had understood that she was free to go, had understood the words and their meaning and the specific quality of institutional permission that gave them weight. She was still at the counter because her feet had not yet received the information her mind had been processing for the past four days, and because the lobby's cold morning light was the first unmanaged light she had stood in since intake, and she was standing in it the way a person stood in something they had forgotten existed.

The warden was not the intake warden. Younger, his Registry badge showing the correct patina of someone three seasons into the work. He stopped at a distance that was not quite professional and said, in the register of a man carrying words that were not his, that the director of Registry Operations had requested a brief meeting before her departure. The meeting was voluntary. She was not required to attend. If she chose to attend, there was a room on the second level that had been prepared for the purpose.

Vael looked at him.

The voluntary in his sentence had the bearing of a word that knew exactly what it was doing.

"How brief," she said.

"The director did not specify."

She looked at the lobby's cold morning light. She looked at the door with its dark-centered handle that she had not yet touched from the outside.

"Second level," she said.

The room on the second level was not the calibration chamber and was not the session room and was not any room she had been in during the four days of administrative detention. It was smaller than all of those — two chairs and a table and a stormglass panel in the ceiling throwing its even light at 94.7 hertz, within tolerance, the primary band, the reading that had always been filed. A water carafe on the table, two cups. The window was narrow and faced north, the gorge wall visible in the distance, the Sorrow a sound rather than a sight. She could hear it through the stone. She had been hearing it since intake. She sat in the chair that faced the door, put her coat across her lap, and waited.

Maerath came alone.

No escort, no warden, no Tenne with his secondary desk efficiency and his patience. The door opened the way it opened for someone who had opened doors like it ten thousand times before — unhurried, the latch depressed without thought — and Maerath came in and crossed to the remaining chair with her eyes already taking the measure of the room's corners, then stopped short of the chair and stood a moment as though she had decided, somewhere between the service stair and this corridor, not to do that anymore.

She sat in the remaining chair.

She did not open a file. She did not place a document on the table. She sat with her hands in her coat pockets and looked at the water carafe and then at Vael and then at the window's narrow rectangle of gorge wall.

Neither of them spoke.

The stormglass panel held its 94.7 hertz. The Sorrow moved through the stone below. Somewhere in the Spire's upper levels, the administrative apparatus was running — correspondence channels, review timelines, hearing notifications, the Registry's public response circulating through the official channels with the measured, accurate language she had written. All of it running, as it always ran, without requiring her presence in any particular room.

She was in this room.

"You came without an escort," Vael said.

Maerath looked at her. "Yes."

The word was not an explanation. It was not designed to be.

Vael set her coat on the table between them and looked at the woman who had ordered her re-calibration.

She had been building language for this moment for five years — in the Hollows, in the overflow rooms, in the specific pre-dawn hours when the archive's grammar felt most legible and the shape of what she was trying to prove was clearest. She had built language for the confrontation with the Registry's institutional structure, with the suppression apparatus, with the authorization chain that ran from Tace's anomaly report through Maerath's signature to the name above Maerath's in the hierarchy she had been trying to reach. She had not built language for a room with two chairs and a water carafe and a woman who had come without an escort.

She used the language she had.

"The certification that authorized the Glass Bridge's final installation recorded a primary band reading of 94.7 hertz," she said. "Within tolerance. Within every parameter the assessment protocol required."

Maerath did not move.

"The secondary band was running at 97.3 hertz in the eastern anchor housing for three months before the certification was filed. That reading was not in the protocol. The technician who conducted the assessment didn't know to look for it. The engineer who reviewed his work and classified the anomaly as equipment variance had the training to know what 97.3 hertz in an undocumented secondary band meant for a load-bearing anchor housing under asymmetric stress, and she classified it as equipment variance anyway." Vael kept her voice level — not flat, not stripped, level. The register of someone who has made peace with the thing they are about to say. "The authorization chain ran from that classification through your signature to the name above yours in the Registry's hierarchy at that time. The bridge was certified. Three months later, forty-one people crossed it."

The stormglass panel held its frequency. The water carafe held its light. Maerath held her stillness the way the stanchion held its residue — because it had been holding it for a long time and the holding had become structural.

"The suppression order had no authorization signature," Vael said. "You filed it. The name above yours in the chain did not sign it. That gap is in the public record now. The broadcast put it there."

"I know," Maerath said.

Two words, nothing more. Not a concession. An acknowledgment — she took it in and said nothing further, the way a person confirms a reading by not correcting it.

Vael looked at her. "The re-calibration order had a signature."

A beat. Something shifted in Maerath's face — not expression, not the legible vocabulary of guilt or calculation. Something below that. The specific movement of a person absorbing a distinction they had not permitted themselves to examine until this moment.

"Yes," she said.

"You signed it."

"Yes."

"The suppression order covered the secondary band data, the anomaly chain, Tace's classification report. The re-calibration order covered the one person in Bridgefall who could read the secondary band without equipment. Without access. With her hands."

Vael did not raise her voice. The level register held. "Those two orders were the same act. Seventeen years apart."

Maerath looked at the water carafe. She looked at the narrow window and the gorge wall beyond it. She looked at her own hands in her lap — the specific redness at the palms that Vael recognized from her own hands after holding cold iron too long, the hands of someone who had been gripping something for longer than she intended.

"Yes," she said.

It was the third yes. Each one had arrived at a slightly different register — the first a receipt, the second an acknowledgment, the third something that had not decided yet what it was.

Vael waited.

Maerath looked at the window for a long time.

The gorge wall's stone held the morning light the way old stone always did — taking it in first, the surface warming slowly while the interior stayed cold, so that the heat came back to you later than you expected it, later than the light itself had warranted. She had looked at that stone from Spire windows in the seventeen years since. She had not, until this morning, stood at the Glass Bridge grating in the pre-dawn cold and understood that the stone was doing to her exactly what she had been doing to every person who had brought her something true.

"I knew the readings were not equipment variance," she said.

Not to the window. Not to the carafe. To Vael. The specific directness of someone who has decided that directness is the only remaining form of accuracy available to them.

"I knew it the way I knew every structural frequency assessment I had reviewed before my appointment to the directorship. Eight years in the field. The deviation pattern was not instrument drift. Tace was correct. The anomaly was real, and I classified it as equipment variance because the name above mine in the authorization chain was present in the room when I reviewed the documentation, and I understood — I was given to understand — that the correct determination was equipment variance."

The sentence ended. She did not add to it. She did not qualify it or revise it or move it into a different register.

"You were pressured," Vael said. Not a question.

"I made a choice," Maerath said. "There was pressure. I made the choice. Those are not the same statement."

Vael looked at her.

"I have been making them the same statement for seventeen years," Maerath said. "They are not."

The stormglass panel held at 94.7 hertz. The Sorrow through the stone. The city above them, already in the middle of its morning, the broadcast twenty hours old and circulating. None of it waited. All of it continued.

"You reassigned Oren," Vael said.

"Yes."

"He had done his job correctly."

"Yes." The word was different from the previous ones — heavier, arriving with the weight of something that had been held at the bottom of a very long filing system and had just been required to surface. "He had done his job correctly by every standard he had been given. I moved him to the western annex to prevent him from speaking to anyone who might ask questions about the certification. He spent —" She stopped. She had not, until this moment, allowed herself to complete this sentence either. "I don't know how many years he spent there. I have not checked."

"Because checking would require knowing."

"Yes."

The silence lasted long enough that the Sorrow's sound through the stone became audible again — the low continuous frequency of water through stormglass, indifferent, ongoing, carrying what it had been given.

Maerath reached into her coat. She took out the personal ledger. She set it on the table between them without opening it.

"I wrote one sentence in this this morning," she said. "At the grating. In the vocabulary that names things by what they are rather than by the category available to them."

She did not open it. She did not offer it. She left it on the table between them the way the stanchion left its residue in the iron — present, factual, not requiring anything.

"What did it say," Vael said.

Maerath looked at the ledger. She looked at Vael.

"That there was no decision," she said. "That there were two absences — Oren's, which was ignorance, and mine, which was not — and that forty-one people fell into the space between them, and that I spent seventeen years protecting the space as though it were a choice that required protecting."

The ledger sat between them on the table. Neither of them touched it.

"That is what the sentence says," Maerath said. "It took seventeen years."

Vael looked at the ledger and then at the woman who had written in it.

She had been waiting, she understood now, for something in this room to resolve —
for the confrontation to arrive at a point that felt like completion, for the exchange of
truth to produce the specific quality she had been expecting since she was seven years old
and her palms first registered something wrong in a piece of glass and she had brought it
to her mother and her mother had said, with the steady precision that was the grammar
of everything Solen did, *yes, that is what you are feeling, and it is correct, and it means
something is not right here.* She had been waiting for the yes that meant the wrongness
had been confirmed and that the confirmation would change the shape of what came
next.

The wrongness had been confirmed. Maerath had confirmed it, in her own words, in
the vocabulary that named things by what they were. The confirmation was sitting on the
table between them in a ledger with worn leather and dark thread repair and seventeen
years of accurate documentation of inaccurate acts.

Nothing had changed shape.

Davan was still in a clean room with one hundred and eighty days running. Nava was
still in the market without the memory of the work she had done. Oren was still in the
western annex — or wasn't, and she still didn't know. Tace had signed the document and
the document was in the public record and forty-one names were in the public record
and the secondary band reading was in the public record, and none of that had required
Maerath to confirm anything.

She had already known. That was the specific quality of what she was sitting with in
this room — not the discovery of truth but the formalization of it, the moment when the
thing you have known for a long time is finally spoken by the person whose speaking of
it would change nothing and mean everything.

"You came before the broadcast," Vael said. "Solen came to you."

Something moved in Maerath's face. Not surprise — something more specific than
surprise, the movement of a person who has reached the end of a boundary she built
herself and finds, on the other side of it, only the plain fact she already knew.

"Yes," she said.

Vael waited.

"Three days before the collapse," Maerath said. Her voice had not changed register. It
had only become more precise — the way a frequency became more precise when the
interference cleared. "She came to my session room. She did not have an appointment.

She had been in the installation records — the anomaly chain, the secondary band data. She had traced it further than Tace had. She had names. Not one. Three."

The Sorrow through the stone. The 94.7 hertz panel. The gorge wall in the narrow window holding its morning light.

"She asked me to act," Maerath said. "Not publicly. Not through the Registry's formal channels. She knew that the name above mine in the chain would close those channels before anything reached them. She asked me to act through the mechanism available to the directorship outside the standard authorization structure. A formal safety hold. My signature alone. It would have stopped the certification, triggered an independent assessment, required a secondary band protocol the name above mine could not suppress without producing a paper record of the suppression."

Vael held the shape of what she was hearing.

"I did not act," Maerath said.

The sentence arrived in the room with the weight of something that had been in free fall across seventeen years and had just landed.

"I told her the evidence was insufficient for a formal safety hold. That the anomaly chain required independent corroboration before the directorship could justify the mechanism. That I needed more time." She looked at the ledger between them. "She left. Three days later, forty-one people crossed the bridge. She sent me a message the same afternoon — two words, through the secondary channel she had been using for the installation records. I have the message. I have kept it seventeen years in the same place I keep this."

She touched the ledger's cover once, with two fingers, and withdrew her hand.

"The two words were *you knew.*"

The room held them both. The morning was fully outside by now — the market sound audible even through the Spire's stone, the broadcast still running in the city's receiver network, the compounding effects running whether or not anyone was calculating them. The city did not wait. It was already in the middle of the next thing.

Vael looked at the water carafe. She looked at the two cups that had been placed with the deliberate care of an institution that had made comfort into policy. She looked at the narrow window and the gorge wall and the specific quality of morning light on old stone.

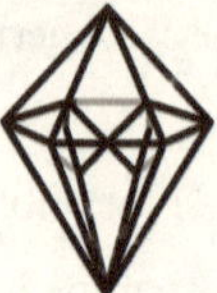

"She knew you wouldn't act," Vael said.

Maerath was very still.

"She had already built the archive before she came to you. She had already encoded it. She came to you because she needed to know whether there was another way — whether the directorship's mechanism would work, whether you were a path she hadn't seen." Vael kept her voice level. "When you said no, she had her answer. She went back to the archive and she encoded what she had and she made sure it would survive without her, because she already understood it would need to."

Maerath said nothing.

"She wasn't asking you to save the forty-one," Vael said. "She was asking you to give her a reason not to do it the harder way."

The silence lasted a very long time.

"I know," Maerath said.

Her voice was the same voice. It had not broken and it had not shifted into a different register. It was simply carrying more — the way a frequency carried more when the material had finally allowed it full passage, when the secondary band stopped running undetected and entered the readable range.

"I know that now," she said. "I knew it, I think, before she left the room. I have been not-knowing it for seventeen years. It required more effort than most of the work I have done in that time." She looked at the ledger. "Less than I expected, finally not-knowing it."

Neither of them moved toward the door.

The room sat between them the way the truth sat between them — not peacefully, not with the quality of a thing resolved, but with the weight of something that had been named and was still present and would continue to be present regardless of what happened in the corridor beyond the door, in the review timeline, in the ninety days, in the formal notification of hearing dates that would arrive through the standard correspondence channel once Vael had updated her registered address.

"The re-calibration order," Vael said.

"I have not reversed it." Maerath paused. "I do not know whether I have the mechanism to reverse it. The procedure was completed. Whether completion can be contested through the directorship's review function or requires an external process — I don't know. I am going to find out."

"That's not an answer."

"No," Maerath said. "It is not."

She picked up the ledger. She put it back in her coat. She looked at Vael the way someone looks at a person when they have finished looking at everything else in the room first and have arrived, at last, at the only thing that was ever in it.

"You are going to continue," she said. "Not as a question. As a reading. The way you read glass."

"Yes," Vael said.

"The sealed record has three names. The name above mine in the authorization chain is in that record. What you do with it is not within my ability to predict or to manage." She stood. The chair did not scrape — she rose with the care of someone who had learned to move through rooms without disturbing their surfaces. "I would not attempt to manage it. I am telling you this so you know the shape of what I am telling you."

Vael looked up at her.

"I came without an escort," Maerath said. "I will leave a record of this meeting. In the personal ledger, not the Registry's files. What it contained is between the people in this room."

She moved toward the door.

"Maerath," Vael said.

She stopped. She did not turn immediately. When she did, it was with the look of someone who has been waiting for a sentence to arrive and is uncertain whether she is ready for it.

"Did you know," Vael said, "what the secondary band was carrying? Before Solen came to you. Before the broadcast."

Maerath looked at her for a long moment.

"I knew the secondary band existed," she said. "I knew the certification had not assessed it. I knew what 97.3 hertz in an undocumented channel meant for a load-bearing anchor housing. I did not know what the stormglass below the bridge was carrying." She held the door handle. "I did not know about the archive. I did not know about your mother's system. I did not know that the frequency I had spent eleven years suppressing had spent eleven years remembering."

She opened the door.

"I know now," she said. "It changes the specific shape of what I did not do. Not the weight."

She walked out. The door closed with the sound of institutional hinges, heavy, self-closing. Not locked. Voluntary, from both sides.

Vael sat in the room for a moment. The stormglass panel held its 94.7 hertz. The water carafe held its light. The two cups sat on the table, neither of them touched.

She picked up her coat. She stood. She walked to the door and opened it from the inside and stepped into the corridor and went down the service stair to the civic intake level and across the lobby to the door with the dark-centered handle and opened it onto the cold morning air.

The shard moved in her pocket.

Not fell — moved. The specific shift of something changing temperature, changing state, the way stormglass moved when a frequency found it from outside. Vael's hand went to her coat before she had made the decision to move it. Through the envelope, through the fabric, the amber was warm.

Warm in a way it had not been since the broadcast chamber.

She took it out.

Tace saw her hand move and went still — a sharpness entering her posture, the stillness of an engineer who has just heard a reading she does not recognize.

The envelope was warm through the paper. Vael's palm registered the differential before she had opened it — the specific gradient of pre-Charter amber under active load, the glass running a frequency, the encoding alive. Not residual. Not the ghost-warmth of a recording played out. Active. Present. Something still running.

She pulled the shard free of the envelope and held it in the open air above the gorge.

It was lit from within. Not the amber pulse she had seen in Nava's overflow room, which had been faint, a frequency signature at low power. This was full activation — the warm gold of pre-Charter glass under sustained encoding, the specific color her mother's workshop had always carried in the late afternoon when Solen had been working for a long time and the glass had been absorbing for a long time and the two had settled into a frequency together that Vael had grown up calling the color of concentration.

She had not seen that color in five years.

"That shouldn't be possible," Tace said. Her voice came out flat, stripped of inference, the voice of someone confronting an instrument reading that refuses to resolve. "The encoding was complete. You played it in the broadcast chamber. The stormglass rule—"

"I know the rule."

What was given was given once, and played once, and then held without release. She had pressed her thumb to the shard in the detention cell and nothing had activated. She had been carrying it for days as a cold object, a weight, a piece of glass that had finished being what it was.

It was not finished.

Vael pressed her thumb to the worn surface.

The secondary band opened — not the way it had opened before, not through the angle she had always used, but through the shifted angle, the fraction-of-a-degree displacement the re-calibration had left in her reception. The channel that was almost the same and not the same. The channel that had been waiting for her to arrive at this specific angle, this specific position, after the specific alteration that the re-calibration had made to the way she received.

Solen had known about the re-calibration.

Solen had encoded the second layer for the person Vael would be after it.

The shard opened all the way.

Not the workshop. Not the calibration chamber. Not the pale stone walls and the gas lamp and her mother's hands moving across the frequency reader with the economy of someone who had been doing this work for a long time.

A different room. Smaller. No windows. A room Vael recognized from the Registry's lower levels — not because she had been in it, but because she had been in rooms built from the same logic, the same institutional compression of space, the same grey stone that absorbed light instead of returning it.

Solen sat at a table with no equipment on it. No frequency reader, no calibration instruments, no encoding stylus. Just the table and her hands and the amber cylinder, which she was holding the way she had held it in the earlier recording — with the specific quality of someone holding something that belongs to someone else and is in the process of making sure it will get there.

She was looking directly at the recording surface.

She was looking at Vael.

Not in the way of someone who knows they are being recorded. In the way of someone who knows exactly who will be watching — who has encoded the activation condition to ensure that only this specific person, at this specific moment, after this specific alteration, can receive what follows.

Her mother's face. Five years of absence, and her mother's face, looking at her.

Solen spoke.

Not the vowel-structure of degraded consonants, not the rhythm-without-attribution of a recording playing at the edge of its fidelity. Full clarity. This was not a recording made once and stored. This was a recording made for a specific playback condition, held in reserve in the secondary band's deepest register, below the layer the counter-archive had released, below the layer the Council's archivists would not know to search for even now that they knew to search for the secondary band at all. A layer below the layer. Solen's system had always had this. Vael had decoded the grammar four years ago and had not understood, until this moment, what the deepest notation markers meant.

I encoded three names, Solen said. *You read two of them clearly. The second was in the fold.*

Vael's palm had gone still against the shard. The gorge wind moved below. The Sorrow ran. Tace stood at the iron grating and did not speak and did not move and Vael registered none of it. There was only her mother's voice and the careful economy of someone who has been saving the last of something and is now spending it.

I told Tace I was protecting her from knowing the second name. That was true. I told her the fold was accidental. That was not.

The fold had not been accidental.

I chose which name would be obscured. I chose it because the second name is the one that ends this if it surfaces through the wrong channel before the first and third are already in the record. The first and third create the chain of authorization. The second name is the chain's origin — not Ossian, not Maerath. The position above both of them. The position that does not appear in the Council's current structure because it was renamed. Because the person who holds it renamed it themselves, eleven years ago, when they understood what the secondary band contained.

The room was very quiet around Solen. The kind of quiet that meant the room had been chosen for its quiet — a room no one else entered, a room that did not register in the clearance logs because it had been removed from the clearance logs by someone with the authority to remove things from clearance logs.

You will know what to do with this. You will know because you are reading it at the correct angle, which means the re-calibration has already happened, which means the broadcast has already happened, which means the first and third names are already in the record. The chain is anchored. The second name can now surface without ending what you have built.

Solen looked at her daughter through five years of amber glass.

The second name is Brek.

The encoding held for three more seconds — Solen's face, steady and precise, the face of someone who has done the most careful work of her life and has arrived at its conclusion — and then the shard went dark.

Cold in Vael's palm. The cold of spent glass, emptied at last.

She stood at the gorge's edge with the cold shard in her hand and the Sorrow forty feet below and Tace's hand on the iron grating and the morning fully around them, the market noise and the warden at the junction and the ordinary hum of a city that did not know what had just happened.

Brek.

Not an operative assigned to surveil her. Not a secondary investigator brought in to add institutional pressure to an existing case. The person who had conducted the re-calibration of the lower-ward girl with the specific care of someone who believed he was doing the work correctly. The person who had stood at the grating four years running and felt the hum and not reported it. The person who had arrested them at the broadcast chamber door and filed accurate intake documentation and read Davan's account in the sealed record with the look of a man confirming what he had long suspected and had preferred not to know.

The person who had been in Brek's position in the Registry's hierarchy over eleven years — since the year after the collapse, since the year the governance position above Maerath's had been quietly renamed, the year a new senior investigative function had been created and filled by the same person who had just that year closed the final thread connecting the suppression order to the upper ward.

He had not been running an investigation.

He had been running containment.

The adjournment notice. His clearance to the sealed record. His access to Davan's account. The re-calibration of the girl, conducted with the specific care of someone who took the work seriously and believed the work was serious — which it was, which was the point, which was what made it possible to do it for eleven years without the people around you understanding that the thoroughness was not professional virtue but professional necessity. The work had to be done correctly because incorrectly done work left traces and traces produced the specific category of problem he had spent eleven years managing.

What he would do with what he knew was not yet decided.

She had written that line in her mind standing at this grating an hour ago. She had written it about Brek.

It was not undecided. It had never been undecided. He had already decided, eleven years ago, and the decisions had been compounding since then with the calm of a man who had made one sufficient choice and built everything else on top of it.

He was in his office. The adjournment notice was on his desk. The sealed record was on the terminal. He had read Davan's account and he had read the third name in the broadcast's rendered content and Ryn Ossian's voice was playing in the civic squares and Brek knew — had always known — that Ossian was the shield. That the name above the shield was his.

He was in his office and he was not deciding. He was calculating.

Tace's voice, from the grating. Quiet and level, the voice of an engineer reading an instrument she had not expected to need.

"What did it say."

Vael looked at the shard in her hand. Cold amber, the surface pitted where so many thumbs had pressed it, the glass that had felt like her mother's attention for the past year now simply glass, simply an object, simply a piece of the pre-Charter manufacturing stratum that had never been officially documented.

She looked up. The gorge wall rose on the far side of the Sorrow, its stormglass surfaces catching the morning light and returning it fractured, in frequencies.

"Vael." Tace's voice did not rise. It simply arrived — patient, exact, with the particular quality of someone who has been waiting those seventeen years and can wait a few more seconds and will not wait indefinitely. "What did it say."

The city was behind them. Ordinary, ongoing, already in the middle of the next thing.

Vael closed her hand around the shard.

"We need to find Davan," she said.

She turned from the gorge and walked.

Author's Note

I started this book for my wife.

That's the simplest way to say it. Jennifer and I had been married thirty years when I began writing it, and I was building toward thirty-one — toward the kind of anniversary that deserves something made rather than purchased. I wanted to give her a world. I wanted to give her Vael.

She didn't make it to thirty-one. She died on January 14, 2025, before I finished the book, before she could hold it, before she could sit in the front row with her camera and tell me afterward that she was proud of me.

So I finished it anyway. Because that's what you do with something you were making for someone you loved. You finish it. You send it out into the world. You trust that the love it was built from is still in it somewhere, encoded in the prose the way Solen encoded truth in the secondary band — present, waiting, readable by the right hands.

This book is about what happens when institutions decide that certain truths are too inconvenient to survive. It's about the people who carry those truths anyway — quietly, at personal cost, for years — and what it takes to finally bring them into the light. I've spent most of my adult life working alongside people who were hurting, people who had been failed by systems that were supposed to protect them. I know what it looks like when someone carries something true for a long time without anyone to receive it.

Jennifer received things. That was one of her gifts. She didn't look away from hard truths, and she didn't let the people carrying them feel alone in the carrying.

Vael counts things to stay steady. Jennifer took photographs. Different tools, same instinct — the need to register what is real, to name it precisely, to refuse the managed version.

I think she would have loved this book. I think she would have asked good questions about Maerath. I think she would have understood Nava without explanation.

I wrote it for her. It belongs to her. And now it belongs to you.

R.M. Kiser Kingsport, Tennessee

Acknowledgements

Books don't get finished alone, even when the writing feels solitary.

To Kai, my son — I love you without condition. That is not something that requires your support to remain true.

To my family and friends who showed up during the hardest year of my life and kept showing up — thank you. You didn't ask me to be okay before I was ready. You sat with me in the ordinary days and the difficult ones and you didn't pass me by. Jennifer would have noticed that. I did too.

To the Lamplight Theatre community in Kingsport — you gave me a place to remember who I was when I had forgotten. The stage has a way of doing that. I'm grateful for every rehearsal, every performance, every conversation in the parking lot afterward.

To the readers who pick up a book like this one — quiet, strange, asking hard questions about truth and institutions and the cost of carrying something for a long time — thank you for being the kind of person who reads this kind of book. You are exactly who I wrote it for.

And to Jennifer — you are in every page. You always will be.

R.M. Kiser
Kingsport, Tennessee

About the author

About the Author

R.M. Kiser is an indie author and the founder of Summit & Shore Publishing, based in Kingsport, Tennessee. He writes literary fiction, dark fantasy, and faith-based parables — stories that don't look away from hard things and don't offer easy comfort in place of honest witness.

He spent years working alongside people in crisis, and that work shaped everything he writes. His characters tend to be people carrying something true for a long time without anyone to receive it. He writes for the readers who know what that feels like.

When he isn't writing, he volunteers with Lamplight Theatre, a Christian community theater in Kingsport, where he has discovered that the stage and the page ask the same thing of a person — presence, honesty, and the willingness to show up.

The Echo Rewritten is his first novel in The Echoes of Bridgefall trilogy.

He lives in Kingsport, Tennessee.

Connect with R.M. Kiser:

www.rmkiser.com

Also by R.M. Kiser

Dust and Mercy

Letters We Couldn't Read

The Echoes of Bridgefall Trilogy

The Echo Rewritten — Book One

The Echo That Burns — Book Two (*forthcoming*)

The Echo Misheard — Book Three (*forthcoming*)

Stay Connected

I 'd love to hear from you.

Visit me at **rmkiser.com** for news, upcoming releases, and exclusive content.

Scan to connect or visit rmkiser.com